Elizabeth,

It has been great to get
know you these past few
weeks. And thanks for letting
Erica be part of the book club!
You said you liked books that
are mind fucks and this is
one of them. Hope you enjoy it!

AJ

# STONE'S MISTAKE

Book One of Agent Morgan Stone

Adrian J. Smith

Supposed Crimes LLC • Matthews, North Carolina

Published in the United States.

ISBN: 978-1-952150-16-6

www.supposedcrimes.com

This book is typeset in Goudy Old Style.

STONE'S MISTAKE

# More by Adrian J. Smith

**Romances**
Memoir in the Making
OBlique

**Quarter Life**
Unbound (#1)
De-Termination (#2)
Release (#3) (2021)

**The James Matthews Series**
Forever Burn (#1)
Dying Embers (#2)
Ashes Fall (#3)

**Spirit of Grace**
For by Grace (#1)
Fallen from Grace (#2)
Grace through Redemption (#3)

**Detective Grace**
Lost and Forsaken (#1)
Broken and Weary (#2) (2021)

**Agent Morgan Stone**
Stone's Mistake (2021)

# CHAPTER ONE

HEADPHONES CLAMPED tightly over her ears, and the wind whipped flakes of snow around her. Lollie heaved with each step she took, continuing her run even though it was difficult. She had on little other than her jogging clothes, windbreaker, and arm warmers as she jogged through the streets. The snow had only lightly been falling when she'd slammed the door of her house without looking back and going for a run.

Clearing her mind and getting away—those had been the only two thoughts spinning through her head when she'd roughly pulled her workout clothes on. She'd gritted her teeth and bit back the tears as Katie watched her every move with precision. It had been like that for the entire time of their relationship. Katie watched, and Lollie hoped something would happen. Tension and walking on eggshells, nothing but wanting out of the cage she had created.

Breaking free had been her best bet. Slamming the door had been more satisfying than she had anticipated. When she'd first stepped out into the brewing blizzard, her heart had soared in a way she hadn't expected. Lollie was leaving. She'd already emotionally left, but physically, she was ready to get out of the damn dungeon.

When she took in a deep breath, her nose and throat froze. The wind slapped against her cheeks, and she huffed. Lollie stumbled down a curb, raced across the street, and ran partway down the next block. She was certain this time. She was leaving. Katie had thrown her last fit, and Lollie couldn't handle it again.

Coughing and sputtering, Lollie stopped in the middle of the block and put her hands on her knees, gasping for air. She shivered and choked on her spit, the exertion too much with the weather. She shouldn't have run. Catching her breath, she stood up straight and stretched as cold seeped into her limbs. She wasn't sure she could run again. Turning around, Lollie screamed and jumped away.

The sleek black car turned into the driveway she stood on the edge of, the bright lights blinding her. Lollie put her hands up, protecting her eyes. The tire on the passenger side of the vehicle hit the slush puddle at the edge of the street and splashed it all over Lollie. She swallowed and stumbled backward as the car barreled forward, nearly knocking her down.

Brakes ground to a halt as the driver slammed on them, the car sliding on the ice formed in the below freezing temperature. Lollie shivered and bit her lip to prevent the curse words from slipping and the screaming from beginning. She'd already shouted enough that day—she didn't need to do it anymore.

She expected the driver to be a man, for him to be wearing a business suit and rushing home for a dinner his stay-at-home wife was making him and he was late for. Instead, when the driver stepped out of the vehicle, her dark hair danced around her face, her baby-blue eyes locking on Lollie. Lollie gasped, clutched a hand to her heart as the woman raced around her vehicle, sliding on the ice and shouting.

Lollie shook her head, trying to hear what the woman was saying, but she couldn't make it out over the whistling of the wind. She grabbed Lollie's cheeks and tilted Lollie's face toward her. Lollie's eyes widened when she stared into the woman's pale blue ones, seeing the woman's lips move but hearing nothing. Finally her voice broke through.

"Are you all right?"

Lollie nodded.

"I didn't see you at all." The woman put a small amount of space between them, futzing with her jacket and trying to button it up. "The snow is so bad. What are you doing out here?"

"R—running," Lollie answered. Her stomach flipped and twisted, the beauty of the woman before her knocking her for more of a loop than almost being hit by the car. She would have taken the hit—it would have proved she was still alive, still could feel, and probably would have been a better ending to the night she'd already deemed a total loss and failure.

"It's ten below!"

Lollie nodded. "I—I needed to get my head straight."

"God, you must be freezing. Come inside."

She ushered Lollie toward the front door of the house. She could barely see through the snow as it raced in circles and sideways. The click of the lock had her thinking again, and Lollie stepped into the warmth of the house, shivering and running her hands up and down her arms for added warmth.

Lights flickered on in the living room, and Lollie stayed put. Water slid down her legs onto the front rug, and she didn't dare step off it onto the nice hardwood floors. More lights came on. When Lollie looked around, she was greeted with a beautiful house, finely furnished, and definitely well lived in. A newspaper rested half open on the coffee table, along with a few empty and half-full glasses. Blankets lay over the top of the couch, half folded. Taking a deep breath, Lollie exhaled. Heat seeped into her limbs first, and she clenched and unclenched her fingers so she could try and feel them again.

"Here you are."

Lollie looked up in time to see the woman hand her a few towels. She grabbed the top one and pressed it to her face and then her chest, reveling in the warmth she hadn't known she'd lost. Lollie's teeth chattered as she tried to dry the rest of her body.

"Stay here. I'm going to get my stuff from the car and be right back."

All Lollie could do was nod her head and look over her shoulder when the brunette ran out into the storm again. The car came to life as she drove it the rest of the way up the driveway and unloaded grocery bags from the back seat.

Heart pounding, Lollie waited for her to come back in. Katie's blank stare as she left the house, the sound of the door slamming echoed in her mind, and she had to get it out. Whoever this mystery woman was, Lollie was sure she could do that. When she came into the house with the bags in her hand, tiny white snowflakes were stuck in her hair and eyelashes, her cheeks were pink from the bite of the wind, and she huffed.

"Sorry. I'm so sorry, again, really."

"Don't worry about it," Lollie answered. "I'm Lollie."

The woman took Lollie's extended hand and shook it, her cheeks reddening even more than they were before. "I'm Andrea. Again, sorry about almost running you over."

"There's zero visibility. I shouldn't have been jogging in the first place."

"Well, that's for damn sure," Andrea said with a light chuckle. "Let me stick these in the kitchen, and I'll get you some dry clothes to put on. There's no sense in being drenched and cold."

Nodding, Lollie toed off her shoes, jacket, and arm warmers while Andrea disappeared. Shivering, with her hair dripping onto the front mat where she'd put her shoes, Lollie waited patiently. She knew Andrea would be back soon. It was not like she could run away in her own house. Once Andrea came around the corner with more clothes, Lollie let out a sigh.

"Come on. You can change in the spare bedroom."

Lollie stepped off the mat into the living area. The nerves in her stomach calmed, and for the first time since setting eyes on Andrea, she was at ease. Licking her lips, she followed Andrea to the back of the house and down a hallway. Andrea opened the door on the left and went inside, setting the clothes on the bed and giving Lollie a wan smile.

"I'm really sorry."

"You can stop saying that," Lollie answered with a shrug. "I know you're sorry, and it's not going to change anything. It's not as though you tried to hit me or splash me."

"You're right." Andrea's cheeks were red again. "Bad habit. My ex didn't like it either. I blame it on being Canadian."

"You're Canadian?"

Andrea grinned and nodded. "Born and raised. I moved to Chicago for a job and a girl and never left."

"I grew up constantly moving."

"That's a shame."

Lollie nodded her agreement and fingered the pajama bottoms and top Andrea had brought her. They were soft and fuzzy, but most importantly, they were dry and warm. Andrea must have noticed because she backed out of the room, saying she'd let Lollie change.

Shimmying out of her drenched workout clothes, Lollie put them in a heap on the floor. She took off her underwear and bra, noting they were as soaked through as her pants and shirt. It wouldn't do her any good to wear them and get sick, not if she was going to stay there a while. She was dressed in no time and picked up her wet clothes, walking out of the bedroom.

Andrea was in the kitchen, putting away the food when Lollie walked in. Her gaze skimmed Andrea's body, admiring the jeans and shirt that clung to her curves. Lollie licked her lips and stepped forward, warmer than she should have been from simply changing.

"Dryer? I can dry these and head home."

"Nonsense. You're not going home in this. You'll get run over by some other insane driver who insists on going to the grocery store in the middle of a blizzard."

Lollie chuckled and shook her head. Lifting the clothes again, she smiled. "In that case, I'll do a full wash on them."

Andrea's eyes crinkled at the corners when she turned to look at Lollie. "Down the hallway, third door on the left."

"Right. Thanks."

Lollie took her time putting her clothes in the washing machine. She measured the detergent carefully. When she stuffed her clothes into the washer, she noticed something on her pants. It was sleek and dark on the black material. Picking it up, she brought it closer to her face and narrowed her eyes to try and see what the stain was.

Running her finger over it, she pulled it away and saw the red stain. Lollie sighed and looked around for a stain remover. Moving up onto her tiptoes, she grabbed it from the top shelf and rubbed it into the black material, making sure most of the stain lifted before she dropped her running pants into the wash. It was a good thing she'd had the opportunity to wash instead of only drying them.

She set the washer to run and went to the kitchen. Andrea was finishing putting all the groceries away. Lollie leaned against the doorframe, crossing her arms and watching the way Andrea's hips swayed from side to side. She licked her lips and trailed her gaze up Andrea's back just in time for Andrea to turn and face her. Lollie's cheeks flushed, but she smiled and lowered her gaze in an embarrassed pose.

"Would you like something to drink?" Andrea whispered, a husky tone lacing her voice.

Lollie detected it as easily as she detected her own attraction. She was built for listening and reading people. "Coffee?"

"Yeah."

Andrea turned her back, and Lollie resisted walking up behind her and wrapping her arms around Andrea's middle. She wanted to smell her neck, see if she had any special perfume on. Lollie sauntered over to the kitchen table and sat down as Andrea went to work on the coffee.

"You live here alone?" Lollie asked, wanting to know for sure what she was up against.

"Yeah. Have for the last five years. Not really interested in living with anyone either, but I don't mind visitors." Andrea shot a look over her shoulder.

"I just got out of one of those that I haven't really been into for a while, if you get what I mean."

"Finally take the plunge to leave?"

"I did," Lollie said with a sigh. "I should have done it ages ago."

"How long were you two together?"

"Umm...longer than we should have been, that's for sure."

Andrea nodded and leaned against the counter, her hands framing her pose. Lollie's heart rapped twice in her chest, and she stood up straight out of her chair, the feet screeching on the ground as she moved.

Lollie bit her lip and remained still. Her legs wanted to propel her forward and into Andrea, but she couldn't bring herself to do it quite yet. They didn't know each other. They had only met moments ago, and while Lollie wasn't one for wasting time, she did need to build the flirtation up. Glancing over at Andrea, she noticed the strained shirt as Andrea's breathing increased, the dampness of her lips when she licked them, the way her own gaze cast a longing look over Lollie's trim form. Swallowing, Lollie stayed put.

"Coffee?" Lollie whispered.

"Almost ready. How old are you, anyway? I know it's rude of me to ask, but you seem so young."

"Twenty-eight."

Andrea nodded wordlessly before turning to her cupboard and grabbing two mugs. Her shirt rode up when she reached for the glassware, and Lollie's insides turned to jelly, the sweet tingling of arousal pooling between her legs and in her stomach. When Andrea turned back to the coffee maker, Lollie made sure she was standing right next to her.

"And you? How old are you? It's only fair."

Andrea blinked and poured the coffee. "Forty-nine."

Lollie put her hand on Andrea's upper arm, heat searing through her skin in the exact way it had when she'd done the same to Katie. "Age doesn't really matter. You know that, right?"

"Sometimes," Andrea answered, filling her cup with milk at the same time. "What do you like in yours?"

"Black."

Andrea handed the mug over, and they locked gazes. Lollie pulled her lip between her teeth and bit down harshly. It was obvious Andrea was uncomfortable with the age gap, but if anything, it only spurred Lollie on. She stayed close, not moving when Andrea slid to lean against the counter again.

Seduction—it would take seduction and a breath of patience, but Lollie knew she would win Andrea over. She had to. Resting her hand on Andrea and squeezing only once before relaxing her fingers, Lollie drank her coffee with her free hand, not letting Andrea's form leave her line of sight.

"I—I've never..." Andrea swallowed and shook her head. "I haven't been with someone your age since I was much younger."

The side look Andrea gave Lollie incited her. Lollie remained rooted to her spot but entwined their fingers together. It meant Andrea was thinking about them. Lollie had neither said it nor implied it, but Andrea was thinking about being tangled in the sheets. Smiling into her mug, Lollie took one last sip before setting it onto the counter, away from the edge.

"I've always been in relationships with an age gap." Katie's cold eyes flashed through her mind, and she closed her own to force the image away. It wasn't one she wanted when she was trying to start a new relationship. She didn't want to think of the woman who had nearly ruined everything. It had all been Katie's fault anyway.

Andrea looked Lollie straight in the eye, and Lollie's stomach flipped. She was so close to having her. So close to wedging Andrea into the one place she wanted her to be. It was Katie's fault she had left the way she did, and right then and there was not the time to dwell on it.

"Why didn't your last relationship work out, then?"

"Not because of our age difference," Lollie answered. "She had problems that couldn't be resolved, no matter how hard I tried to resolve them."

"I'm sorry."

"Me too."

Lollie switched hands on Andrea's. Scooting her other around

Andrea's back and slipping in closer, she played with Andrea's right hand with her own. She stared down at their fingers, looking at the way they moved as she touched Andrea's soft skin.

"I'd like to kiss you," Lollie whispered, her heart rapping against her ribs and her cheeks flushing. Usually she just kissed, but something was different about Andrea. She usually courted her dates for days or weeks before they let her take them home. Andrea had all but shoved her into the house.

Andrea's lips parted. Lollie knew she was about to protest, so she squeezed Andrea's fingers again and shook her head. Taking a breath, Lollie worked to figure out a backup plan. Being forward with Andrea obviously wasn't working as well as she had anticipated.

"Think about it this way. The storm is supposed to last through the night and into tomorrow. It's Friday. I'm stuck here, unless you kick me out, until at least Sunday. What would a whirlwind weekend of fun and relaxation do for you?"

"N—nothing." Andrea cleared her throat and tilted her chin down to look Lollie in the eyes.

"I'm not asking for forever. At least not yet, and I may never ask for it. But what's the harm in having a little fun?"

Andrea shook her head. Silence lingered between them, the wind howling outside as they stared into each other's eyes. Lollie's muscles ached from running and then from standing still, waiting in anticipation of something bigger. It would be Andrea's decision in this moment, but if Lollie did end up staying longer, she could always try again later.

The hand on her cheek surprised Lollie. She smiled up at Andrea, her eyes widening when Andrea took it a step further. Bending her neck, Andrea brushed her ruby-red painted lips over Lollie's. Lollie closed her eyes, the touch alighting her skin in ways it hadn't done since she'd met Katie—actually, since she'd left Katie.

The urge she didn't want yet blossomed. Lollie ignored it as much as she could. She threaded her fingers into Andrea's dark locks and brought her closer, keeping her there as their mouths gained momentum. It wasn't much longer until Lollie took Andrea against the counter. She made it slow and sensual, wanting to lavish in Andrea's pure body. It wasn't until she tasted Andrea that she realized she had tasted heaven one more time.

## CHAPTER TWO

MORGAN HIT the button on the coffee pot to set the dark liquid brewing. It took a few minutes, but the scent wafted over to her, and she shuddered. She needed that dark brew at her lips immediately. Tapping her short fingernails against the counter, she stared down the coffee pot and willed it to brew faster.

Her day was going to be a busy and boring one, and while she didn't relish going into the office in the middle of a snow storm that was supposed to hit them midday, she knew she had no other choice. There was paperwork to be done, research to be looked into, and conspiracies to test. Swallowing, Morgan glanced down at the coffee, glad to see there was finally enough in the pot for one cup. She'd need at least three to get her brain spinning gears fast enough to work.

She grabbed her favorite mug her mother had given her with *The Golden Girls* on the side of it and jerked the pot back. The hiss of coffee falling directly onto the warmer underneath didn't phase her as she poured her cup. One teaspoon of sugar later, and she was leaning against the counter, sipping the coffee and groaning as its dark roast hit the front of her tongue. It was heavenly.

It was going to be a hellaciously long couple weeks at work. She was due to leave the Chicago office and head south into Kansas on Friday and wasn't planning on being back for at least seven to ten days. Clenching her jaw, Morgan looked around the tiny apartment she was so pleased to call home for less than half the year and sneered. She should probably clean up before she left, that way when she returned she'd have time to relax.

Snorting as the thought ran through her head, she rolled her eyes. Who was she kidding? She didn't relax. The next sip of coffee hit the back of her throat, and Morgan felt the dregs of sleep pushing from her brain and clearing her thoughts. Perhaps she could get a cat. That could be good company for when she was actually at the apartment, and while she was gone, the cat could easily take care of itself.

Morgan shook her head. No, what she needed was a date. It was nearing on a year since she'd gone on her last tried and true date, which had been an utter disaster. Getting called in to help with a homicidal maniac in the middle of a first date wasn't exactly the best way to begin a relationship. She shook her head. Dating apps had failed her and going to the bar had failed her. She was left with little else to make connections for her except friends, which she was severely limited on.

Her coffee mug was halfway empty before she slipped from leaning against the counter and headed for her small bedroom off the side of her living area. The bedsheets were strewn about after she'd forced herself to exit the warmth. She had clothes all over the floor that she had yet to pick up and wash, but it didn't matter. She wouldn't have time until the weekend anyway, which she wouldn't be home for.

Clucking her tongue, Morgan set her coffee down on her night stand and tugged off her loose shirt and pajama bottoms, shucking them to the floor right by her bedside. That way when she returned in the wee hours of the night, she wouldn't have to stumble around to find them. With a fresh pair of undies, the bra she'd worn the last week, Morgan dressed.

The slacks she pulled on were tan and barely fitting as she'd gained a few pounds recently while out of the city for work. Eating out didn't always fare well on her health, but it was necessary in her line of work. Sucking in her stomach so she could button them properly, Morgan moved to her closet to find a blouse. White. She'd go with white today since next week it'd be impossible to keep it clean.

With the material over her shoulders, she buttoned it rapidly, misaligning them and having to start over again. Once that was done, she pulled down a matching suit jacket and laid it on the bed. It had taken her years to get used to dressing in suits for work. She much preferred a uniform. Easier and less thinking.

Morgan left the jacket alone and moved back to her coffee. Holding the mug in one hand, she reached down into her nightstand with the other and pulled out her weapon. She checked it over deftly and slid it onto the bed next to her jacket. Then she took out the shoulder holster after setting the mug down and slipped her arms through, making sure it sat flush to her skin. She preferred it to the holsters that kept her weapon at her hip. This way her gun was always on her, and she didn't have to sit awkwardly in chairs.

Once again, she checked her weapon and slipped it into place on her right side, making sure she could easily access it if she needed. With one more sip at her coffee, Morgan set the mug down once more and finished out her morning routine.

By the time she left her small apartment, her mug had been refilled twice, her thin coat of makeup was in place, her door was locked, and the cold bit at her cheeks. She shivered. Winter used to be one of her favorite seasons until she'd started her job and had to fight crime in the middle of all kinds of weather. After that she much preferred spring and fall.

It took no more than her standard twenty-two minutes to get to the office. The caffeine jittered through her hands as she parked in the underground garage and stepped out into the chill air once more. She locked her vehicle, shouldered her satchel, and headed for the elevators along with the rest of the throng of federal employees.

It'd been her routine for the better part of five years since she'd begun working for the Chicago Office of the Federal Bureau of Investigation. Before that she had been in Houston, which had been sweltering and her least favorite place to live in her entire life. The elevator up to her floor was long, and she desperately wanted another cup of coffee to tide her over. She was about to be nose deep in detective work for the better part of a day, and she'd need her best thinking forward in order to finish it.

As soon as she got to her floor, Morgan stepped out and sniffed. Good, someone had already put a pot on. She dropped her bag onto the chair at her desk in the open office format and headed straight for the coffee pot in the small kitchenette off the west wing and in between two conference rooms. She saw the glorious brew, waiting for her taking.

Morgan filled the mug she'd brought from home near to the brim, added her one teaspoon of sugar, and sipped carefully as she walked to her desk. By the time she reached it, her partner was already waiting for her with a file in his hand.

She smirked up at him and shook her head. "That better not be a break in the case."

"It's not," he chided at her. "It's a potential witness file."

Narrowing her gaze at him, she took a long sip of her coffee before settling at her desk. Pax leaned over her shoulder, sliding the folder in front of her. Morgan popped it open and skimmed the very thin file. In fact, it was only one sheet.

"All this for one flipping piece of paper? Jeez, wasteful much?"

"Says the woman who drinks an ocean of coffee every day."

Snorting, Morgan read the name and age. The girl was young but old enough to at least remember—hopefully—life before her pimp. Morgan rubbed her lips together. "She pregnant?"

"Six months."

"Well, that's an unexpected bonus." Turning to look up at him, she raised an eyebrow. "Why her over Nicoletta?"

"I think this one is more reliable. She's also higher up the chain."

"Really? Pray tell."

Morgan turned in her chair to focus on him, her coffee still blessedly perched between her hands as she sipped at it. The one sheet of paper he'd given her said nothing about where Reilly was in the chain of command. It hadn't even shown she was pregnant, that'd just been Morgan's lucky guess since most girls wanted out of trafficking when they found themselves knocked up. Many, it seemed, didn't want to raise a child in that environment. She couldn't blame them. She wouldn't either.

Focusing on Pax, she let him talk and explain to her why he thought this girl was a much better informant than the last one they'd been contacted about. The field agents were the ones who handled most of it, but she and Pax were in charge of making a lot of connections, and seeing as how this trafficking ring went north to Canada and south to Mexico, there was no one better to deal with it than them.

"She's pregnant," Pax started, stumbling when she'd put him on the spot.

"You said that." Another sip of coffee slid down her throat to warm her belly. "You're gonna have to give me more than that."

"She came to us."

"Oh?" Morgan raised a brow at that and looked over the piece of paper still sitting on her desk top.

Pax leaned against his desk which was right next to hers and rolled his eyes. "She, I guess, made the connection through Nicoletta, at least she claims she did. She's says she's been looking for an out for a while now."

"She's seventeen."

"Yeah, seventeen but experienced. She's been with this guy for ten years."

Morgan froze. "She's the pimp's?"

"Yeah."

"Oh, well...that changes the conversation a bit."

He raised his thick brows at her in a "no duh" stare. Morgan set her coffee down and read the paper he'd given her. There wasn't much to go on in it. No statement, no way to verify whatever Pax was telling her, not to mention nothing of what Pax was telling her.

"Where's the rest of the file?"

"Topeka office is supposed to be emailing it shortly. I just got off the phone with them before you came in. They gave me her name, and this was what I pulled up since you didn't take more than five seconds to get your morning cup of joe."

She sent him a sarcastic look and shook her head. "Excuse me for wanting all the information you claim to have."

"I have it." He jerked his head and then grinned. "I just haven't seen it."

"So you don't even know if this girl is legit."

"Oh, she's legit."

"Whatever. Talk to me with facts."

Pax snorted and pulled out his chair to plop down in it. Morgan watched him out of the corner of her eye as he stretched his arms over his head before hitting the buttons on his mouse to pull up his email. She could readily see he had no new emails. Laughing inwardly, Morgan focused on her own computer and some real hard true facts they did have—from Nicoletta.

They'd been working this case for the better part of a year, amongst other cases. Thus far all the others had come to a completion, and they were left with this one for now. Morgan was ready for some new work to focus on. Human trafficking, especially when it involved young kids, was hard for her to stomach.

The rest of the office filled up slowly with those who were still in Chicago. Other agents from around the country would pop in and out for whatever they were working on and ask for advice here and there. Morgan didn't pay them much mind as she finally got hold of the paperwork Pax had been promised. She wanted to read through the girl's statement with a fine tooth comb, but really, she wanted to meet her in person and get a sense for how truthful she was being and how willing she was to cooperate.

## CHAPTER THREE

MORGAN HAD spent the entire day searching for the girl by some other name than the one she'd given to the agents in Topeka. She'd found nothing. The next morning, she was back at it with a steaming cup of coffee she'd freshly brewed before Pax had arrived.

Blinking at her screen, Morgan bent over and typed onto the computer. The files they'd gotten from Topeka—finally—had indicated Reilly was from somewhere out west in the Seattle area. If she had been part of the pimp's enterprise since she was seven there had to be a missing persons case on file somewhere. She was determined to find it.

Filtering through case after case, Morgan ignored the tedium. She'd worked child abductions before, serial rapists, serial murders, and she'd worked several human trafficking cases. Her preference was anything other than rape. She never enjoyed those cases. Sure, she enjoyed catching the bad guy and locking them up, but the entire topic of rape or sexual assault always felt like a rain cloud covered her head.

Sighing, Morgan glanced up as Pax jerked his chair back and plopped his briefcase heavily on the desktop. She shot him a questioning gaze before leaning up to focus on her obviously angry partner. "What happened?"

"Mel. Mel is what happened." He huffed out a breath and sat next to her, grumbling something she couldn't hear.

"Care to elaborate?"

Pax and his wife had been married fourteen years, and it still wasn't unusual for him to show up miffed about a fight they'd had just before he'd left for the office. Morgan, in some ways, reveled in his life. Married, twin girls, stability, a home. It was everything she didn't have and only some things she wanted.

She'd known Pax since before he married Mel, had been the best man at his wedding even, so she knew the ins and outs of their issues. When he shot her a look, Morgan chuckled. "Forget to take out the trash?"

"One flipping day, that's all I wanted."

"Wanted for what?" Morgan turned to her computer screen, deciding she wouldn't waste all her energy on placating him in his foils.

Pax grunted. "I wanted to go golfing."

"Since when do you golf?" She furrowed her brow and pursed her lips. "And who the hell do you golf with?"

"None of your business."

"Wait. Hold on. You don't golf. What did you really want to do?"

"It doesn't matter," he muttered, powering on his computer and clenching his jaw.

Morgan turned her lips to the side as she debated whether or not to pursue the topic. Giving in, she pushed slightly away from her desk and faced him. "No. What did you really want to go do?"

"I was trying to set up a renewal of our vows."

"Oh..." Morgan pulled a face. "Really?"

"Yes." He glared.

She laughed softly. "Didn't figure you for the sentimental type."

"It's a surprise, for our fifteenth. Thought it might be nice."

"You thought it would get you out of some hot water for something you did, or you thought it'd win you some bonus points for the future when you screw up."

The look he gave her told her the latter was correct. She laughed again. If he was going this deep in his planning, he was going to have to lie better than trying to go play golf when the man had never swung a club in his life.

"Pax, you're gonna have to learn to lie better."

"I can't lie to Mel, you know that."

"You're going to have to if you want this to be a surprise."

"Can't you—"

"Absolutely not. This is your own fresh hell you welcomed into your brain. You do it. I am not the best friend who plans vow renewals. You're lucky I dressed up for your wedding and showed up."

He grimaced. Ending the conversation, Morgan turned to her computer and continued searching for Reilly's real name and face. She was another hour deep into search when her phone buzzed. Frowning at it, she knocked her head to Pax to see if he was paying attention or not. When he wasn't, she slipped away from their desks and down the hall to a quiet and empty conference room.

"This is Agent Stone," she said, her voice full of confidence.

"Agent Stone, this is Detective Fiona Wexford with the Chicago Police Department. I don't know if you remember me or not."

Oh, Morgan remembered her. She remembered her fondly, the short brown hair that sat just at her shoulders, her deep brown eyes that she knew she could fall into, her slim form, lithe in its athleticism. She'd had crush on her since they'd met over a year before when Morgan had given a talk on identifying serial murderers.

"I remember," Morgan rushed, her voice cracking so she coughed and repeated herself. "I remember. What can I do for you, Detective?"

Morgan stared around the room, silently praying Fiona would drop a case in her lap and she could run with it, that or she was calling to ask her on a date because there was no way Morgan had the courage, even a year out from meeting the tantalizing woman.

"I had a case come up, and something about it reminded me of some things you said in your talk last year."

"Oh?" Intrigued, Morgan sat down and pulled her ever present notebook and pen from her pocket. She definitely wanted to jot down notes for this one.

"Would you be able to meet sometime this week to go over it?"

Morgan rubbed her lips together and stared at the television screen at the end of the room that was turned off. She could meet with Fiona, though she only had two days until she was set to leave for Wichita to deal with Reilly and Nicoletta.

"Are you asking for assistance on a case or an outside opinion on it?"

"For now just another opinion. We're a bit stumped by it, honestly, and could use some fresh thinking."

Nodding, Morgan shoved her notebook into her pocket after clicking her pen closed. "I can meet for lunch in—" she glanced at the watch on her right wrist "—an hour? Does that work?"

"Yes. That would be fine."

Phones rang in the background of the call and the general chatter of a detective's office as people moved around doing their jobs. She thought briefly of a place to meet before shaking her head and going with her usual.

"There's a pizzeria off 66 and Taylor."

"Yeah. I've been there before. Good food."

Morgan smirked. "See you soon."

She hung up and headed to her desk. Pax was still bent over his computer. Morgan slid into her chair and grinned at him. "What?"

"I may have just caught ourselves another case."

"Do tell." He sat up and brushed his arms over his chest.

She shook her head. "I'll know more in a few hours. Going to meet with CPD and see what they have first before I let you in on it."

He frowned. "Fine, but you bring me back a slice."

"That predictable?"

"Oh yeah."

Shaking her head, Morgan did what she hadn't thought of before and took the mug shot of Reilly they did have and put it through their system to reverse her age ten years. Once the rendering was done, she'd run an image search and see if she came up with any hits on that.

While the computer whirred, Morgan gnawed on her lip. Meeting up with Fiona for lunch might have been a bad idea. She could keep it professional for sure, but the problem was on one level, she really didn't want to. Fiona was an enigma, young, dreamy, and probably just like her. Women didn't just go into law enforcement without certain personality quirks. Deciding pursuing any type of relationship between the two would no doubt end in disaster, Morgan shoved the thought from her mind and looked at the image of Reilly at approximately seven years old.

She turned her head to the side and then to the other side as she studied it. She'd seen her before. Where, she had no idea, but she would readily find out. It wouldn't take too long for the computer to do its work. Checking her watch, she realized she'd have to jet from the office to meet up with Fiona. Bidding her goodbyes to Pax, she grabbed her jacket and left everything else behind as she walked to the elevator.

Morgan arrived first, as she had planned. She grabbed a seat near the back where she could look out the front windows and know who was coming and going. Frankie pulled up a chair next to her, grinning when she smiled at him over the menu.

"Why bother?" he asked.

"Bother with what?"

"You know what you're getting."

Smirking, she blushed. "I come here too much."

"Not enough. Waiting on someone?"

"Yes, she should be here soon." His eyebrows rose and fell twice in rapid succession. Morgan shook her head. "Not that kind of lunch date."

"Sure it's not. I'll make sure to put on my best waiter face and cook the best I ever have."

"Shove it," Morgan muttered, smirking when Fiona walked into the restaurant.

Morgan's heart stuttered. Her cheeks heated with a flush, and she had to run her hands through her short and spiked hair to try and cover it and get hold of herself. Fiona gave her a small wave, files in her other hand, as she walked over and slipped into the booth across from Morgan.

"Thanks for meeting me." Her voice was soft spoken, but Morgan remembered her from the talk—she asked direct and good questions.

"Any time. Frankie should be by in a sec...speak of the devil."

"Ma'am." He bowed low, and Morgan gaped at him. This had not been her brightest idea. "What can I get you to drink today?"

Morgan watched as he turned his charm on with Fiona, pulling the pencil from behind his ear with a flourish and spinning and putting it to his notepad to wait for her order. Fiona shook her head.

"Only water please."

Swallowing, Morgan sent Frankie a glare and a roll of her eyes as she ordered her standard coffee in the biggest cup he could find. He snorted at her and went to fill their orders.

"Come here often?" Fiona asked as her hands folded neatly in front of her, her dark eyes cascading down to Morgan's lips and back.

Morgan blanched. "Too often, apparently."

"I always love to find a good hole in the wall place to eat and relax. Makes it that much better when I get to know everyone who works there."

Humming her agreement, Morgan jumped for joy that Frankie was already coming their way with drinks in hand. She took her coffee, glad to have something to do with her hands rather than clenching and unclenching her fists six million times. He had his pencil to his pad again, staring directly at Morgan.

"Huh? What?"

He shook his head. "Eat. What do you want, hunny buns?"

Morgan tossed her head up at an angle and shook it at him. "Not funny. The usual."

Rolling his eyes, Frankie wrote it down. "You could try something new, you know."

"I'm sorry," Morgan interrupted. "Weren't you just here two seconds ago asking why I even bothered looking at a menu and told me to order what I normally do?"

He shrugged. "And for the lady?"

Fiona looked between the two of them, a smile tugging at her lips. "I'll just have what she's having."

He didn't wait a beat before he left again. Morgan growled and sipped her coffee. "Sorry about him. He tends to get moody when I take all his coffee."

Fiona waved it off. "Don't worry."

"So this case you have...?" Morgan asked, leading them away from Frankie and toward the real reason they had met up.

"Yes. It's odd. We can't find any motive or any connection or really any idea of who or what might have happened."

"Mind if I see?" Morgan indicated the file Fiona had brought with her.

Fiona slid it across the table, and Morgan flapped it open. The images inside were certainly gruesome, but they were still done with care. Morgan flipped to the next picture. A middle-aged woman, probably no older than fifty, lying in her bed completely naked.

"Sexual assault?"

"Sex, yes. We haven't been able to determine if it was assault or consensual."

Morgan nodded and filed the information in the back of her head. "Forced entry, anything?"

"No. That's just it. There's nothing. It's like whoever was there is a ghost. They just up and vanished or really never existed before this."

"Any other cases similar?"

"Not in the Chicago area."

Morgan sent her a look over the top of the file and nodded. "Have you checked elsewhere?"

"That's where I was hoping you could help."

Morgan set the photos down. "I could. I'm about to leave town for a case. I'll be gone a week, but I can hand it over to my partner, and he can look into it."

"I'd rather keep this between the two of us for now, if you don't mind."

Morgan's heart fluttered. She couldn't be sure why, but something in the way Fiona said it she thought there might be another reason for their reconnection. "I don't, but you'll have to wait until I get back before I can look into it any further."

"I can wait. We won't be stopping our investigation while you're gone."

"Surely not." Morgan smiled as she saw Frankie round the corner with their two plates, heaping with fresh baked ziti and a slice of everything meaty pizza. "Thanks, Frank."

"Don't call me that," he ordered before turning on his heel and walking away.

Morgan chuckled. "He says Frank is his dad. Hates it."

"Ah." Fiona took a small bite of the pasta while Morgan dove right in to her meal. "I'm not sure if this is a serial case, but something about it says it's happened before."

Morgan opened the file again and stared at the one picture that had the full body of the deceased on the bed. Her eyes were wide open, there was a definite strangulation pattern on her neck, but the way her body was laid set off warning bells for Morgan as well. She flipped to another photo that also showed a full image of the body.

"It was someone who knew her."

"Why do you say that?"

Morgan flipped the photo around and pointed. "She's covered with the blanket, and her hair is not a mess, though I'm sure she probably struggled."

"She did. There's DNA under her nails along with blood."

"Any other injuries we're not seeing in this?"

Fiona nodded and pointed to the deceased's chest. "She was stabbed three times in the heart."

Morgan grunted. "Crime of passion, then."

"Perhaps," Fiona muttered. "Maybe it's just a feeling."

"I always say follow your gut." Morgan glanced up at Fiona, their eyes locking as the pasta was positioned two inches from her open mouth. Morgan's stomach flopped and then flipped before she forced the food between her lips and chewed. She'd seen the heat rise in Fiona's cheeks, noted the blush that ran to her face and down her neck. Holding back her own shudder, Morgan focused on the photos. She would keep it professional, even if it was the last thing she did.

## CHAPTER FOUR

WAKING CLOSE to noon the next day, Lollie stretched her legs and arms, turning on her side to watch as Andrea slept almost soundlessly in the bed next to her. They'd had sex almost all night. Tracing a finger over Andrea's cheek and breast, Lollie watched each movement carefully.

Andrea took deep breaths, a small wheeze coming from her nose every fourth one. Sighing, Lollie got up from the bed, her fingers itching to stop the noise in her annoyance. She tamped down the feeling and threw on the pajamas Andrea had given her the night before. She then headed to the kitchen to make coffee.

She opened each cabinet, her gaze skimming over the contents. Andrea had the good stuff. Whatever she did for work, she must be decently well off. The plates and bowls all matched, the food was packed neatly and organized. It was rare Lollie found a lover who was so meticulous. Perhaps it would last this time.

Biting her lip, she reached for the coffee she found in the cabinet just above the maker. She measured and poured the grounds into the filter before filling the carafe with water. Setting the liquid to percolate, she leaned against the counter and sighed. She could live here. This could easily become a place she called home. Grinning, Lollie went to the refrigerator and grabbed milk and sugar and made herself at home in the open kitchen. She was setting it on the counter when Andrea's bare feet padded on the wood floors and arms wrapped around her middle, tugging her gently.

Lollie sighed and leaned into Andrea's sleep-warm body. Andrea's lips were at her neck before she rested her chin on her shoulder to look over at the counter. Lollie turned slightly to face her. "Hope you don't mind. I'm dreadfully unpleasant without my morning coffee."

"Me as well," Andrea whispered. She pressed a heavy kiss to Lollie's cheek and reached over to grab two mugs from the cabinet Lollie knew they were in.

Once they were on the counter, Lollie turned so they could face each other. Andrea was pressed to her front again, and Lollie breathed a sigh. If Andrea was this clingy after one night of romping, perhaps they weren't a good match. Giving in to what Andrea obviously wanted, Lollie rubbed her lips over Andrea's in an unexciting embrace meant only to satisfy not entice more lust.

"Want breakfast?" Andrea asked.

"Sure." Lollie shifted away as she stared down at the pot of coffee and willed it to speed up its process.

Andrea chuckled. "I don't think glaring at it is going to make it work any faster."

"You know they make ones that have timers. You set them up the night before and then it starts up before you wake up."

Andrea pulled out bacon from the fridge. "I've seen those."

"We could get one." The look Andrea shot over her shoulder told her she'd misstepped. Swallowing, Lollie shook her head. "I meant you could get one. I already have one, obviously."

The grin she sent Andrea smoothed the ruffled feathers, and she focused on the coffee pot, once again willing it to finish so she could drink her elixir of life. After a few more minutes passed, Lollie bounced on her toes as the coffee was finished. She poured them each a cup with a flourish, putting sugar and milk in Andrea's.

The batter was mixed in the bowl, and Andrea put round dollops onto the hot skillet. Pancakes. Lollie's stomach twisted. Classic breakfast. She leaned against the counter until Andrea was finished. Each with a plate in hand and mug in the other, they walked out to the living room where they reclined on the couch, sipping at coffee and nibbling on their breakfast.

The television was on in the corner of the room, and Lollie sat moving her gaze from the screen to Andrea. She was double-checking, wanting to make sure Andrea's focus was only on her and not on anyone else. She kept her eye on every reaction Andrea had to any woman who graced the screen.

As soon as the news anchor came on and her voice rang through the room, Lollie pivoted her gaze back to Andrea's face. She seemed nonplussed, thankfully, so Lollie took another bite of her pancake, but she could already feel the tendrils of jealously raging in her belly. She wished she could turn the television off, but Andrea seemed engrossed.

Swallowing hard, Lollie popped another maple syrup-coated bite between her lips. She wondered briefly if she could distract Andrea with some food play. She'd done that before but hadn't really enjoyed it. Perhaps Andrea would, and then her entire focus would be on Lollie and off the prissy woman on the screen. Lollie wouldn't have their relationship be tainted with infidelity—even infidelity by thought.

When her coffee had run dry, Lollie stood for a refill, making a production of it to get Andrea's attention. Leaning down and kissing Andrea's cheek, she slid her hand to Andrea's fingers and squeezed. "Want more coffee?"

"Yes, please."

Smirking, Lollie took Andrea's cup and headed to the kitchen, the whispers of the news echoing throughout the eerily otherwise quiet house. The wind hadn't stopped pounding against the front door yet, snow falling hours beyond what had been predicted.

She stopped to look out the window in the dining room to the front yard, at least what she could see of the front yard. There was a large mound where Andrea's car was parked, but other than that, everything was white. If she wanted to get out, she'd have to trudge through feet of snow. Tree limbs bowed down from the weight of the wet snowflakes, and there was an odd snow drift that swung around Andrea's front yard and ended—Lollie presumed—on the other side of her car after it wrapped around the back.

There was no way they were going to get the car out without some serious shoveling. Heaving a breath, Lollie filled their mugs with warm liquid. Lollie was glad Andrea had invited her to stay. They could get to know each other while Lollie decided if they were a good match or not. The blizzard was only an added bonus.

With two full mugs, Lollie went into the living room. Andrea had stopped eating and was staring at the television screen. Anger welled up in Lollie's chest, and she dropped the mug in her left hand to get Andrea's attention before she jumped in mock-surprise and spilled the second cup of coffee all over her arm.

The burning sensation hit her fast, but Lollie ignored it as much as she played off it. Immediately her gaze was on Andrea, who jumped up and ran over.

"Damn it!" Lollie said. "I'm so sorry. I just—I tripped and dropped it. God, I'm such an idiot."

"It's fine. It's just coffee." Andrea paused briefly as she surveyed the mess. Walking over carefully, she made sure her bare feet avoided the shattered ceramic and the pool of hot liquid. Andrea disappeared behind Lollie and into the kitchen.

When Lollie looked up to see who it was on the television screen that had captivated Andrea so much, she was stunned into silence. There was a picture of a beautiful woman on the screen, her name scrawled across the bottom. The news anchor's voice echoed, but Lollie couldn't see who was talking.

The woman's picture was of her smiling, her eyes crinkled in the corners as her age betrayed her, and her dark cold eyes staring gracefully at anyone who was watching. Lollie turned her head to the side as she listened carefully. The screen flashed to a video of cops and medics bundled together as the news story broke.

The beautiful news anchor was back on the screen, and Lollie's heart clenched. She spoke rapidly about the victim of a heinous crime. "Ms. Jenkins was a teacher, much beloved. Her students will dearly miss her."

Lollie wildly looked around to see if Andrea was paying attention. Her heart rapped in her chest as fear built in a way it hadn't in years. Worry and fear hit her at once. They weren't supposed to be there yet. Something had happened.

Andrea arrived with towels in hand and bent down by Lollie's feet as she pressed a towel to the hard wood floor, soaking up the spilled coffee. Lollie stepped forward, not watching where she was walking. A shard of ceramic bit into the bottom of her foot, but she was unphased by the pain. She lifted her foot carefully as she took another step.

"Lollie! Be careful," Andrea ordered behind her.

Lollie stopped, but her eyes were still glued to the television screen.

The news anchor continued, "The police were called to the residence after a tree fell in the storm, landing on both sides of the duplex. Ms. Jenkins' neighbor found her and called authorities immediately."

The image went to the news anchor who had a sad look on her face. Her co-host shuffled some papers as he spoke. "They have no solid leads at this time, but they are continuing their search for Ms. Jenkins' murderer."

Lollie's heart fell as relief washed over her.

"It's so sad, isn't it?" Andrea commented. "She lived around here. I guess I should make sure the doors are locked just in case whoever killed her is still in the area."

Lollie nodded. "Yeah, that'd be a good idea. We don't want to end up in the same situation she did."

Andrea stood next to Lollie and touched her arm briefly. "You're bleeding."

"What?" Lollie looked down at her foot. "Oh! I must have cut it."

"Go sit down. I'll look at it in a minute when I'm finished cleaning up here."

Lollie nodded. Her shoulders relaxed as she hobbled over the couch, letting Andrea clean up the mess she had made. Once she was seated, she seemed to catch her bearings again. "Sad that it's still a dangerous world for a woman to live by herself. You'd think our society would have grown beyond ruthless and random attacks by this point. We're supposed to be the world's greatest country, after all."

"One can only hope for that in the future, along with working and fighting for our rights and equality."

Andrea got down on her hands and knees as she cleaned the spilled coffee and broken ceramic. Lollie was only half-focused on the mess and what Andrea was doing as she listened to the news anchors move from the murder story and to the blizzard.

Lollie cursed her luck. She would need to head to a new town sooner than she had thought and hoped. While the house Andrea lived in was nice, it wasn't perfect, and she could already tell she and Andrea weren't hitting it off as well as she had once hoped. The extra rooms in the house were completely unnecessary, furniture didn't match or go well together from room to room, and Andrea still had issues of her own. Lollie bent her foot up on her knee and stared at the blood pooling around her cut. She'd have to take care of that and clean it well before she left. It would only be a matter of time.

Andrea had patched up Lollie's foot with a few butterfly bandaids, and Lollie had hobbled around for hours afterward before she dared put the full weight on it. Andrea had eventually nestled back into the couch with the throw blanket tossed over her legs to keep the chill away while Lollie settled next to her.

A book balanced precariously on Andrea's knee as she read. Lollie tried to distract her by pressing kisses to her neck and sliding her fingers under her shirt. Andrea had giggled, kissed her, but always went back to the book. Giving up, Lollie headed for the kitchen to start in on dinner for the both of them.

As soon as Andrea came in, she knew their night would be perfect. Andrea slipped into the chair at the table, and Lollie dropped a kiss to her shoulder. "Dinner is served."

"How sweet."

Andrea waited until Lollie sat before she grabbed the spoon and sipped the stew. She hummed her pleasure. Lollie took her own sip. It had been far too long since she had eaten a full dinner made at home. She longed for that type of relationship. She watched carefully as Andrea ate, wishing their last meal together wasn't one so filled with good memories. It had been easier with Katie, the arguing and the pain as they fought through that last night.

"Where do you work?" Lollie asked, realizing she didn't even know.

Andrea hummed and nodded as she swallowed. "I work in finances. Simple, but lucrative."

Lollie nodded. "I lost my last job just before the end of the month."

"I'm so sorry." Andrea's hand found hers and squeezed.

The sympathy had been exactly what Lollie wanted. It would deepen their connection, allow their trust to build. Perhaps their relationship could last.

"How's your foot?"

"Much better, thank you. It doesn't hurt at all."

Andrea nodded and took another bite. Lollie mimicked Andrea's movements, but she no longer tasted the sweet stew she'd spent hours making. Instead, she focused entirely on Andrea. The breath in her chest, the way her eyes closed, the sound as she breathed in.

Each wrinkle on Andrea's face told a story. She was over two decades older, but Lollie loved older women. She didn't need to teach them, they just knew how to follow her, please her. They didn't want to play games or ruin a good thing.

Lollie set her spoon down and curled her fingers behind her own ear to brush the hair from her face. She sent Andrea a coy look, knowing it would set her on edge. Older women liked the attentions of a younger woman. They enjoyed her as much as she enjoyed them.

Reaching out, Lollie grasped Andrea's free hand. She set about eating her dinner, wanting to make sure she had a full stomach before she left. They finished eating with Andrea continuously touching Lollie under the table. Before they got to the end of dessert, Lollie pulled Andrea up and pressed a deep kiss to her lips. She swallowed as she ran her hands down Andrea's arms and twined their fingers together.

They only had one more day left, and Lollie planned to make the most of it. Sighing, Lollie nipped at the base of Andrea's neck.

"Bedroom?" Lollie breathed into Andrea's ears.

"Yes, please," Andrea answered, her voice deep with desire.

"I'll meet you there. I just want to start the dryer with my clothes in it."

Andrea pouted, and Lollie's stomach churned at the move. She hated women who used their wiles to get what they wanted. Andrea skimmed her hand down Lollie's side, and Lollie moved into her, wanting it to seem as though she was still completely into Andrea.

"You're staying until tomorrow, though, right?"

"Yes. Until tomorrow. And then the real world beckons."

"It does," Andrea whispered. "I'll have to dig my way out of here."

Lollie bit her lip. Andrea wouldn't be leaving. She liked a woman who stayed home where she could keep an eye on her at all times. Kissing Andrea again, this time quicker than before, she sauntered out of the kitchen. Calling over her shoulder, Lollie ordered, "Bedroom!"

"Yes, ma'am." Andrea giggled as she walked down the hallway, following Lollie until they reached her room. Andrea turned, and Lollie went straight until she got to the washer and dryer.

She picked each piece of clothing out of the washer and checked it over. Everything looked clean, the red stain in her track pants gone. Katie had been damn close to being exactly what she wanted, but it wasn't meant to be. Neither was Andrea. The way she continuously ignored Lollie, her obsession with the news anchor, and her inability to do exactly what Lollie expected was beyond any fixes. Andrea wasn't the woman for her.

Knowing their relationship would be ending, Lollie put the clothes into the dryer, and set the timer to eighty minutes. Pressing the start button, she let out a breath, anticipation making her fingers and toes tingle while her stomach clenched. She had eighty minutes—the timer had been set. It was like it had been with Katie, only then she'd had ninety minutes.

Lollie sauntered to Andrea's bedroom. Andrea was already on her back, completely void of all clothes, legs splayed with her hand between them. Lollie bit her lip and swallowed; the sexy sight almost made her want to change her plans. However, with the timer set, there was no turning back.

Crawling onto the bed, Lollie covered Andrea's belly with kisses. She hummed deep in her throat, drawing in the scent of Andrea's body wash. She swallowed as she moved farther down and bit lightly at Andrea's thigh. "You're so beautiful," Lollie whispered.

Andrea's breath hitched.

"Perfect in every way. I knew we would be good together." Lollie licked the inside of Andrea's thigh and nudged her nose into the soft hair between her legs. She took in a deep breath and grinned. "Smells so good."

"Just...just taste me already," Andrea begged.

Lollie sent her a look and shook her head. "I always like a wanton woman."

Andrea reached down to brush her fingers through Lollie's hair. Lollie dashed her tongue out before swallowing the juices that hit her tongue. "Amazing."

Andrea shivered as Lollie dipped down. Lollie spent the first forty minutes lulling Andrea into a false sense of security. She praised Andrea's body, making her muscles pull and relax in the many ways she had done the night before. They rose and fell on the bed in an age-old rhythm that had them both heaving.

Once the sixty mark hit, Lollie had Andrea right where she wanted her—exhausted and lax in her arms. Straddling Andrea's hips, Lollie bent down and kissed her red lips gingerly. She started slowly, deepening the kiss every few seconds until Andrea's hands were tangled in her hair, and Lollie could feel nothing but the way Andrea squirmed between her legs.

Pleasure ratcheted up a notch, and Lollie couldn't control herself. She swirled her hips against Andrea's stomach, the grinding motion adding so much to the movement Andrea already made. Lollie was on the cusp of her orgasm, the timer was almost up, and Andrea was ready. Skimming one hand up from Andrea's breast to her neck, Lollie latched her fingers hard. Her second hand followed moments later, her grip tightening. Andrea's lips parted in surprise, and her hips bucked up, causing a wave of pleasure to pull through Lollie's stomach to her core.

Andrea clawed at Lollie's hands as she pressed more of her weight down onto Andrea's body and spread her thighs even more. Lollie gritted her teeth, keeping the pressure on Andrea's neck as hard as she could. Andrea turned her body, her hip digging between Lollie's legs, making pleasure coil deep within her. Lollie ground herself against Andrea's hips as she tried to escape. Lollie breathed through the pleasure as she kept her fingers locked in place.

Blue lips greeted her when she opened her eyes after Andrea stopped moving. Minutes had passed, and she continued to grind until the waves of her orgasm pulled her over the edge. The timer on the dryer went off, resounding down the hallway, through the open door and into the bedroom. Lollie stayed seated on Andrea's stomach, her core pulsing and her fingers still around Andrea's neck.

Bending down, she pressed a kiss to Andrea's forehead and smoothed out her hair so it wasn't in her face. Lollie touched their lips together before she got off the bed and wandered around the house, cleaning up her mess. It took her two hours to finish.

After dressing in her jogging clothes, Lollie went into the bedroom where Andrea stared at her, unseeing. Lollie pursed her lips and walked over to the bed, running her fingers over Andrea's chest and cheek.

"It's not because you're not beautiful. You're just not right for me," Lollie whispered. "I'm sorry, but I do have to go."

Andrea didn't move, but Lollie didn't expect her to. Every time she broke up with someone, they always gave her the same cold, blank stare. Taking a deep breath, Lollie walked out of the bedroom without a glance back. She was thankful her departure from Andrea's wasn't as loud or angry as leaving Katie's had been.

She headed to the kitchen and grabbed a knife from Andrea's pristine collection. Heading into the bedroom once more, Lollie straddled her lover and fisted the knife. "You should know better than to break my heart."

Stabbing down in Andrea's chest, Lollie gasped. Joy flooded her belly. It was one of the few times she ever felt true happiness. She brought her hands down again and again and again, making a total of four knife wounds to Andrea's once-beautiful chest.

"Now you'll be marred like I am."

Grunting, Lollie got off the bed. She cleaned the knife good and well, wrapping it in a kitchen towel to bring with her. Lollie then went around the house and collected a few things she might need. She went through Andrea's purse, found her cards and the cash she had missed before. Shoving them into her pockets, she went through the photos Andrea had on the wall in the hallway. Most of them were of other people, but there were a few with Andrea and another woman.

Punching the glass with her fist, Lollie took the picture out. She ripped it in half, dropping the piece of the other woman and pocketing the half that had Andrea smiling at whoever took the photo. It was her memento of their relationship. They hadn't had time to take photos of the two of them together. It had been a whirlwind romance at that.

Sighing, Lollie grabbed Andrea's winter coat and wrapped it around herself. She toed on her shoes and picked up the keys Andrea had left on the hook by the door. Opening Andrea's front door, Lollie stepped out into the falling snow. She locked the door behind her and stared longingly at the car.

It'd take her hours to dig it out, if not another day entirely. Grimacing, Lollie bypassed the car and tossed the keys in the middle of the snow covered yard. They would not find them easily. Trudging through the fifteen inches of snow that had fallen in the last two days, Lollie went to the end of the driveway. She knew the bus wasn't far, and if she could reach it, she could get to somewhere safe and warm. Somewhere she could call her own. Stretching her muscles, Lollie headed down the road, putting her relationship with Andrea behind her.

## CHAPTER FIVE

RUBBING THE end of her pen against her lip, Morgan stared at the image search she'd run. She'd gotten a hit. Opening the file, her heart thudded. Pax was out somewhere dealing with the Topeka office, and she was blissfully continuing their work in a conference room so she'd have to revel in her joy by herself. She bit her lip, dropping the pen onto the table as she stared at the image of seven-year-old Haven Dunne, born August 31, 2004. She was abducted the day before her seventh birthday from the front yard while her father, Rob, had been bringing in the groceries.

It was a story Morgan had read and seen before. It wasn't uncommon for traffickers to follow their prey home from a store once they'd gotten a whiff of an easy take. Rob probably hadn't even known what had hit him. Morgan pulled up the second image that was of an age-advanced Haven Dunne. She compared the image to the mug shot of Reilly. They looked similar enough.

Only a DNA test would prove Reilly was Haven, or Reilly remembering when she'd been abducted, but being at the mercy of her trafficker for the better part of ten years, Morgan had her doubts she'd willingly remember the family she'd left behind. Morgan picked up her phone as it rang and rolled her eyes when her mother's name appeared. Hitting decline, she set the phone down and went to get the papers she printed.

Her phone rang again when she returned. Cursing under her breath, Morgan declined the call. If her mother couldn't understand she was at work and unable to answer every call, she'd have to make sure her mom understood it. The third time it rang, she gave in. Maybe three phone calls in a ten minute window meant there was an emergency.

Answering on a huff of frustration and shoving the phone between her shoulder and ear, Morgan filed papers while she spoke. "Ma, what's wrong?"

Her mother's voice filtered through, her pitch high. "What? Nothing's wrong, baby. I was just calling to check in. I haven't heard from you this week."

Morgan couldn't resist rolling her eyes again. "I'm at work."

"Oh, are you?"

Morgan imagined her mom was pulling the phone away from her ear to look at the time. "I thought I'd caught you before you went in."

"It's eleven. I get to work at eight every day unless I'm out on a call or out doing something else. Really, though, now that I answered, what did you need?"

"I wanted to check in. You know how I like to hear from all my kids every week."

Morgan slapped the paperwork down on her desk. She caught sight of Pax coming through the doors. Perfect. He could be her reason for hanging up. "I'm fine. Sorry I didn't call. Got busy."

"Your sister might be getting married soon. She says she's expecting a proposal any day now."

Narrowing her eyes, Morgan shook her head. "Which sister?"

"Amya, of course."

Morgan snorted. There was no way Amya was getting engaged. Holding back her laugh, she shook her head. Her mom and her wild thoughts were known throughout the family. She always had her hopes up that each of her kids would get married and have two-point-five kids—or preferably nine since that's what she'd done—stay home and stop putting their lives at risk.

None of them had followed their mom's not-so-silent expectations. Licking her lips, Morgan focused. "Well, when Amya does get engaged, I expect I'll be one of the last to hear about it, but I will be there for the wedding."

Chuckling, she smiled at Pax, who walked around the desk and gave her a questioning look. Morgan grabbed the papers and handed them over so he could catch up. Morgan shifted the phone.

"Mom, Pax just showed up. Why don't you call me again when Amya's planning the wedding and let me know when I need to request off, okay?"

"Okay, baby. Just know I love you and miss you. Please come visit your poor old mother soon."

Holding her tongue, Morgan smiled. "I will, as soon as I can plan a vacation."

It was a lie. She knew it. Her mom knew it, whether or not she wanted to admit it, but it was a game they played each and every time they had a call like this...which was every week. She hung up and set the phone down before turning to Pax and crossing her arms.

"Yeah. Did you see this?" Pax asked, eagerly.

"See what?"

Pax flipped the paper he was looking at so Morgan could skim it over. It was a record of all the identifying factors on young Haven's body, which were slim to few since she didn't have tattoos or piercings at seven, but she did have a birthmark on the back of her right calf muscle that spread upward to the back of her knee.

"Well, that'll be helpful."

"Hey, what happened with that detective yesterday? I forgot to ask."

Morgan pursed her lips. "Not much. She wanted an opinion on a case. She doesn't have much to go on. She was at my talk last year about profiling, guess she thought I might be interested, but with only one murder in the books, it doesn't look like a serial case."

"Did you search for similar?"

"It wasn't highly specialized. There could be similar cases, but nothing stood out that would make it special."

"Ah." He leaned in his chair and crossed one ankle over his knee. "So did you look?"

Morgan narrowed her eyes at him. "Yes."

"I knew it." He grinned. "Did you find anything?"

Sighing, Morgan brushed a hand through her short hair and popped open the briefcase at her left. She flipped her fingers through a couple folders before pulling one out. "A few cases that could match up, but not much, really. If this is a serial case, whoever it is hasn't done it much before, if at all. This might just be the first escalation."

"You sure?" Pax took the file from her and flipped through the pages.

"Yeah. It's not anything that's making my radar go off."

He hummed until he got to the second to last case. "I remember this one."

With the paper back in front of her, Morgan nodded her agreement. "Yeah. That one was tough, but they found the killer."

"You're sure?"

"They are."

"But are you?"

Morgan shrugged. "I'd have to look deeper into it and get the rest of the files, something I am not wanting to do right this very minute."

He scoffed. "Special Agent Morgan Stone turning down a potential case? Since when has that ever happened."

"Better buy a lottery ticket. Today's your lucky day."

Morgan grabbed the file and shoved it away. She was done talking about the murder. Fiona hadn't sent her any more information, and it wasn't what she needed to be focusing on. However, Fiona had her interest, whether she wanted to admit it or not.

With a bullet proof vest strapped over her chest, Morgan kept her gun firmly in her hand. The pimp was holed up in the house in the suburbs of Wichita, there were at least a dozen girls inside that they knew of, Reilly being one of them, and quite a few more johns. Clenching her jaw, Morgan waited for the go ahead.

SWAT was in place, FBI had its agents settled around the house, local PD joined them. The joint task force was about to make national headlines—hopefully. It had been a long drive to Wichita the morning before, but Morgan had made it gladly. They were going to take some bad people off the street, and she couldn't be more excited.

Her radio clicked once and then twice. It was go time. SWAT went to the front door and surrounded the house. Side doors and windows were covered. Morgan followed slightly behind them with her vest that identified who she was and gun drawn. She'd let the experts move in ahead of her and do their thing before she did hers.

Her heart pumped wildly as she took each step. Shouts rang through the air as SWAT called forth their presence. The bangs of the entry ram at the front door shocked through her chest and reverberated down to her toes. It was two hits, and they were in.

Screams echoed into the cool dusk air, women and men. Bullets fired. Morgan stepped forward, keeping her eyes pierced for any runners. She waited with baited breath as some women were led out and screamed at to lie down face first on the grass in the front lawn.

Morgan gripped the zip ties at her waist, keeping her gun in one hand as she threaded the hands of the first girl through the loops and jerked it tight. "Stay here. Don't move."

The girl nodded, tears streaming down her cheeks. She couldn't have been more than fifteen. She went down the line, detaining anyone who was brought out of the house. More bullets fired. Morgan dipped her head down and pushed her weapon up to aim it at the front door.

She knew the sound was coming from inside, but without being there herself, she couldn't see who was firing or why. Grunting, she stayed put, one knee pressing into the damp grass as it soaked through her slacks. She kept her arms firmly raised. She wasn't going to give any of the perps a chance to shoot at her.

It took time, but SWAT filed out of the house, one after the other with perps already restrained in front of them. One of them, Morgan recognized as Reilly's pimp. He wasn't the one who had taken her all those years ago, but he was the one she was bonded to.

The captain of the SWAT team came out last. "House is clear."

Sneering, Morgan stood up and holstered her weapon. She let out a breath and glanced down to the girls in front of her and the men who were essentially raping them. Her heart rate slowed. Now they just had to go through the house.

The pimps were shoved into separate vehicles to keep them apart after they'd been patted down. The girls were debriefed while Morgan strolled into the house. It was a disaster inside, not that she expected any less. Trash was strewn about, there was a heavy scent of cigarette smoke that permeated everything, and no matter how hard she tried to see, it was so dark she knew she was missing something along the way.

Toeing her way through the living room, Morgan noted the lines of coke on the coffee table, the bags of it in the kitchen stacked high, no doubt ready to be packaged for resale. She let out a breath and headed up the stairs to the second floor. There were three bedrooms up there, each of them had housed three girls. Reilly had been given the downstairs bedroom where she and her pimp lived. No one else was allowed to touch her.

Pushing the sickening feeling from the pit of her stomach, Morgan went into the first room. It was definitely a kid's room. There were toys around it along with dress up clothes. The bed was unmade, but there was a stench of sex to it she tried to ignore. Letting out a short breath, Morgan squashed the sensation of bile rising from her stomach to her throat. She would not allow herself or them the courtesy of that much disgust.

It took them another seven hours to search the house and bag all of their evidence. By the end of the night, which was really the next morning, Morgan was beat. She crawled into her bed in the hotel room, closed her eyes, and relaxed into the soft covers. She was expected in the office in the next four hours, dressed and ready to start in on the evidence collected, interrogations, and even more investigations as they continued to make connections to the higher ups in the trafficking ring.

She just had to catch a few hours of sleep. That was all she needed.

Morgan lay on the bed for a good two hours before she gave up. Not only had the extra coffee wired her for the night, but she couldn't shake the images of the girls they'd taken into custody. Getting out of the bed, she sat at the small desk in the corner of the hotel room and pulled out her computer. If she couldn't sleep, she might as well make a profile for Wexford.

She pulled out the file from her bag. Taylor wouldn't be happy she was spending time liaising with the Chicago PD on a case that wasn't going to end up being hers, but she wanted to do it anyway. Morgan stared at the file, full with whatever Wexford had given her. She analyzed all the evidence before she even wrote down one word of the profile for the potential murderer.

"Man, most likely in his mid-thirties."

She typed it into her computer and clenched her jaw.

"No previous criminal history."

Morgan pulled the picture out of the woman dead on her bed with the blanket up to her chest. She cocked her head at it and bit her lip, gnawing on the inside before she sighed.

"Possibly romantically involved with the victim."

Throwing the picture onto the desk, she leaned back. This was near hopeless. She didn't have the full case file, and it was impossible to write up a profile without one. She didn't have forensics, and there'd been barely any time passed since the murder itself. She honestly couldn't fathom why Fiona was insisting there was more to this than a crime of passion. Giving up, Morgan headed to the bathroom to shower and get ready for her day. She'd just get a jumpstart on her own paperwork rather than someone else's.

After a week in Topeka and Wichita, Morgan was done with Kansas. There'd been a storm to hit Chicago over the weekend, and she struggled to keep her car on the road as she drove back to the Chicago office two days before she'd originally planned. Taylor wanted to talk to her. Reilly was safe in custody, and her parents were coming in from Tacoma, and Pax...well, he'd jumped ship and took a plane home to see his kids sooner.

As she crossed the border into Springfield, Illinois, glad to finally be back in her home state, her phone buzzed. Glaring at it, Morgan didn't answer. When it rang for the fourth time, she cursed under her breath and picked it up daring it to be her mother again.

"What?" she answered with a bite, her tone far more angry than it should have been.

"Did I catch you at a bad time?" Fiona's smooth voice hit her ears.

Immediately, Morgan's shoulders eased, and her stomach jumped with anticipation. Backtracking, she white knuckled the steering wheel and took a deep breath. "Just driving back to Chicago-land. What's up?"

"There's been another murder."

"You're kidding."

"No. I told you I had a feeling about this one."

Morgan really wanted to curse, but she and Fiona didn't have that kind of relationship yet. Keeping it professional would be best. Heaving a breath, Morgan glanced at the clock on the dash of her car. "I'll be back in like four hours if the roads stay clear, but if they're not—"

"They're not."

"Wonderful," Morgan muttered. "Then it'll be longer before I'm back. I can meet with you tomorrow at the crime scene if you want, but I'm going to have to let my superior officer in on what I'm doing."

"I don't want you to take over this case."

"You might not have a choice. If there are other murders outside the state, it's my jurisdiction."

"You said yourself there were no other murders."

Morgan snorted. "That we've found yet. This could very well be more than just the second one."

Fiona hummed. "It's mine until I say so."

Clenching her jaw, Morgan steered through a pile of slush. "Sure, whatever you say. Tomorrow?"

"I can get you in."

Morgan held back her retort. If she wanted in on a crime scene, she would be there without anyone holding her back. Honestly, that'd been why she'd gone with the bureau instead of becoming a local officer—that and profiling was her preferred placement.

Realizing she hadn't answered Fiona, Morgan cleared her throat. "Tomorrow morning."

"Yeah."

Morgan let out a breath about to hang up when Fiona's voice caught her attention.

"Forensics came back on the rape kit for Jenkins."

"Anything interesting?"

"She had sex before she was killed, we knew that."

"And?" Morgan sensed there was more to the story. Why she hesitated, she had no idea, but she didn't relish staying on the phone while driving through the ends of a snowstorm any longer.

Fiona sighed. "She had sex with a woman."

"No joke. That changes some things in the profile I was building for you."

"I thought as much."

"I'll bring it with me in the morning."

"Sounds like a plan."

Morgan hung up without saying anything else. Her mind whirred with the new information Fiona had ditched in her lap. A woman—that certainly changed things. If this person was a serial murderer and not just doing this in a crime of passion, then her whole profile would have to change.

Building it in her head, now that she had a little more information to go on, Morgan drove the rest of the way home. By the time she got to the bureau's office, she was warmed from the heater in her car, sore from sitting for ten plus hours, and ready to dive face first into a vat of coffee.

Taylor waited for her as soon as she pushed through the elevator. Groaning inwardly, Morgan bypassed the coffee and went straight to his office. The verbal report she gave him was far longer than the one she'd given on the phone. They talked the ins and outs, what they could improve on next time. He nodded at her to dismiss her, and Morgan was just about to leave before she turned around.

"Hey, actually, I may have another case that's coming our way."

"Oh?" he prompted, resting in his chair with his arms folded.

Morgan sat back down. "Week or so ago I was contacted by CPD about a murder. They wanted a second opinion, nothing more. I just got a call on my drive back there was a second one."

"You think it's the same person?"

Morgan shrugged. "I haven't looked at the new case yet, but I plan on meeting up with CPD tomorrow to go over the crime scene and the evidence they've collected so far."

He nodded. "When?"

"In the morning. I'll leave Pax here. He can get a bit bullheaded if we don't have the case yet."

Taylor nodded. "CPD think it's the same person?"

"I'm not entirely sure yet. I think they might suspect it, but I don't know what evidence they have connecting the two."

"Check it out. Meanwhile, this trafficking case isn't closed."

"I know. I'm still on it."

"This one takes priority, Stone."

"Got it." She half-saluted to him before bowing out of his office and going to her own desk. She was about to spend the next five hours writing reports and working up what she could of a profile on this murderer without seeing a second crime scene. It would no doubt take her into the middle of the night.

## CHAPTER SIX

WHEN SHE pulled up outside the address Wexford had given her, police tape still surrounded the house. She was first to arrive. There had clearly been a car parked in the driveway, but it was gone, leaving a gaping hole with no snow.

Morgan headed up to the front door. She loved when she was the only one at crime scenes, when she could spend the time in thought. She walked from window to window peeking in. It was clear CPD had been through the house, but other than the standard search, it looked decently intact.

"Find what you're looking for?"

Morgan jumped and put a hand over her heart as she spun around. "Jesus! You scared the shit out of me."

Fiona grinned, and Morgan's heart skipped a beat. Her smile was near perfect. She had a little dimple to the side, but her grin was uneven, the right side pulling tighter than the left. Morgan echoed her smile and shook her head.

"Don't you know better than to sneak up on law enforcement?"

"Well, I called your name. You must have been really focused on whatever you were thinking."

Morgan turned to the house. "Got the code? It's still freezing out here."

"Yeah." Fiona pushed the buttons on the door lock CPD had put on the house. She handed Morgan shoe covers before she donned her own and walked in. Morgan leaned against the door frame, shoving the covers over her shoes.

Even with the door shut, it was cold. Morgan tried to avoid looking at Fiona's ass as she walked ahead. Wexford led the way into the kitchen, and Morgan followed. "There wasn't anything out of the ordinary except where the body was found."

"Which was where exactly?" Morgan peeked in the cabinets with a gloved hand, letting the doors snap shut.

"In the bed. Body wasn't moved."

"Rape kit?"

"Done, but again, not sure if it was rape or consensual."

Morgan walked toward the living room. Fiona had been right, not much had been touched in the common areas. Two people had been in the house, that was clear. Morgan walked around to the other side of the couch, looking from the couch to the chair. She imagined their victim would sit on the couch with the book and the blanket strewn over her lap, and their murderer would have potentially sat in the chair. It gave them more power. They could see everything from there, what the victim was doing, outside the windows, into the kitchen, and the front door.

"Suspecting the same woman?"

Wexford shrugged. "I am, but my captain wants to wait until there is physical evidence to back it up."

Morgan grunted and pointed down the hall. "Bedroom?"

"Yeah, this way. The knife used to stab the woman in both cases is also unaccounted for."

"So whoever murdered them took it."

Fiona nodded. "But Jenkins wasn't stabbed to death."

"Oh?"

"Strangulation and suffocation."

Morgan pursed her lips and nodded. She pushed the door open to what she assumed was the main bedroom. Walking in, it looked far more like an actual crime scene than the rest of the house. The bed had been stripped, but the mattress was still there and stained with blood. Drawers were pulled out and strewn on the floor.

Fiona stopped next to her. "Most of the mess is from CSU."

"Wish I'd been here the other day. The body, how was it found?"

Wexford grabbed her phone, pulled up a photo, and shifted so Morgan could look. Morgan took it from her fingers, their skin brushing and sending shockwaves up her arm. Morgan ignored it and looked at the image and walked around to the side of the bed so she could better visualize the body.

The victim was much like the other, this time no blanket on top of her, but if she wasn't dead, she very well could have been sleeping. Her eyes were closed, there were obvious strangulation marks on her neck, and the stab wounds to her chest were dead giveaways.

Furrowing her brow, Morgan counted. "There's four."

"Four what?"

"Stab wounds. There were three last time."

"Yes."

Morgan made a noise in the back of her throat. She handed the phone back to Wexford and stepped closer to the bed. "What's missing from the house?"

"Nothing really. The knife, some credit cards, probably some cash if she had any. Look, are you going to let me in on what you're thinking or was it a total waste of time to bring you out here?"

"She knew whoever it was," Morgan ignored Fiona's question.

"The woman."

"If the test comes back, yes, the woman."

"It's the same person."

Morgan sighed. "It could very well be, or it could be someone else. Did this victim have anyone in her life? A boyfriend or something?"

"No. She was single, worked her forty hours a week, had very little life outside of that. She wasn't a busy body like Jenkins."

"So how did they meet?"

"What?" Fiona's voice was sharp.

Morgan closed her eyes. "How did they meet? Where's the connection? If it's the same killer, how are the victims chosen?"

"You can't deny that these cases are similar."

"I'm not." Morgan put her hands out. They'd reached the hallway between the kitchen and the living room. "I'm not denying these cases are similar, but there's a severe lack of connection between them, lack of evidence."

"I'm working on it," Fiona growled, her face set in anger.

"I know. I know you are. These things take time. If this is the same killer, and we are assuming it is the woman who had sex with Jenkins prior to her murder and sex with this victim, then we also have a type. Middle-aged, brunette women who live alone."

Fiona bopped her head from side to side. "They both also wouldn't have been found for weeks."

"What do you mean?"

"Jenkins had a tree fall on her duplex. The victim here, Andrea Phillips, had a scheduled maid service yesterday—which was only scheduled monthly. The worker found her."

"Some shit morning for that job."

"Yeah. Agreed. But Andrea had taken the week off for vacation, so really, it's our luck she was found so soon."

Morgan hummed. "Whoever this is, they are meticulous. There's signs there is a second person here, but everything is so domestic it could be the killer or it could not be. There's hardly anything missing from the house, only necessities. If it is one in the same, then whoever is killing these women is doing it for the basics—shelter, food, heat. In the middle of a snow storm this weekend? I have no doubt the killer needed a roof over their head to wait it out."

Fiona cocked her head to the side and nodded. "I was thinking the same."

Morgan headed for the door, opening it and walking outside. She pulled off her booties and gloves, shoving them into her pocket along with her hands. Wexford locked up the house and turned to Morgan.

"Who took the car? You are the suspect?"

"We have it. Took hours to dig it out."

Morgan snorted. "Figures."

"Thanks for coming."

"Any time, but I gotta tell you, if there's a third one, we're working together fully. If there's a third one out of state, it's mine completely."

Fiona grinned. "I'd expect nothing less."

Morgan's heart rose to her throat again. She coughed to clear it, sputtering as she tried to find words. Business she could talk, but she wanted so much more than business with Fiona. Wexford took a step closer, her hand on Morgan's arm.

"You okay?"

"Uh, yeah. Just a frog. It's been a long week."

"Where'd you go? You said you were driving back yesterday."

"Had an operation to do."

Wexford's eyes widened. "Were you in Kansas? Was that your case?"

Morgan's eyebrow lifted. She didn't answer as Fiona stepped even closer. Her heart thudded hard. She didn't know what possessed her, but leaning to her side, Morgan pressed her mouth to Fiona's.

The kiss didn't last long. Morgan jumped back, her eyes wide and fear settling in the pit of her stomach. Looking wildly to her car, Morgan begged for a phone call, a distraction, something, anything.

"That was...I don't...Uh..." Morgan bit her lip. "I don't know why I did that. I should...I should go."

Booking it for her car, Morgan escaped and didn't wait for a response from Wexford. She didn't want to hear or see the reaction. Putting her car in drive, Morgan headed to the bureau, ready to dig in to some old case files and see if she could find another one that matched the two here.

Morgan's head took a beating as she stared at her computer screen for the fifth hour in a row. She'd finished up her report of Wichita and had sent it in to Taylor. However, since returning from her little excursion with Wexford, she was doing her damnedest not to think about it.

Sighing, she rubbed her neck, her muscles tense from leaning over the desk and staring at a screen, not to mention the horrible mistake she'd made hours before as they were leaving the crime scene. Who kisses someone at a crime scene? Who kisses someone they don't even know is single? It was unbelievably unprofessional of her to do that.

Cursing, Morgan doubled her efforts on the computer. She needed one more case to take it over from Chicago Police and make it hers. That would not be a fun conversation with Wexford. In fact, it might be the most awkward conversation she'd ever had considering that morning, but after seeing the crime scene, Morgan was convinced whoever had done these two murders had acted before.

Clearing her throat, she stretched her back, thankful when Pax slipped her a refill on her coffee. She grinned at him and shrugged, turning in her chair. "Man after my own heart. You better be careful, brother. I've got some mean claws."

"I think Mel might have something to say about that."

Morgan chuckled as she took a sip of the piping hot liquid. "She might, or she might not."

"What's that mean?"

Grinning broadly, Morgan flushed. "Wouldn't you like to know?"

"Stone..."

She laughed out loud. "It's nothing. You find any cases that might match up? I'd really like to take over the investigation if we can."

Pax shook his head. "Not yet. I've mostly been going over Reilly's interview."

"Oh...that was an interesting one." Morgan set her coffee down and focused on the computer.

"It was. You did an excellent job getting what we needed."

"Aww, thanks, big guy."

He glared. She grinned again. Teasing him was far too much fun, and she never wanted to miss an opportunity to do it. Morgan clicked at her screen, closing down the current cold case she'd been staring at and opened the next one.

"Oh, now this is interesting." Shifting in her seat, Morgan moved closer to the screen and pulled up her reading glasses she was supposed to wear but refused half the time.

"What is it?" Pax leaned over her shoulder.

"Murder, mayhem, lust. What else?"

"Shove it. What's the case?"

"Woman murdered in her apartment. Very similar to these other two. She was left on the couch, though, not the bed. Strangled after sex or during—that's unclear in any of the cases."

"Yeah, get on with it."

Morgan shot him a glare. "Shush, and I will."

Pax wisely kept his trap shut.

"Stabbed once in the heart."

"That's different."

"It is, but is how many times they've been stabbed really relevant or more the fact they've been stabbed after being strangled?"

"Point taken."

Morgan returned to the screen. "I think this might be it."

"Why?"

"Knife is missing. Credit cards missing. Witness—who was the woman's neighbor—said she'd had a girlfriend move in with her a week or two before and had never seen her before."

"Girlfriend?" Pax sneered.

"Fuck off. I don't want to hear any damn comments about lesbians otherwise I will send you straight to Taylor's office for sensitivity training...again."

Pax put his hands up. "I haven't said a word."

"It was your tone."

"You said the first victim here had sex with a woman prior to her murder."

"Yes."

"So that's a pretty good connection, and if it really is because these women are gay, then it's a hate crime."

Morgan swiveled her chair so she could look at him, her hand not moving from the mouse. She cocked her head to the side. "Never thought I'd hear you start that as the conversation."

He smirked. "Old dogs can learn new tricks too, you know."

"Mmmhmm," Morgan answered, unconvinced. "If this killer is targeting lesbian women, then yes, it's a hate crime as well as a serial murder. If this is the third case...well, the first, actually."

"Really?"

"Happened over three months ago. They have no new leads according to this report, but that doesn't mean much. Filed reports are so behind sometimes."

Morgan straightened her back and printed out the file. Laying the papers out, she stared down at them as she stood.

"What is it?"

"I don't know...something feels different about this one."

"What about it?"

"I don't know, Pax. That's why I just said I don't know." Morgan rolled her eyes. "I think it's enough to take over the investigation, especially after we call the detectives in...oh...Grand Rapids, Michigan. Yup, this will be ours."

"I see that glint in your eye."

Morgan turned to him, bouncing in her boots. "This could be the case of the decade, you know."

"It could be. Or it could be a dud. Why don't you focus on finding the killer first?"

Morgan snorted. "Always the party pooper. Want to go with me to talk to Taylor after we call Grand Rapids?"

"Absolutely." He grinned. "We need something new to entertain us for a bit."

She picked up the phone sitting on her desktop and dialed the number for the detective on the case.

It had been three days since she'd seen or heard from Wexford. Fiona had called her—once—and she'd promptly sent the message to her voicemail. Wexford had wanted to know if she had any updated information on a profile yet. Morgan had finished her profile, but she'd had far more information than Wexford did, unless Fiona had managed to find the case in Grand Rapids, which she had her doubts. Drawing in a deep breath, Morgan parked her car outside Wexford's building and let out a breath. Pax was just behind her in his government issued SUV. He was out of the car first, shivering in the cold as he came around to her car.

"Ready?" he asked.

"No," Morgan confessed. She looked warily at the building, and Pax narrowed his gaze at her.

"Why? You've never been one to avoid a case."

Sighing, Morgan put her head against her headrest and turned off her vehicle. "It's not the case I'm avoiding."

"What?"

Ignoring him, Morgan got out of her car, locked it, and walked toward the building.

"You can't just say that and walk away."

But she could, and she knew it. Morgan plowed through the front doors, checked in with the front desk, and went to the elevator. She hit the button for the floor she knew Wexford's office was on. What would she even say to Fiona? She couldn't fathom all that coming out in front of Pax. Sure they'd been best friends for twenty years, and as much as he loved his wife, she knew Mel was not as straight as Pax thought she was. They never talked about it, and thus Morgan never talked about herself. Pax only heard stories of her dates with men, she gladly skipped over dates with anyone else: queer, lesbian, trans, non-binary, or otherwise without labels. And there had been a lot of dates.

Drawing in a deep breath, Morgan wished the elevator would drop to the basement and swallow her. Normally when she went into a relationship, she had a plan. It was typically a one month stint, have some fun, and come out it the other side with some entertainment and no broken hearts in sight. Fiona was different. She'd had a crush on her from a distance for the better part of a year. Having the chance to work with her had only intensified her feelings. After her divorce, there was no way she was going to enter into a relationship with another woman on the long term and certainly not a woman who was easily twenty years her junior.

The elevator doors opened. Pax walked out in front of her and turned back with a questioning gaze when she didn't move right away. Jerking to a start, Morgan stepped through the doors, her stomach twisting. She had to calm and control herself. She trained for things like this, trained to go into situations no one else would dare to dream of entering, and yet, here she was a mess of emotions because of one stupid and impulsive kiss.

Pax grabbed her arm as the got to the door to the offices. He pulled her to the side, towering over her. "Okay, seriously, what is wrong with you?"

"Nothing. Just drop it." She growled and shifted around him.

Wexford saw her immediately, her lips parting and her stare hardening. Morgan grimaced. Fiona knew why she was there. The FBI didn't just show up in a lowly homicide detective's office unannounced without good reason. Holding her breath, Morgan strolled to Wexford's desk. Wexford stood up, her back rigid, and her cheekbones high and set with defensiveness.

"Detective Wexford..." Morgan started.

"Special Agent Stone, to what do I owe the pleasure?"

Holding the breath in her lungs, Morgan looked to Pax. "We found another case."

"You're taking my case, you mean."

Inwardly cursing, Morgan shifted her weight to her left foot and attempted to soften the blow. "In essence, yes, we are taking over your investigation."

Wexford slammed her palm on her desk and leaned over, her nose close to Morgan's as her anger permeated the room. "We'll see about that."

She took off to the next office over. Morgan drew in a deep breath and let it out slowly as she turned to Pax and gave him a wan smile. "Well, that went better than I expected."

"Really?" He raised an eyebrow.

"Yeah. I thought she might hit me."

"Why would you think that?"

"Long story." Morgan crossed her arms, indicating she didn't want to talk about it. He took the hint and dropped the subject.

They both stood in silence while they waited for Wexford to reappear from her captain's office. Morgan could readily make out Wexford shouting and her supervisor attempting to calm her down. She knew when Wexford came back out of that room it was not going to be pleasant no matter what happened. Any chances she had at a relationship—which she had probably ruined days before—were certainly out the window now.

Wexford came out and glared Morgan down. Morgan's heart

plummeted. Yup, there was no chance in hell they could even fathom a relationship. Wexford stomped over to her desk, pulled out a box and shoved papers into it, glaring at Morgan every time she looked up.

Pax remained—thankfully—silent. Once Wexford finished, she shoved the box into Pax's hands and stepped back. "There. You have everything I have."

"I would like to talk to you for a minute," Morgan chanced. "In private, if we could."

"No."

"Please, it'll only take a minute."

Snorting, Wexford spun on her heel and headed toward a conference room. Morgan shot Pax a glance, telling him to stay put. She followed Wexford, her head hanging toward the ground. As soon as they were in the room again, Morgan put her hands together in front of her so as not to piss Wexford off any more.

"I'm sorry it happened this way, but you knew if we found another case it would become ours."

"Where's the case?"

"Grand Rapids."

Wexford's lips thinned tight in anger. "That's the only other case?"

"For now. Look, I don't want bad blood—"

"Should have thought about that before the other day."

Morgan's heart clenched. "I...I'm sorry about that. I don't know what I was thinking. Well, I know that I wasn't thinking is more like it. It was unprofessional and uncalled for."

Wexford let out a sigh. "What's the profile you have? I'm assuming you've finished it out."

"Yes, I have. Woman, somewhere around twenty to thirty, not a lot of ties to home. Most likely abused as a kid by an older woman. She may be a lesbian, but that's unclear. She targets older, single women, women in their forties to fifties. Women who are open to lesbian relationships, women who may reflect an image of her abuser."

"So this is a hate crime."

"It could be, but again, I'm not convinced she's killing those in the community because they are in the community. I think it's likely she's a lesbian."

Wexford's shoulders loosened, and she leaned against the conference table with her arms crossed. Her eyes locked on Morgan's when she asked her next question. "Think she's still in Chicago?"

"No."

"Where's she headed?"

"Out of state would be my guess. She's had two close calls here and needs to move again."

"What does she want?" Wexford put her chin in her hand. "What's her motive?"

"It's as simple as shelter, food, and heat. She needs a place to stay, she uses the space until she has to leave, and then she moves on to the next place. She's trying to find a home."

Rocking back, Wexford shook her head. "She could go after anyone."

"Yeah, she could, and she will." Morgan stood still, not quite sure where their conversation was going, but at least Wexford wasn't raging mad anymore. "About the other day, I'm sorry. I shouldn't have kissed you."

Fiona's gaze shot to the open door. Morgan swallowed, following her gaze and then looking back at Fiona.

"I wanted to apologize."

"Don't," Fiona said. She stood and walked closer to Morgan. Carefully and subtly, Fiona reached out and grabbed Morgan's fingers, squeezing. "It was unexpected but not unappreciated. Thank you."

Without another word, Fiona left the room. Morgan let out a breath she hadn't known she was holding and followed Wexford. It didn't take her long to round up Pax and the box and head back out to their vehicles. She'd easily spend the next eight to ten hours going over all Wexford's notes.

## CHAPTER SEVEN

LOLLIE TURNED the heat down in the car as it sweltered. The roads cleared up decently in the last day or two, but there was still snow on the ground. The farther south she drove, the less of it she saw. She'd stopped a few times on her drive, trying to find some new fling that may hold her attention. Her break up with Andrea had been rough. She'd held out hope until the last minute that they'd be together.

It had been a whirlwind of an almost perfect weekend. Sighing, she pulled into a coffee shop on the outskirts of St. Louis, hoping to juice up on caffeine. Parking and heading inside, Lollie waited in line at the counter. There were very beautiful women inside. The barista worked behind the counter at a break neck speed. Lollie must have come in during an unexpected rush hour or something. Glancing at her watch, she noted the time. It was early afternoon, but still, the line was unexpectedly long.

The woman in front of her smiled as she watched Lollie check her watch again. "Are you going to be late somewhere? You can go ahead of me if you need to?"

"Oh, no!" Lollie gave her a gorgeous grin. "I was just wondering why the line was so long at two in the afternoon. I didn't think there would be that many people here."

"I know, right?" the woman smiled, a flush tinging her cheeks.

Pleasure built in Lollie's belly. Swallowing, Lollie extended her hand forward. "I'm Lollie, by the way. I just moved to town."

"Oh really? I'm Samantha. I've lived here my whole life. If you need any tips on where the best places to eat are, I'm your girl."

Lollie chuckled. "I'll certainly take you up on that offer."

The line moved up, and there was only one person in front of

Samantha to order. Lollie, eyed her up and down. She was beautiful. In shape, for certain, her curves slight. The parachute pants only added to her mystery and intrigue. Samantha had her long dirty blonde hair pulled back into a pony tail that sat in the middle of her head. Lollie's fingers itched to tug on it. She wondered if Samantha would cry out in pleasure if she did.

"You're up," Lollie whispered as Samantha moved to the barista.

"Thanks." Samantha grinned.

She was a bit younger than Lollie's normal interest, but she was still older than Lollie herself. Lollie bit her lower lip as she listened to Samantha place her order. Before she could pay, Lollie stepped up. "I'll get hers as well."

"Really? You don't have to."

"It's my pleasure. New connections."

The barista waited expectantly. Lollie turned to her with a smirk.

"I'll have a coffee, medium. Anything to warm my cold bones."

After paying with one of the cards she kept close in her purse, Lollie stepped to the end of the counter where Samantha already waited for her drink. She stood next to her, once again eyeing her up and down. "What do you do for a living?"

"Oh, um, I'm a store manager over at one of the grocery chains. It's my day off, so I thought I'd come and get some work done here rather than sit at home alone."

"You live alone?" Lollie's interest piqued.

"Yeah, my, uh, ex-girlfriend just moved out a few weeks back."

Lollie tried to hide her grin, but she couldn't. Rolling with it, she licked her lips. "How could anyone break up with you? You're drop dead gorgeous."

A blush rose to Samantha's cheeks. Lollie was pleased with herself. She grabbed Samantha's coffee and handed it to her before taking her own.

"I'll let you work, then. Don't want to distract you."

"No, wait." Samantha put her hand on Lollie's arm. "I could use the company. That's really why I came here. Needed to get out and see people, remind myself there are good people in this world. Come sit with me. I can give you the low down on St. Louis, and you can tell me where you're from."

"Sure." Lollie swallowed. "I'd love that."

The two of them sat down together at a small table in the corner. The cold from the window behind her chilled Lollie's back, but this way, she had a view of the front door and a wonderful view of Samantha. Lollie spun her coffee cup in her hand, waiting for it to cool slightly so she wouldn't burn her tongue.

"You said you've lived here all your life?"

"Yeah. Born and raised. Never wanted to move."

"I can't imagine not moving. I've lived so many places."

"Oh? Whereabouts?"

Lollie bided her time, taking a sip of her steaming cup. Samantha mimicked her move. Lollie rested on the small round table, pressing her elbows into the wood top. She rubbed her lips and sent Samantha a grin. "Well, most recently I'm coming from Chicago. But I've lived north, south, east, and west. Literally, all over the country."

"Army brat?" Samantha smirked. "My sister is military. She and her family move every couple years. I can't even begin to imagine what it would be like."

"It's not so bad once you get used to it, and hey, if you don't like a place, it's super easy to just pack up and go somewhere new."

"Very true. I think I'll stick with right here, though. I've got all my favorite spots. My coffee joint..." Samantha put her hand out to the room like she was showing it off. "I've got my mechanic, my best friends, my parents, my doctor who has been my doctor since I was born."

"That's a bit odd." Lollie wrinkled her nose.

Samantha shrugged. "I guess it could be."

Lollie hummed around another swallow of coffee. "Where's the best place to get comfort food, like the best burger joint in town?"

"Oh!" Samantha's eyes lit up, and Lollie's stomach clenched. "There's this place just on the other side of the river. It's seriously the best. They've got all different kinds of burgers, but I have never had a bad one there. Here." She took a napkin and wrote the name of the place down.

"We should go there sometime."

Samantha furrowed her brow. "Yeah, I guess we could."

"I'm just new to town and all. Gotta make some friends somewhere."

Nodding, Samantha slipped the napkin closer to Lollie. "Ain't that the truth. I firmly believe everyone could use another friend or two in their lives."

"I've had a hard time making friends lately. It seems to never work out in the long term. Things go really well in the beginning, but once we've been around for a while, they tend to fade into the background."

"I'm so sorry." Samantha covered Lollie's hand with her own. "That must be so hard. I don't know where I'd be without my friends. They got me through some really tough times."

Lollie nodded, playing into the sympathy Samantha was no doubt feeling for her in the moment. The more she got to know Samantha, the more she imagined they might work well together so long as they had the time to explore a relationship. Lollie swallowed and gave Samantha a weak smile.

"I guess. I've had to go most of it alone. I left home when I turned eighteen, never really had family to fall back on. No degree, so I worked my way up the ladder by being the go-to girl, but now, I really just want to settle a bit and be a homebody."

"Seems you've done a decent job at life."

"I have, thank you. I'd love to go back to school, though. I started once but never finished."

Samantha nodded. "Me too. Well, I did finish, after about fifteen years of starting and stopping. I needed the degree to get the position as store manager. It was not a very pleasant experience. School is not for me."

"Me either! But I get tired of working dead-end jobs here and there and not being able to have a career. Do you know what I mean?"

"Yeah, I get it."

Lollie warmed even more, and she knew she was getting closer. "Want to get that burger tonight? I have to drive by and get keys to my new apartment." Lollie checked her watch. "But I'm sure I could meet tonight. Girls gotta eat, right?"

"Yeah, I think I could swing that. Eight?"

"Sounds perfect."

Lollie leaned over and pressed her lips to Samantha's cheek. She lingered a little longer than would normally be considered appropriate for a first time meet up, but she wanted Samantha to know she was amenable to a different kind of relationship, perhaps a permanent one.

"I'll see you tonight, then."

"Eight." Samantha reiterated.

"At eight, yes."

Lollie slid out of her chair, grabbed her coffee cup, and went to her car. She glanced through the window to see Samantha still sitting at their table. Her heart warmed at the sight. Samantha may be perfect for her. They definitely had chemistry, and she was willing to take the risk to get to know her. Licking her lips, Lollie pulled out of the parking lot to drive by the burger joint. She wanted to know where she was going later so she didn't get lost.

Lollie had waited in the parking lot all afternoon until Samantha showed up. She watched as she walked inside. Samantha had changed into a new outfit, and it made Lollie smile. If she'd changed clothes to something tighter, something sexier, it was because she had been thinking about Lollie and their dinner together.

It was perfect. Lollie waited another five minutes before stepping out into the cold air. She rushed inside the restaurant, immediately looking around for Samantha. When she found her in the corner, waiting for the host to tell them a table was ready, Lollie's heart skipped. She sauntered over and grabbed Samantha's hand with her own, squeezing lightly.

"I like what you're wearing."

"Yeah? Thought I needed a change."

"Yeah. It's sexy." Lollie grinned. Samantha was damn sexy in her tight jeans and even tighter shirt. The washed out navy blue spread across her chest, accenting her breasts, and her leather jacket cut around her curves perfectly to accentuate her body.

"Uh, thanks." Samantha blushed.

Lollie squeezed her fingers again, not letting go. She didn't want to lose the contact if she could avoid it. Seducing Samantha would take a bit more than Andrea. Andrea had been easy, too easy in a lot of ways. That's why they would never have worked. Katie had almost worked, though. Lollie had lived with her for a couple weeks before they broke up, one of her longest relationships to date.

"What are you thinking?" Samantha leaned in and whispered in Lollie's ear.

"That I'm starved."

"Me too." Samantha chuckled. "How do you like your new apartment?"

"It's nice. Not the nicest place I've lived, but it's not bad. I need to get some stuff for it."

"Don't we always when we move?"

"Yeah." Lollie raised her eyebrows. "I need basic things. Like a bed. It'll be interesting to sleep on the wood floor tonight with only blankets. Hopefully, I'll be able to get one tomorrow."

Samantha clucked her tongue. "Oh look, I think the host is headed our way."

Lollie turned to see a man in loose jeans and t-shirt come their direction. "Sam."

"Oscar."

"Table's ready."

"Good. By the fireplace?"

"Always for our best customer."

Samantha grinned and tugged Lollie's hand. "Come on. This is the best seat in the house."

"I didn't realize you knew everyone who worked here." Lollie commented, her stomach churning at the fact Oscar may see her and remember her. She wasn't sure she was ready to be public about her relationship with Samantha yet. Groaning inwardly, Lollie shook her head. She supposed she should have thought about that before inviting Samantha out for dinner on the town.

Samantha led her over to a high top table right in front of a roaring fire place. Lollie smiled at it, pulling herself up onto the high stool. Samantha had a good six inches on her, so she easily sat down. Lollie tugged her jacket off and rested it over the back of the chair.

"What's good to eat?"

"Burgers." Samantha giggled, the sound echoing kind of like a chipmunk. "Try the lamb one. It's perfection on a plate."

"I'll take your recommendation."

It didn't take long for their meals to arrive, and Lollie moaned as she finished her burger. She looked directly at Samantha, moving back and forth on her stool in a happy jive.

"That was excellent. I think I'll take your food recommendations any time."

Samantha chuckled. "I know where all the good stuff is. I told you."

"You certainly do." The look Lollie sent her was heated. She wanted to try this, to see if they would be a good match for each other. She had subtly been attempting to seduce Samantha all night with flirting here and there, listening to her all about her life and her navy sister. She knew it was time to step up her game.

Leaning in, Lollie slid her hand across the table and gripped Samantha's fingers. "Really, thank you for bringing me out tonight. It's just what I needed to feel welcome in a new place."

"My pleasure." Samantha's voice had a husky tone to it that sent pleasure straight to Lollie's core. They shared a long look, and Samantha eventually broke the gaze, staring down at her fingers. "I can't stop thinking about what you said earlier."

"What did I say?"

"That you're going to be sleeping on the floor."

"Ah." Lollie's lips turned to a frown. "Don't worry about it. It's not the first time I've had to sleep on the floor, and I'm pretty sure it won't be the last."

Samantha turned her head slightly to the side. "But you don't have to. I mean, you could crash on my couch if you were comfortable with that."

Excitement bubbled in Lollie's stomach, but she knew she had to hold back on it for now. "No, I think I'll be fine. I don't want to impose."

"You're not. I have to be up early in the morning for work, but I promise I won't bother you. You can stay until you want to leave to start unpacking your new place."

"You're sure? I really don't want to cause any problems."

"It's not a problem. It'd be my pleasure, really. Us women have to stick together."

"That we do." Lollie grinned. "Since your offer is so generous, let me pay for dinner tonight."

"Oh no, I couldn't let you do that."

"Really. My treat. It's the least I can do."

"All right."

Lollie brushed her thumb against the back of Samantha's hand before she reached into her purse to grab her card. After she paid for their meal, Lollie guided Samantha out to her car and refused to let go of her fingers.

She did not what to lose the connection they were building.

Once they reached Samantha's car, Lollie turned Samantha to face her and grinned, bringing their lips together. It was soft at first, tentative with a dash of fear and worry. But when Samantha carded her fingers through Lollie's hair, Lollie moaned. This was near perfect.

She didn't want to push Samantha too hard, so after pressing her hand to Samantha's waist, Lollie pulled back. "Thank you again for tonight. It's been one of the most perfect nights of my life."

"I don't know what to say to that."

"Don't say anything, then." Lollie pressed her lips briefly to Samantha's. "Should I follow you?"

"Yeah."

"Let's go then. It's getting cold out."

## CHAPTER EIGHT

PAX WAS in the middle of an interview, and Morgan had been chained to her desk for the better part of the day. She needed a stretch, and probably some food, too. She phoned in an order to the pizzeria and told them she'd be picking it up. Morgan left a note on Pax's desk to let him know where she'd gone and she'd ordered for him as well.

It didn't take her long to walk down there. She slipped up to the counter and waited for Frankie to notice her. He gave her a cockeyed grin and shook his head as he sauntered over and threw a towel over his shoulder. "Twice in one week? Should I be flattered?"

Morgan snorted. "Hardly. Just a rumbly stomach and you're quickest on the list for delivering an edible product."

He grasped his heart in mock hurt. "You wound me, sister."

Laughing, Morgan leaned on the counter. "Honestly, it's the feel of this place that keeps me coming back. Always a joy, Frankie. Where's my grub?"

"Coming up, boss. Where's the girl?"

Morgan froze as she reached into her pocket for her wallet. "What girl?"

"The one you brought the other week."

Pulling a face, Morgan shook her head. "I didn't bring a girl then."

"Sure, you did. Yous sat right over there." He pointed at the booth. "And yous ordered the same thing. It was so sweet and girlish for you."

"I repeat, I did not bring a girl last time. We had a work meeting and decided over lunch would be best."

Frankie rolled his eyes as big as he could make them. "You were all googly-eyed over her, practically drooling."

"Shut it." Morgan slapped her card onto the counter, signaling an end to the teasing. Normally, she probably could have helped it, but with the last week under her belt, the last thing she wanted to do was talk about Fiona and her crush and the kiss and taking her case. She wanted to push it all from her mind's eye. "The food, Frankie."

"It's coming. It's coming." He slid her card off the counter and swiped it through their semi-ancient machine. She'd tried to get them to upgrade at some point, imagining the security issues they were exposed to by not having updated tech. Frankie had promptly rolled his eyes and walked away without another word.

He handed her card back and then handed her the food. She smiled as it sat warm in her palms. Morgan walked to the bureau and brought the food to her desk. Pax was still gone, her note untouched. She grabbed her ever-present coffee mug and went to refill it, needing the extra juice to push her through to the end of the day.

Morgan plopped down at her desk, dug into the bag with her food and took a bite of calzone as she stared over the screen of her computer. She'd watched the interview with Reilly a dozen times before, but she still wanted to see if there was anything else to glean from it. Reilly was now in the custody of the FBI at a safe house while she reunited with her parents and worked on her transition to motherhood.

An agent had been in and out of the house daily to check on her and see if there was any other information to learn. Morgan went over those files as well but found little to nothing in them. It seemed as though the girls were not privy to as much information as they'd once thought. Sighing, she took another bite and worked her way through the notes on other interviews.

She got to the third or fourth one and narrowed her eyes. "Interesting," she muttered to herself. Clicking open the video, Morgan put on her headphones and relaxed in her chair. She ate while she watched.

"How old are you?" the interviewer asked.

"Twelve," the young boy answered, not looking up and boring a hole into the table.

"What's your role, Dimitri?"

Dimitri looked at his hands. "I'm a runner."

"Which means what?"

Dimitri took in a deep breath. "I take things from one person and give them to another person."

"Like who?"

Biting his lip, Dimitri shook his head. Morgan swallowed right along with him, raptly watching the video. He shook his head again, clearly not wanting to answer.

"Dimitri, we can't help you if you don't talk to us. Who is it you give things to?"

Morgan's heart clenched. She'd used the tactic before, but she didn't like it, especially when used on kids. Dimitri looked so small in the large interview room. He had no lawyer, no adult, no one to advocate for him. Morgan cringed. It'd be a nightmare if he confessed to anything, and they pressed charges.

"I don't know," Dimitri muttered.

The interviewer's hands pressed down onto the table. "Then I think we're done here. You can go—"

"You can't send me back. They'll think I snitched."

"You haven't said anything."

"Don't matter. They'll think I snitched."

"All right, then answer my question."

Dimitri took a large breath and leaned into the chair, his demeanor opening. He was resigned to the conundrum he found himself in. "I take stuff to the girls."

"Is that all?"

Shaking his head, Dimitri toyed with a pen on the table. "I take stuff to the boss."

"Which boss?"

"The one above mine."

"Who is your boss?"

"P-dog."

"Who is P-dog's boss?"

Dimitri swallowed, his shoulders tensed, and he was clearly uncomfortable. The pen between his fingers flung to the floor. "Mr. Jimmy."

Morgan's heart sank. She'd heard that name before. He was one of the highest up that they knew of in the ring they were investigating. If it was true, and this boy had more information to prove that, he would need immediate protective custody not to mention a second and probably third interview.

"What kind of stuff do you run from P-dog to Mr. Jimmy?"

Dimitri shrugged and shook his head. "Dunno. Don't look."

"How are you paid for your work?"

Dimitri paled. His already white skin went whiter. Morgan's heart broke again. She knew how he was paid, or rather not paid. He'd get a bonus for bringing stuff, but Mr. Jimmy obviously preferred young boys to the girls P-dog kept. She let out a breath, blinked back a few tears, and then bolstered herself with coffee for Dimitri's answer.

"He usually gives me cash."

"How much?"

"Depends."

"Depends on what?"

"What I bring him."

The interviewer paused a moment before asking the next crucial question. "Does Mr. Jimmy ask you to do anything else for him in order for you to get paid?"

Dimitri hesitated, but he nodded.

Morgan turned off the video. She closed her eyes, rubbed the bridge of her nose, and turned to her abandoned lunch. Pax popped over the back of the desk with a grin on his face. She pulled off her headphones and threw them onto her desk, thankful for the break before she watched the rest.

"What'd you find out? You look all happy," she commented.

"I did. I got a name!" He walked around and sat down in his chair, handing her the file.

Morgan put it to her forehead, closed her eyes. "Is it...Mr. Jimmy?"

Pax's jaw dropped. "How the hell did you know that?"

Morgan giggled. "Magic."

Snorting, Pax rolled his eyes. "No, really. How'd you know that?"

Turning back to her computer, Morgan pointed. "Interview with a twelve-year-old detainee. He's a runner, would bring stuff from Reilly's and Nicoletta's pimp to some Mr. Jimmy. Reilly mentioned him too, albeit briefly."

"Reilly did?"

Morgan nodded. "She said his name in connection with who P-dog would go to when he needed a new girl."

"Hmm." Pax licked his lips. "Where's your kid?"

"Uhh..." Morgan looked over the file. "Wichita."

"My kid is here."

"Does that cross interstate again?"

Pax shrugged. "We can't prove it yet."

"But it's close." Morgan took a long sip from her cooling coffee. She'd have to top it off soon to keep it warm. Pax looked at the food on her desk. She shoved it toward him. "It's for you."

"A girl after a man's heart."

"Anyone knows the way to yours is food."

Pax shot her a look but dug into his pasta. Morgan continued to mull over the information she'd gleaned from watching Dimitri's interview. She read over the highlights of Pax's. There were some similarities. She'd have to ask some different questions to make sure it was the same Mr. Jimmy and to make sure the kids had enough information for them to make a move. She was tired of sitting on her hands and waiting for the right evidence to fall into their laps.

"Your kid a foster kid?" Morgan furrowed her brow as she turned suddenly to Pax.

"Uh..." he looked down at the papers. "Yeah."

"Mine too. Wonder if that's how he's picking his kids."

"Maybe."

"They are more at risk, but Nicoletta said something about being in the system, too."

Pax shuffled the papers on his desk until he found the right file. He opened it up and shook his head. "She wasn't when she was brought into P-dog's house, but she had been when she was two or three."

Morgan took a bite of her cold calzone and debated whether or not to warm it up. Deciding it'd probably end up cold again before she had a chance to finish it since she didn't shove food down her throat like Pax did, she opted to eat it cold. "Something to look into."

"Absolutely. You find anything on the murder case?"

"Yes and no." Morgan closed down the tabs on her screen and pulled up the second file. She switched over her papers and slid them so Pax could read the words. "Here's the full profile I've done up. There's been one hit on the first victim's credit card, first one in about a month. It was for a car rental. I've got an APB out on the car, but nothing has come up as of yet."

"You think it's a woman?"

Morgan turned to him, narrowing her eyes and straightening her shoulders. "Yes."

"Why?"

"There's a reason I'm the profiler and you're not. Just trust me."

"No. Why?"

"She seduces them before she kills them."

"What?"

Morgan rolled her eyes. "Didn't you read the brief?"

"Kind of?"

Shaking her head, Morgan let out a heavy sigh. "This killer is killing solely for food, shelter, clothing, etcetera. She's trying to find a place to live, essentially. The people just seem to get in the way. But each one has had sex with a woman prior to being murdered...well, prior or during, that is still unclear."

"Wait, wait, wait." He wiped his mouth with a napkin. "She kills them while she has sex with them?"

Shrugging, Morgan nodded. "It would seem so. You really need to read the brief. Seriously."

"I'll get on that."

Focusing on the computer, Morgan listened to the rest of Dimitri's interview. He gave specific details about Mr. Jimmy raping him, multiple times, and how he got paid extra for certain things. Morgan had to pause the video several times to gather her wits before continuing.

She checked for flags on the car that their killer had presumably rented. There were none. Unfortunately, she could be anywhere. It was going to be a while before they caught up with their killer unless they found a more specific connection between the victims, which Pax told her he was supposedly working on.

With a glance at his computer, she could see him looking through financials on their first victim. Good, so he was at least doing what he said he would do. Financials were more his thing while she focused on profiling and behavior analysis of their perps and victims. That was why they worked so well together as a team. Fifteen years being partners, twenty years knowing each other, and Morgan wouldn't have it any other way, except perhaps someone who was a little more comfortable with her sexuality.

Grunting, she went back to the video. She'd have to go to Wichita and interview Dimitri herself. She wasn't lead on the case, but she was the best at profiling, and she needed to get a good one down of Mr. Jimmy—whoever he was in real life. She wouldn't be surprised if Mr. Jimmy had nothing to do with his actual name and instead it was a euphemism.

One more glance at Pax, and she dove into her own work. It wasn't long until the day was over. She'd made arrangements to fly this time to Wichita and to leave the next day. It'd be a short trip, only two or three days this time. Pax vowed he'd have the rest of the financials gone through and at least three connections between all of her victims by the time she returned.

Nerves wrangled in her belly as she headed home. Her bedroom floor was littered with the laundry she'd vowed to do last weekend and never got around to. The trash desperately needed taking out, but she had no energy to do it. Plopping down on her couch, Morgan dragged the blanket over her legs and tried to get Dimitri's small voice out of her head. She didn't want to listen to him tell his story over and over again. She wanted to think better of humanity, but she couldn't. Human beings were assholes and most of them perverted, especially the ones she dealt with.

Grimacing, she turned on the television to watch the *Hallmark* channel's Christmas special and their twenty-million Christmas romance movies they had on. When her phone rang, she glanced at the caller and groaned. Morgan shifted farther under the covers and gritted her teeth as she answered.

"Clyde."

"Sis."

"What do you need?"

"How dare you ask that? I'm offended!" His fake offense was evident.

Morgan chuckled. "You don't call unless you need something. What do you need?"

"I was just calling to check in on my big sis. I saw the bust in Kansas. Was that you?"

"You know I can't answer that. Make national headlines?"

"It did. Don't you watch?"

"No. I see enough of that shit at work." Morgan glanced back at her television, missing a pinnacle moment in the show but knowing she'd likely be able to figure out what happened since it wasn't a plot heavy movie.

Clyde paused before he spoke again. "I need a favor."

"When do you not?"

"It's a legal one."

"No."

"Morgan, you don't even know what it is!"

She shook her head even though he couldn't see her. "The answer is still no. I'm not doing anything illegal for you."

"It's not illegal. It's legal."

"What? What trouble did you get yourself into this time?"

He sighed. "I got another DUI."

"Jesus Christ, Clyde. That's the third one."

"I know. That's why I need some legal help."

"I can't help you with that. You need rehab and a swift kick in the ass."

He didn't say anything. Morgan rubbed the bridge of her nose and closed her eyes, wishing she'd let it go to voicemail instead of answering.

"Fine, what legal help do you need?"

"Well, it's my third. So...that means jail."

"How long?"

"One-hundred-twenty days," he said softly.

"Jesus, Clyde. What's Lauren going to do?"

"I don't know. That's why I need your help."

"I can help her. I can't help you. You need to get your shit in order and get your ass straight. I'm serious. You've got to stop with this nonsense."

"I know."

"I'll help Lauren any way I can, just let me know."

"Thanks, sis."

"When do you have to report?"

"Next week."

"Call before you go in, will ya?"

"Yeah."

"Talk to you later. And don't call Amya. She's got enough of this drama going on."

"Wasn't planning on it."

Morgan hung up and glanced to her television screen. Letting out a heavy sigh, she let herself be enveloped in the love story on the screen and push all the chaotic things in her life away from her for just a little longer. The laundry could wait one more day.

## CHAPTER NINE

MORGAN HAD gotten to Wichita only an hour before and her phone was buzzed non-stop. She'd made it to the police station where the bureau was holding up waiting for her to interview Dimitri again. But her phone would not stop ringing. Glaring, she pulled it from her pocket and rolled her eyes.

Her mom. Again. For the billionth time.

Sighing, she glanced at her partner for the day and issued a silent apology. Morgan knew if she didn't deal with her mom then and there, she'd have six hundred voicemails by the end of the day. She stepped into a quiet part of the hallway, not knowing where there was anywhere else more private, and answered.

"What is it, Ma?"

"Are you going to do something about Clyde?" Her mother's shrill voice echoed in her ear.

Morgan took a deep breath and calmed her anger. "No, and neither should you. The bonehead got into his own trouble, and he needs to get out of it."

"I can't live with him in prison."

"Ma, he broke the law, multiple times. Don't call your kid who works the law to bail out your kid who breaks it." She knew it would fluster and likely piss off her mom, but after three years of Clyde's drinking and driving, Morgan had enough. He needed to grow up and deal with his own shit.

"Well, I guess I know where you stand on family loyalty."

Scoffing, Morgan looked down the hall at her partner for the day who was waving her to come. "Don't start with me. You know I'm loyal as anything to our family. Clyde needs to learn from his mistakes. Look, Ma, I got to go. I have a case I'm about to break, and I really can't talk. If you want another opinion, call Amya. She'll tell you the exact same thing."

"I already talked to her."

Morgan snorted. "Then there you go. I'll talk to you later."

Hanging up, Morgan put her phone on do-not-disturb and headed for the interview room. Dimitri looked so much smaller sitting at the table than he did on the video. He was twelve, but he was a scrawny twelve. It was obvious he'd missed a few meals and even more obvious he had suffered immeasurable trauma.

She would have to carefully toe the line. This time, Dimitri had an advocate with him, something Morgan was extremely grateful for.

Morgan slipped into the uncomfortable metal chair. She set her papers down and stared right at him. Once again, her heart shattered into a million little pieces. She didn't bother with her papers yet, she'd use them later. For now, she needed to make a connection with Dimitri, and she imagined being a woman unlike his previous interviewer may work to her advantage.

"Hey, kid."

He didn't answer.

Morgan took a steadying breath. "I guess you know why we're here, for the most part, anyway."

He nodded.

Morgan relaxed her posture in hopes it would reflect back on him and open him to talking more about what he had done for Mr. Jimmy and P-dog. "We're here because of some stuff you told our other interviewer. Do you remember what you said to him?"

"Yeah, I remember." There was fire in his voice, but Morgan knew that was a good thing. Anger was an emotion, and she could work with it.

"We're trying to find Mr. Jimmy and take him into custody, put him in jail, but we need your help to do that."

"Why?"

Morgan shook her head. "We don't have anyone else right now who can help us."

Dimitri pursed his lips but didn't say anything. Morgan figured he might be a bit harder to break than others. He'd been in the sex ring for quite some time, foster kid before that, he had walls to back up is other walls to back up even more walls. She would have to take each one down at a time.

"You told my friend the other day that you were a runner for P-dog."

"Yeah. I run."

"What kind of things did you run?"

"I already told him."

Morgan nodded slowly, keeping her body loose and calm. She knew it was what he would need. "I know, but I need you to tell me again. That way we can make sure you're telling us the truth."

"Why the fuck would I lie?"

Morgan stiffened, but then she calmed herself. She had to keep her cool. "It's for my bosses, you know? It's not something I want to make you retell. It's for them."

He nodded like he understood. He stared at his advocate, who encouraged him to talk with a nod. Dimitri leaned forward, his palms flat on the table top. "I'd run whatever they asked me to. Drugs, papers, money. Anytime P-dog had something for Mr. Jimmy he'd send me 'cause Mr. Jimmy liked me."

"Did you ever look at what you were running?"

"Not really."

"Hmm." Morgan paused for effect. "So you did look sometimes. What did you see?"

Dimitri shrugged, and his advocate leaned closer to him. "You can tell her, Dimitri. She's only here to help you stay safe."

"She can't keep me safe."

"Sure, I can," Morgan added. "That's my job. I'm here to keep you safe and to put Mr. Jimmy away in prison."

Dimitri snorted. "He ain't going to prison. You can't touch him."

"Why would you say that?"

"He's rich."

Morgan swallowed. It was a common misconception by a lot of people that the rich weren't arrested, and while they did tend to evade arrest a bit longer than normal on occasion, she could—in fact—take them down. And she planned to do it with Mr. Jimmy, especially after watching Dimitri's first interview.

"That doesn't really matter in the long run. I'll find him, and I will arrest him."

Dimitri shook his head. "You won't, but whatever."

"Let's get back to what you saw of what you were running. What did P-dog send to Mr. Jimmy?"

"He sent money, a lot of it. He'd send photos sometimes."

"Photos of what?" Morgan resisted the urge to write. If Dimitri had been an adult, she would have grabbed her notebook and taken copious notes, but she didn't want to lose any credibility she'd gained.

Dimitri looked from his advocate to Morgan and then to the door behind Morgan. "Pictures of girls, mostly."

"Young girls?"

Dimitri shook his head. "No, the girls P-dog would put on the street to make them money. Mr. Jimmy liked to inspect the merchandise."

Morgan's stomach churned. "What else did you run?"

"Drugs, sometimes, but they don't trust me with them much. It was only when Tuck wasn't around."

Letting out a breath, Morgan refocused. "You said to my friend the other day that Mr. Jimmy liked you. Did he like the pictures of the girls, too?"

"No. He only likes boys."

"Okay. Okay. So when you would run for P-dog, where would you go to give the stuff to Mr. Jimmy?"

Dimitri got quiet. His cheeks paled, and his nose reddened. Morgan knew she was walking into dangerous territory, but she needed a location, somewhere she could send some people to meet with Mr. Jimmy or at least search him out some more.

"Dimitri, I know this is hard, but I really need you to tell me everything you can about Mr. Jimmy."

He nodded in the slightest way possible. "What do you need to know?"

"Where did you go to meet him?"

"A hotel."

"Which one?"

Dimitri shook his head. "I had to get on a plane to go there. It took a long time. Big John always went with me."

"Who is Big John?"

"My boss."

"Okay. What did the hotel look like?"

"It was nice. Had gold doors, and white floors, lots of trees inside. We'd drive right up to the entrance, then I'd go in, up the elevator to the top floor, and I wouldn't come out until Mr. Jimmy was ready to send me back."

"Thank you, Dimitri. I also need to know what Mr. Jimmy looks like."

Dimitri's eyes watered, and his nose got even redder. "I can't."

"I need you to. It's the only way we'll catch him."

It took Dimitri a full minute before he answered, and Morgan let him sit with his decision. He was doing excellent for such a young kid who had been through so much. He was giving her a lot of useful information, and she hoped, he would be willing to testify. The next part of their conversation was her least favorite.

"He has brown hair and brown skin. He's not very tall."

"How old do you think he is?"

"I dunno. Your age?"

"Okay, that's good. I'm fifty."

"Yeah, he's your age."

Morgan filed away every piece of information she could in her brain, thankful they were recording the interview. She would no doubt watch it a couple dozen times in the next few weeks. "Does he have any scars or tattoos or birth marks?"

Dimitri shook his head. "He's skinny and fit. He works out like every day."

"That's good. Thank you! That's really helpful. Anything else?"

"He has a stupid dog he keeps with him."

"A dog?"

"Yeah." Dimitri wrinkled his nose. "It bites. It's a little brown dog."

"Like a chihuahua."

"Maybe. I don't know. It bit my leg."

"Oh no! Is it okay now?"

Dimitri nodded. "Mr. Jimmy had a doctor come and look at it because we couldn't get it to stop bleeding."

"Oh good. I'm glad you're okay." Morgan sent him a smile, hoping now he was talking a little more regularly she was building to having a relationship on good footing. "We're going to put you into protective custody, okay, Dimitri?"

"What's that mean?"

"It means you're going to go live with a family who is going to take really good care of you."

"I've lived with families like that. They always kick me out."

"These people won't. I promise." Morgan licked her lips. "It also means, though, that when we find Mr. Jimmy you're going to have to tell your story again and again and again. That way we can make sure Mr. Jimmy will never get out of prison."

"No."

"Dimitri, I need you to do this."

"No. I won't do it."

Morgan sighed. "I need you to do this, so he won't hurt any other little boys."

That made him pause. Morgan's stomach twisted. She hated pushing him this way. It was too much manipulation, too much pulling teeth and making people do what they didn't want to do. She was good at it, but she did not like it.

"I'll think about it."

"Okay, that's all I could ask for. My friend is going to come in and talk to you about where you're going to stay, okay?"

Dimitri nodded. Morgan grabbed her papers she hadn't even touched and left the room. As soon as the door shut, she let out a breath she hadn't known she was holding. She hated sex crimes. She'd take serial murderers any day of the week over a sex crime.

She'd spent two days getting Dimitri oriented in his new home, double-checking his story, and making sure he would be willing to share it again, which he did twice more. She was confident he was in a good place, although she really wished her sister and her sister's girlfriend were the ones who were hosting him. She trusted them implicitly. This family, she wasn't sure about.

Morgan sat in the airport with her laptop on her knees as she waited for her plane when her phone rang. Wrinkling her nose and praying it wasn't her mom, she pulled it up and smiled when she saw Pax's name. She pressed the phone to her ear and answered with a smile.

"Howdy, partner."

"Don't do that," he snarked. "Did you see it?"

"See what?" Morgan leaned over her computer, checking her email for what she had missed. Sure enough, it popped through as soon as she refreshed the browser. "Oh, now I got it."

"Open it."

"No shit, Sherlock." Morgan opened the email, and her eyes lit up. It was a hit on their stolen credit card they were watching. She scrolled through the data. Restaurant somewhere in St. Louis. "Fuck."

"What?"

"The one time I decide to fly to Kansas instead of driving."

He snickered. "That's what I was thinking."

"You send someone out there?"

"I thought you might want the honors."

As much as she would love to change her flight, the plane was due to board in ten minutes. It also wouldn't be very economical for her to change her flight when they had people on the ground who could check it out for her.

"As much as I would love to," she began, "it's probably best to send someone else this time. I'll catch up to our mystery murderess some other time."

"You're sure?"

He sounded concerned, which was nice of him, but for the time being, she knew she was in the right. It would not likely be approved by Taylor, and she would probably piss him and someone else off in the process if she didn't follow protocol. Not to mention she'd told her mom the other day that she was a cop and followed the law. Rolling her eyes, Morgan shifted into her seat to try and be slightly more comfortable.

"Yeah, just this time. I'm gonna get me this one."

"You do that." He chuckled. "I'll make the call."

"Thanks. How did our kid do up there? Did the information match the witness here?"

"Kind of. Not as well as we had hoped, but it might be enough to try and find Mr. Jimmy."

Shutting her laptop as boarding started, Morgan shoved it into her backpack. "What did he say?"

"Not much, just that he'd go to a hotel, do his duty, and be done with it, and Mr. Jimmy would send him home."

"All right. I'll watch the tape when I get back."

"You do that. See you soon, Stone."

"Back at you, Jones."

Rubbing the ache from the back of her neck, Morgan packed up the rest of her stuff and got on to the plane. It would be a much shorter journey home than last time, but this time, she had a lot more on her mind.

## CHAPTER TEN

LOLLIE SAT on Samantha's couch and peeked through her phone. Samantha was in the shower, the water running, and the door closed. Lollie had made sure to take it slow the night before and didn't push Samantha toward a relationship. There was something she liked about wooing her dates. It made her feel important and as if they actually liked her.

Smiling at herself, Lollie typed in Andrea's name into the search bar on her phone. Swallowing, she looked at the reports out of Chicago. They'd found her decently quick, but it also didn't look like they had any leads. She typed in Katie's name and found the same.

She hated not having access to the police files. That would tell her a whole lot more about whether or not they were going to find her, but sticking with the news outlets was going to have to do for now. Lollie typed in both names to search them together. There was nothing connecting the two.

Breathing a sigh of relief, Lollie leaned into the couch and covered her legs with the blanket Samantha had given her to sleep with. It wasn't the most comfortable blanket, but it had done the trick. That morning, they had shared coffee and conversation, and Lollie had worked on being even closer to Samantha.

With a glance toward the bathroom to make sure Samantha was still in it, Lollie typed in two more names to her search bar. There was nothing new on the first, and the second literally showed nothing at all in the news. They must not have found her yet. Lollie closed and cleared out the search history, setting her phone on the coffee table as she waited.

She had to leave when Samantha went to work in an hour, but she wanted to lay the groundwork for coming back. She liked Samantha. They had a lot in common, but more importantly, they had chemistry. That had been what Lollie was after from the beginning and what had lacked with Andrea. She wanted that deep connection with someone, the trust and the relationship to build on that.

When Samantha came out of the bathroom with only a towel wrapped around her middle, Lollie looked up at her and grinned. She was a goddess. Steam billowed out around her, her hair wet down her back and darker than before, her cheeks rosy from the heat and trails of water dripping down her skin. Lollie licked her lips as she cast her gaze up and down, letting Samantha know she was interested in something beyond mere friendship.

Samantha grinned and pressed a hand to Lollie's shoulder. "I'm going to get dressed, but do you want to grab some breakfast before I head to work?"

"Absolutely." Lollie smiled up at Samantha as she sauntered out of the room. Her plan was working. They were connecting. She saw it in the way Samantha looked at her, felt it in the way Samantha touched her. Lollie brought her hand up to where Samantha's fingers had lingered on her shoulder and kept it there, remembering the slight squeeze of Samantha's fingers, the gentle tug at her lips for a smile. They were made for each other.

Samantha came back shortly, her hair towel dried but still wet as it hung down her back. Lollie grinned at her and stood up, stretching. Samantha came around the last corner, and Lollie grabbed her hand, spinning her until their lips touched. Lollie breathed in and smiled as Samantha pulled away.

"I've wanted to do that for hours."

Samantha giggled. "Me too."

Lollie took the opportunity and leaned in, brushing their mouths together in a sweet embrace. She didn't want to push Samantha too hard or too fast, but she couldn't get over her lips. Something about them was addicting. Once again, she found herself grinning as they kissed.

When Samantha moved and put a finger to Lollie's mouth, her eyes crinkled at the corners. "I do have to work today, so we do need to go get breakfast if that's what we're wanting."

"Right," Lollie answered, looking around for her purse. "And I need to move all my crap into my apartment, at least what stuff I do have. I don't have much. Is there a second-hand store around here?"

"Uh, yeah." Samantha grabbed her wallet and slipped it into her back pocket. With her keys in her hand, she walked to the door.

Lollie stopped and folded the blanket, setting it on the edge of the couch along with the two pillows Samantha had lent her for the night. She couldn't get enough of Samantha. She was gorgeous in a subtle kind of way. Lollie sauntered over to her with an added sway to her hips.

After they walked out, Samantha locked the door. "The second-hand store is just down the road from here. If you go to the corner of Logan and twenty-first, you'll find it."

"Awesome. Thanks. Where are we going for breakfast?"

Samantha snorted. "Donuts."

Lollie wasn't sure how, but she'd convinced Samantha to meet her for dinner that night after she got off work. Lollie had spent the day preparing. She went to the mall, bought herself a new outfit. It was a tight button up royal purple shirt that she conveniently left the top three unbuttoned. The new pair of jeans was still stiff because it hadn't been washed, but light material with fading was perfect for her figure.

It showed off every one of her curves. Lollie had danced in front of the mirror several times before she swiped her card and left with her outfit on. She felt so good. She stopped by a local florist and picked up a bouquet for Samantha. She certainly wanted to woo her. Lollie wanted to make sure this relationship worked. Samantha was damn near perfect.

With the flowers in hand, Lollie headed for her vehicle. She'd wasted away her day, and when she checked the clock in her rental car, it told her she had just under an hour before Samantha would be done with her shift and ready for dinner. They'd already decided on a place.

Lollie drove there and waited. As soon as Samantha arrived, Lollie got out of the car and met Samantha at hers. She leaned in and pressed their mouths together. Samantha didn't hesitate when she deepened the embrace, surprising Lollie. Samantha's hand slid up behind Lollie's neck, holding the two of them together.

The air outside bit at their skin, but the heat they created together was warm enough to keep them in place. Lollie moaned as she pressed hard against Samantha and pushed Samantha into her car. She slid her hand up Samantha's front, cupping her breast. Samantha moaned and tightened her fingers in Lollie's hair.

"Maybe..." Samantha cleared her throat and tried again. "Maybe we should go back to my place."

Lollie grinned. "I thought you said you wanted dinner."

"We can order in." Samantha's mouth was at her neck, and she nipped at the strong corded muscle of Lollie's skin. Lollie moved her head to the side, enjoying the feel of Samantha's teeth against her skin. It sent shots of pleasure straight to her core. If they were this good at making out together, the sex would no doubt be amazing.

"Let's do that, then," Lollie whispered, her fingers carding under Samantha's shirt and jacket until her fingertips met skin.

"Get in my car."

Samantha reached behind her, opening the back door. Lollie giggled as she climbed in and Samantha came in after her. Lollie was waiting with her arms open as Samantha crawled on top of her. They couldn't even wait to get to Samantha's apartment. Lollie tugged Samantha's jacket and shirt off, brushing her fingers along her very practical beige colored bra. This was what she had imagined that morning. Touching all over Samantha's body.

Bending down, Samantha's mouth worked against Lollie's once again. It was awkward, but it was perfect for their first time. Lollie unbuttoned Samantha's pants, working her hand between her legs. She found Samantha warm and waiting as she moved her fingers rapidly. Samantha whispered in her ear how to move and where to move. Each time her breath cascaded over Lollie's ear, pleasure coursed through her chest and her belly.

Samantha moved with the slight of her hand. Lollie brought her leg up to cradle Samantha's body, her lips brushing against Samantha's chest whenever she got a chance. Samantha laughed and leaned down, whispering into Lollie's ear, "I have literally thought about this all day."

"What? Sex in a car?"

Snorting, Samantha shook her head. "No. Sex with you. You naked under me. Me tasting you. Everything you can imagine."

A shudder ran down Lollie's spine. She quickened her fingers, wanting to bring Samantha to the edge over and over again for the rest of the night. This was the closest she had felt with another woman. Their perfection together was insurmountable.

Lollie jerked her hand harder as Samantha's moans echoed in the car. No doubt the car shook as they moved, but Lollie didn't care. She had the love of her life right where she wanted her. When Samantha came, her voice echoed in the still and hot air. Lollie kissed a line up her neck, over her cheek, and to her forehead before back down the other side until their lips met in a deep and sweet embrace.

"Your turn." Samantha grinned.

Lollie didn't hesitate. She grabbed at her brand new jeans and shoved them down her hips. Samantha pulled them even more, past her knees. She spread Lollie's legs and smirked as she stared down.

"So beautiful."

Lollie's heart clenched with joy. "You going to stare all night or you going to do something?"

"Oh, absolutely going to do something." Samantha bent her head and nipped at Lollie's thigh. After that, she didn't wait and brought her tongue straight to Lollie's center.

They were both aware they were in the middle of a parking lot during the height of the dinner rush. If they weren't careful, someone would see them, and if they weren't quick, someone could call the cops on them. That was the last thing Lollie wanted. She grabbed hold of Samantha's pony tail, tugging like she had wanted to do the day before in the coffee shop.

Lollie gave over to every sensation Samantha pulled from her. She careened up and then down, her body rising and lowering as her legs shook with pleasure. She licked her lips as she took in a deep breath, trying to keep her voice from screaming out. Reaching back, she gripped the seatbelt and held on as Samantha took her over.

When Samantha was done, and Lollie's body was still coming down from her high, Samantha crawled up and pressed their mouths together. Lollie tasted her own flavor on Samantha's tongue, and she tried to suck off every little bit of her juices she could. She held Samantha's head to her own until she was done, and when Samantha pulled back, they laughed together.

"Where are we ordering from?" Lollie asked.

"I don't know, and I don't care. I just want to get you back to my bed and do this all over again."

"That'd be perfect."

Lollie sat up slightly, but Samantha didn't move. Pressing one more kiss to Lollie's lips, Samantha reached down to the foot of her car for her shirt. She shoved it over her head, awkwardly moved to button up her pants, and grinned the entire time.

"We're leaving your car. We'll come back for it."

"Okay." Lollie tugged up her own pants.

Stepping out of the vehicle, Samantha pushed Lollie into the side, reminiscent of when they'd met earlier in that very same parking lot. Lollie had to force Samantha away from her, and she licked her lips, looking from Samantha's eyes to her lips to her chest and back again.

"Bed?"

"Yes. Let's go." Samantha moved away from her, awkwardly, before she headed around the car and got into the driver's seat.

Lollie got into the passenger seat and buckled in while Samantha drove. The entire drive home, Lollie whispered exactly what she wanted to do to Samantha as soon as they were going to make it inside. Samantha almost forgot to step on the gas at a stop light she was so distracted by Lollie's descriptions.

Lollie had to gently remind her to go. They were about halfway there, when Lollie gave in and leaned over, once again unbuttoning Samantha's pants and slipping her hand down between Samantha's legs. Groaning, Samantha's knuckles turned white as she gripped the steering wheel and shifted her butt on the seat to give Lollie better access.

"All day, huh?"

"Yes," Samantha answered on a breath. "Didn't you?"

"I've been thinking about this since I met you, to be honest. You're so beautiful, so strong, so confident. It's a glorious mix to witness."

Samantha's cheeks tinged red with a blush, and Lollie's chest warmed. The rest of the drive home, Lollie did her best to torture Samantha as best she could. She didn't come before they made a mad dash for the apartment, but as soon as they were inside, their clothes came off, and they spent the rest of the night wrapped up in each other.

## CHAPTER ELEVEN

THIS WAS the part of her job that she loved the most. It wasn't the most glorious part or the part she got credit for outside of the office, but diving deep into the research, into looking for connections in behavior, that was where her true love was. Morgan scoffed when Pax sat next to her with a paper cup in his hand. She shook her head at him.

"I gave you a washable cup for a reason."

He shrugged. "It's dirty."

"So wash it. Save the planet a little. Yeesh." Morgan turned to her computer. She'd been scrolling through old murder cases in the area, searching for another connection to their woman. She waited rather impatiently for a call back from St. Louis about the credit card charge. She'd already called them twice waiting for a response, and they were not getting back to her.

Morgan tapped her pen rapidly on the top of her desk as she hunched over staring at her computer screen. The caffeine swirling through her veins was almost too much, and she knew she'd over done it that morning. She'd contacted the humane society about a cat, but other than they had a bunch for her to look at, she hadn't made it any further in her quest. She'd chugged an entire pot of coffee before she even left her tiny apartment and another pot after she'd arrived.

Her knee bounced up and down, hitting the top of her desk. It wasn't until Pax gripped her arm and sent her a glare that she stopped. "What?"

"What is with you today?"

"I dunno. Something about this case. It's confusing me. There's like no sign of this woman anywhere."

"Still sure it's a woman."

"Yes." Morgan turned on him. "Women can be serial killers too, just as much as men."

"I'm aware, but this one...you're sure?"

"Yes." Morgan rolled her eyes and glanced at the computer screen. "Why are you so sure it's a man?"

Pax paused and pursed his lips. His dark eyes locked with hers. "Men are more likely to be serial killers. Statistically speaking."

"I know that."

"This person has killed each time by strangulation. It would take a lot of strength for a woman to be able to do that."

"You don't think I could strangle you?"

He narrowed his gaze.

"Seriously. Do you think I couldn't take you on?"

"No, I don't."

"Misogynist."

"Not the first time I've been accused of that." He leaned in his chair and crossed his arms over his large chest.

Morgan shook her head at him and focused on her computer briefly before she turned on him again. "I'm sure it's a woman. A man wouldn't fit the profile."

"Why not?"

"It's not a violent death. The violence happens afterward. It's calculated."

"What do you mean?"

Licking her lips, Morgan pulled out each of the photos of the victims they knew about. She set them in a line in front of Pax so he could see each one. "Here, this one has one stab wound to the heart. It would have been fatal had the victim still been alive, but strangulation."

"Yeah, yeah."

"Here again, stab wounds. This time three to the heart."

Pax shook his head.

"This time four."

"I still don't get it."

"She's counting her kills."

Pax's eyes burned a hole in hers. Morgan raised her eyebrows at him and nodded. He swallowed.

"She's literally counting her kills. We're missing the second one. There might be a first one too, before she started all this—" Morgan waved her hand over the table "—but we're definitely missing number two. It'll only be a matter of time before number five happens."

Pax slipped the photos over so he could look at them more clearly. "Calculated, yes, but you're going to have to do more convincing of me for it to be a woman."

"You're too bullheaded. So far there is no male DNA at any of the crime scenes."

"They've hardly even gotten through the samples yet," he countered.

Her phone shrilled sharply. Morgan twisted toward it, pulled it up immediately, and shoved it to her ear.

"Stone."

"Special Agent Stone?"

"Yes, this is she." Her heart rapped in her chest as she prayed for an answer from St. Louis.

"I'm calling from St. Louis Bureau."

Morgan grinned. "Did you find anything?"

"There's no cameras in the area of the restaurant, unfortunately. The owner wasn't able to give me a description of the individual either. Sorry I don't have much better news."

Clenching her jaw, Morgan stared aimlessly in front of her. "Was there any description of a vehicle or have you found the rental car, yet?"

"We haven't. There's a lot of cars in St. Louis, ma'am."

Morgan held her tongue as much as she didn't want to. She had to play nice with the man, but good Lord, the macho attitude was over the top that day. She swallowed and took a breath. "I'd appreciate an update if you find anything."

"Will do, ma'am."

Morgan hung up, thankful to get off the phone with him. Pax had been watching her the entire time. "That didn't look like it went well."

"They didn't find anything, and I'm pretty sure they're not that interested in finding my rental car, either. Sometimes I hate relying on locals."

"Sometimes you love it."

"Shush. Not today." Morgan gave Pax a gleaming smile and went back to her computer. She desperately needed something she could dig her teeth into and run with. Having a profile for a serial killer was good, but it wasn't much unless she had leads. "You finish the financials?"

"Yeah, but there's no connection between the victims at all other than our killer."

Sighing, Morgan rubbed the bridge of her nose and sipped at her now cold coffee. She grimaced as she swallowed. "Any idea where our killer may have met them?"

Pax shrugged. "Could be anywhere. First victim went to a grocery store, a diner, a coffee shop, work, and church all within the week before she was murdered. Second—"

"You mean third," Morgan interrupted.

"Sure, the third one, Katie Jenkins. She went to work, a coffee shop, a grocery store, a nail salon, a hair salon, and the movies the week before she was murdered. The third one just the grocery store and work."

"So she's meeting them at ordinary places, which basically gives us bubkiss."

"Bubkiss?"

"Again, shush, I'm being nostalgic. Leave me alone." Morgan smirked. "Coffee shop is similar."

"Yeah, so is work. Two of them were teachers."

"Different schools, districts, and states, though."

Pax shrugged. "Still a connection."

"Kind of. Not a strong one." Morgan reached into her pocket and fingered her phone. She had an idea to call Wexford and see what she thought of everything. She seemed to have a brain for the case, but she wasn't sure after their last encounter if Wexford would even answer the phone, or if she really wanted to call her and bring something up both would rather leave behind.

"What are you thinking?" Pax asked.

Morgan shook her head. "That I need more information. That I really want to go to St. Louis."

"We could."

"Taylor would never approve that, not with only one credit card hit and no car. If we found the car, maybe."

Pax nodded his agreement and turned to his computer. "I'm going to work on this trafficking ring. At least we're making progress there."

Snorting, Morgan knew he was right. She had little to nothing on her murderer. She needed something hard, some good evidence as to where she was, but it was as if her killer was a ghost. She made no impact, had no residence, had very little connection to the women other than they were lesbian or at least swayed in that direction of some sort, and Morgan really didn't want to start a panic within the community.

She switched to rewatching her interview with Dimitri one more time. He had been very helpful to them, and she had no doubt he would testify once they brought Mr. Jimmy in. Pax had narrowed their suspect list of who Mr. Jimmy could be to only a handful of people. They were strongly looking at a man who lived in the DC area, who had some traces to trafficking cases of old and certainly had the funds to keep it going under the radar if he wanted.

"I'll be right back. Need a refill." Morgan picked up her mug. She turned at the break room, filled it, but instead of going to her desk, she took a left and headed for an empty conference room.

She couldn't even sit down, her nerves were running like mad. Morgan paced the room back and forth, flipping her phone from side to side. She wanted so badly to make the call, to hear Fiona's voice again, to ask her for her help and her opinion on at least the two murders she knew about.

Nervously, Morgan pulled up Fiona's contact information. She stared down at the number and shook her head. Instead, she called Amya. It rang three times before it switched to voicemail. Cursing inwardly, Morgan stared down at her phone. She didn't dare call anyone else in her family. Amya was the one with the least amount of issues and drama, but she was also the only one who cared to listen to Morgan's own drama.

Pursing her lips, Morgan held her thumb over Wexford's number one more time. Clicking it, she wrinkled her nose and brought the phone to her ear. She listened as it rang. And rang. And rang. Fiona's sweet voice filled her ear. "You've reached Detective Wexford. Leave a message."

Short, simple, and to the point. Morgan hung up before she could leave a message and then immediately regretted that decision, but she wasn't about to call Fiona a second time. Her heart had enough damage to it already. Morgan checked her watch, noted the late hour, and decided it would be best if she headed home for the night. With her hot cup of coffee in her hand, she went to her desk and piled all her paperwork together. She issued a curt goodbye to Pax and walked out the door.

As soon as she got home, she dumped her files onto her kitchen table and laid them out so she could see it all. The first murder, a blank spot for the second one, third, and fourth. There had to be a strong connection between them somewhere.

Standing up and stretching her back, Morgan pulled off her jacket and her shoulder holster, setting them on the back of her couch. She let out a breath and ran her fingers through her hair as she stared down at the crime scene photos and the evidence she had in front of her. Licking her lips, she walked around her table and stared at it from a different direction.

Each woman was murdered either during or shortly after sex. Morgan really wished she knew which, because it would give her strong insight to the mind of her killer. There was no sign of breaking and entering, so they'd known the assailant. They'd met her somewhere, willingly brought her to their place of residence.

Rubbing the back of her knuckles over her lips, Morgan grimaced. Katie had fought back pretty good. They had their killer's DNA. It was being run through their systems to see if there were any familial matches, but that could easily take weeks if not close to months. There were no drugs in anyone's systems. Alcohol in victim one. Each house had alcohol in it.

Morgan swallowed as she leaned over the table. "What the hell is drawing you to these women? It's not like you're going to a damn gay bar to find all the lesbians."

Clenching her teeth, she jerked when her phone rang. Pulling it out of her bag, she smiled at Amya's name, but she didn't answer. She was knee deep in her case, and she wanted to focus on it by herself for a few more hours before she took a break.

Her alarm went off at midnight. Morgan gathered up all the papers with nothing new to break the case. She had just about memorized every piece of evidence she had, but she had no new epiphanies that night. Shoving the papers into her bag, Morgan stripped the rest of her clothes and left a trail behind her as she made her way to her small bedroom off her living room.

She got to her bathroom, naked, and stepped under the hot spray of water. She hated not being able to break a case, not being able to get into her perp's head. It was like she was missing the big picture of everything. Morgan knew this woman was only in it for the basic necessities, to find food and shelter and perhaps even love, but she was unsuccessful each time. The cases that had been found, she didn't use the stolen cards except the once. Morgan wouldn't be surprised if she'd ditched them somewhere.

But the knives. She'd almost forgotten about the knives. Somewhere this woman was keeping the knives she used to stab her victims. She collected them like trophies. Morgan let out a breath. She didn't stay under the hot spray much longer, wanting to put in a full day of investigating the next day and wanting to make sure she was thinking clearly when she did it.

After double-checking the locks on her doors, Morgan slid under the covers naked. She stared at the ceiling, wondering what her perp looked like, what she smelled like, what she was thinking every time she went to find a new woman to murder, what she was thinking as she strangled them. Shivering at the last thought, Morgan turned on her side and willed her mind to shut up and let her go to sleep.

## CHAPTER TWELVE

PAX BOUNCED in his shoes waiting for Morgan. She hadn't really slept the night before, the details of the case churning over in her brain as she laid restlessly in bed and begged for the sandman to show face. She was shit out of luck, though. So when she showed up and Pax looked like a kid in a candy store, she sent him a funny look.

"Take it you didn't check your email when you woke up," he commented.

"No. I chugged coffee. Which I need more of. Why?"

He grinned. "I'll wait for you to set up."

"Coffee?"

With snark, Pax left her vicinity. Morgan dropped everything on her desk and shoved her files onto her desk top. She rolled her chair out so she could sit properly before hitting the power button on her desktop. It was still slowly booting up when Pax came back with a paper cup filled with coffee.

Morgan narrowed his eyes at him. He shrugged. "Your cup is gone."

"My...shit, I brought it home to wash it and completely forgot."

"Guess you'll just have to kill the planet today. You see it yet?"

"No. My computer is taking a day and a half to load. Just tell me."

"No."

Pax plopped down into his chair, turning so he could look over her shoulder at her screen. Morgan glanced at Taylor's office before she pulled up her email. In it were several unread ones, but one in particular that had her attention. It said, "Please read" in the subject line.

"This one, I'm assuming." Morgan opened it up.

It was a case file from three months ago. She opened the attachment and was gobsmacked. "Holy shit."

"Yeah."

"Why the hell didn't you call me?"

"I just got it."

Morgan didn't bother to look at him. She focused on the case in front of her. It was their second victim. Just as she had suspected, this woman had been stabbed twice in the heart post-mortem. The medical examiner's report was thorough. Strangled first and then stabbed—hyoid bone broken. She was left in her bed and found three weeks later.

"Holy shit," Morgan repeated, words not coming into her brain.

"I know, right?" Pax commented next to her.

Morgan shook her head. "How did we not find this case before?"

"Because someone plead guilty, so it's not an open case."

"You're shitting me. Who was it?"

"Some man—" he emphasized the second word "—who claimed he was in love with her. I think he was her neighbor or something."

"But it took three weeks to find her?"

"Stench."

"God, I can't imagine."

"Sure you can."

Rolling her eyes, Morgan stared at her screen. Pax was right. She'd seen bodies three weeks out, and it wasn't pretty, and it did not smell good at all. It was something she could certainly live without witnessing again. "Did he say why he killed her?"

"She had a date, and he was jealous. Look down here." Pax pointed on the screen, and Morgan scrolled the curser down. "There."

Leaning in, she read his confession. Sure enough, he claimed the victim had gone on a date with a woman the night before he went to confront her. He hit her in the process, they fought, and he confessed to strangling her. "He didn't say he stabbed her."

"He didn't. But with a confession and a plea deal, the judge accepted it, and he's in prison."

"The hell? He didn't even tell them what happened."

"Don't talk to me about it." Pax put his hands out in front of him.

Morgan clicked print on the files. She'd completely forgotten her coffee until then, but she chugged it to get the rest of the juices in her brain flowing as she waited for the printer to do its magic. "So she started in Grand Rapids, moved south to Fort Wayne, Indiana, and the northwest to Chicagoland, and back south. She seems to like this area of the country, perhaps she's from around here."

"Maybe. Hey, you coming to dinner for the twins' birthday?"

"Uh...what?" Morgan shook her head at him in confusion. "What dinner?"

"Didn't Mel call you?"

"No. She did not."

"Ugh. I told her to call you."

"Because you can't ask me at work?" Morgan licked her lips and finished her coffee.

Pax narrowed his eyes in a glare. "Now you sound like her."

"When's the dinner?"

"Next week."

"Pax. You gotta give a girl more warning than that."

"What? It's not like you have a date. You're perpetually single."

It felt as though a rock was pressed down onto her heart. He wasn't wrong, although it wasn't for lack of trying. She'd tried with Fiona Wexford, and that had gotten her exactly nowhere. Not that he would know. Grunting, Morgan turned to the printer. Noting it was done doing its thing, she got up to grab her newly printed case file.

When she sat down, he raised a brow at her. "So you coming or not?"

"What day next week?"

"Friday."

"Time?"

"Seven."

"I'll see what I can do." Morgan shoved the papers into a file and grabbed the rest of them, heading for a conference room. She wanted to lay everything out like she had done the night before now that she had the final missing piece to her puzzle, but more importantly, she wanted some space between her and Pax. She loved him dearly, but he was such an oaf sometimes that she wanted to give him a good punch to the nose. She knew Mel would agree.

Pax had picked up her slack for the rest of the day on the trafficking case. She'd gone to assist him in a few quick profiles, but Morgan had focused mainly on her serial murderer. She pulled video footage from the last places Katie and Andrea had gone to see if there was anyone who looked the same between them. She had requested video footage from the Grand Rapids case and from the Fort Wayne case, but she knew that would take days if not a week to get to her. She'd also tried to get the full case files from both, but seeing as the one in Indiana was considered closed, she struggled to convince them to let her look at it.

Her frustration level had risen and fallen several times throughout the day, and the lack of sleep wasn't helping her brain stay sharp and her tongue stay tied when she wanted to make smart retorts to idiots who wouldn't cooperate. She didn't want to take over their cases, for the most part, she just wanted to solve her case and get a murderer off the street.

She was halfway home when her phone rang. Her mother. Groaning,

Morgan answered. "Mom."

"Morgan! You answered this time!"

"I do have a job, and I do have a life, you know. That means I do not and can not always answer my phone. Just last night, I didn't answer Amya's call."

"She called you?"

Cursing under her breath, Morgan scrunched her nose. "Yeah, but she was returning my call. She didn't call to tell me any special news that may or may not have happened, but I'm telling you, Ma. Amya is *not* getting engaged, like ever."

"I think I would know before you."

Morgan really should have had more coffee before she left, especially before dealing with her mother. Sighing, she let her mom think she would know first, when in fact, she would likely be one of the last to find out. Knowing Amya and Grace as well as she did, Morgan would not be surprised if they went to the courthouse, got hitched, and then didn't tell anyone for three or four years.

"What'd you call for? I'm on my way home, but I still have work to do tonight, so I can't talk long."

"You really need to take a break more often. When's the last time you took a vacation? You know you can't keep working hours like this, find someone to marry, and have a family."

Morgan's fingers clenched her steering wheel so hard she swore it would break if she didn't let up. Biting her lip, Morgan took a deep breath and calmed the rage building in her heart. She hated these types of conversations with her mom. Normally, if she was working at full-capacity and firing on all cylinders she would have scouted out this conversation before it even came up and been able to side step it. Instead, she'd practically walked straight into it.

"Ma, please stop."

"I'm not going to stop worrying about you. That's my job. You're my baby, and that's what I do."

Morgan stepped on the brake as she came to a red light. With one more deep breath, she worked out a tactful way to convince her mom to change topics. "I appreciate the concern. I'm not interested in a family. You've known that for years. Please accept what I have decided."

"You'll change your mind when you fall in love."

"Mom."

"What?"

"Please stop. Really."

"Okay, okay."

Stepping on the gas, Morgan took a left turn toward her apartment. "Really, why did you call? I'm tired. It's been a really long week." She may have been over exaggerating, but her mom didn't need to know.

"I'm calling because of Lauren. I don't know what to do with her."

"What does she need?"

"I don't know. I keep bringing her food."

"Have you asked her what she needs?"

The silence on the other end of the phone told her the answer. Morgan turned into her parking garage.

"Look, ask Lauren what she needs and what she wants. She's not your daughter, you have to remember that."

"She is my daughter!"

"By marriage. She is not your daughter by blood, which means she is probably going to react differently to you than her own parents, especially because it's your son who screwed up and put her in this situation. If you want to help, ask Lauren what she needs and what she wants. If you really want to help, convince your son to go to fucking rehab."

"Morgan! Language."

"I'm sorry, but the kid seriously needs some help. This is out of control."

"I know. I agree. I've talked to him about it already, and he's considering it, but he's not sure how to pay for it."

"I'm sure the family can figure something out if he's truly committed to going, but until then, he's not seeing a dime from me."

"He's your brother—"

"Yes, he is. He's also a drunk, and now he's a convicted addict. That changes a lot of things. I love him, but I ain't going to let him walk all over me. Look, Mom, I'm home. I've got some work to catch up on. I'll talk to you later."

Before her mom could say anything else, Morgan hung up and turned off the engine of her car. She rubbed behind her neck. The knot of tension was bigger than she remembered, but to be fair, a phone call with her mom could easily do that.

Morgan grabbed her stuff and headed upstairs. As soon as she got inside, she picked up her phone and dialed Wexford. Folding herself into her couch, she waited as it rang and rang and rang and went, once again, to voice mail. This time she opted to leave a message.

"Detective, it's Special Agent Stone. I was calling to see if I could get your opinion on a case you might be interested in. I could really use some fresh eyes on it."

Hanging up, she put her head down on her pillow and closed her eyes. She really needed a cat. Any friendly face as soon as she walked through the door would be a welcome sight. She'd only ever lived with one significant other in her life. Other than that and a few roommates here or there, but she was finding in her near to middle age if she'd admit it, that she missed the companionship. Perhaps not the nagging, but the companionship for sure.

Morgan let out a sigh and ran her hand through her hair. She had to get a handle on the case. It wouldn't be long before she'd have to focus back on the human trafficking case because they were coming close to finding Mr. Jimmy, and she really wanted to find this killer. The guilt that would come with finding another murdered woman would no doubt crush her to pieces.

Opting not to work even after she'd made the excuse to her mom, Morgan ate a light dinner of leftover takeout she'd ordered sometime in the last two weeks—she forgot when and decided she really needed to label the shit in her fridge but also knew she'd never get to it. She picked up the laundry all over her apartment and shoved it into the stackable washing machine that sat in the tiny-ass what may possibly pass for a closet in her hallway. She picked up the rest of her apartment so it was passable for clean and then she passed out in her bed, finally not dreaming of murder and mayhem.

## CHAPTER THIRTEEN

LOLLIE HAD stayed every night with Samantha, their relationship taking a steamy turn just about any time they were in each other's vicinity. Unlike with Andrea, Samantha clearly had a much higher sex drive, which matched Lollie's. She was pleased with how everything was turning out. It was early in the morning, Samantha had already gone to work but told Lollie she was welcome to stay until she woke up, and they could meet up after she got home from work.

It was clear that while Samantha trusted her enough to stay the night, she didn't want her there all day. It was an odd conundrum for Lollie. She couldn't quite figure it out. Everything seemed to be going well for their relationship, they went on dates together, laughed, joked, flirted, but when it came to Samantha taking the leap to allowing her to stay there more permanently, Samantha always hedged.

Lollie stayed in Samantha's warm bed until she felt the calling to get up. She stretched and slowly walked around the apartment naked. She touched everything. She hadn't had much time to herself there since she'd met Samantha, so she envied this time. Brushing her fingers along the dresser, Lollie pulled open each of the drawers. Samantha had everything folded but haphazardly tossed in the drawers. Lollie pulled open her underwear drawer last and smiled as she found some lacy panties inside it, something she had yet to see Samantha wear, and she figured Samantha probably had worn once and that was it.

Unless it was another woman's.

Picking it up, Lollie brought it to her nose and took a deep breath. She didn't find anyone else's scent on it. Pursing her lips, she folded the article and set it right back where she found it. Lollie opened the small boxes on top of the dresser and peeked inside. She found some necklaces, one pearl and one gold. She pulled them out and shoved them into her purse.

Going into the bathroom, Lollie turned the shower on and stepped under the spray. She picked up Samantha's shampoo after wetting her own hair. Sniffing it, she wrinkled her nose. She scrubbed the shampoo through her hair and then the conditioner. Using her razor, Lollie shaved her legs and her pits, setting everything back right where she found it. When she was done, she wrapped herself in a big fluffy towel and let her hair drip down her back. Using a fist, she wiped down the mirror so she could see her reflection.

She was getting too old to be trying to find someone. She'd wanted to be married and maybe have a kid or two under her belt by the time she was thirty, but her twenty-ninth birthday was fast approaching, and unless Samantha made any sudden moves, which she was beginning to doubt would happen, then she wouldn't be finding a partner in her.

Taking a deep breath, Lollie carded through the baskets under the sink and looked through everything Samantha had there. She looked at her tampons, her blow-dryer, her soaps she hadn't opened. It was all clearance and cheap shit she must have gotten at the store she worked at.

Lollie headed to the bedroom and pulled out a fresh outfit she had bought after she'd arrived in St. Louis. She'd have to go shopping again, especially if she was going to have to try and sway Samantha into letting her stay there yet another night. As soon as she was dressed, Lollie wrapped her hair up in the towel to dry. She grabbed a bowl of cereal and ate at the kitchen table with Samantha's iPad between her fingers.

Running some searches on names of her past girlfriends, Lollie found nothing and deleted the browser history. If they hadn't released any information on the others yet, then she was still golden to stay at Samantha's. Swallowing down the last bit of her breakfast, Lollie did the dishes, tidied up the kitchen, and headed out to her car they had finally gone back to get.

Not having a place to stay was pissing her off. Anger bubbled in Lollie's belly as she drove away from Samantha's house, but she wasn't going to stay there if Samantha didn't want her there. Cringing, she headed off to drive the town. Maybe there was someone better out there for her, someone who was a more perfect fit. All she had to do was find her. She still had another six months before she turned twenty-nine to find the love of her life.

Then again, maybe that was Samantha. Groaning, Lollie ran her hand through her hair and turned into the mall parking lot. She would do some shopping, and then she would see what Samantha wanted to do for dinner. They'd discussed briefly meeting up but not where, although any time they'd attempted to go on a dinner date in the last week they hadn't made it farther than the couch, or the wall, or the front door before they both decided they'd be better off staying in and ordering food for delivery.

After buying some special lingerie for that evening, Lollie got in her car and sent Samantha a picture of her most recent purchase. It was near time for Samantha to get off work, and she wanted to know for sure that night if Samantha was willing to move forward with their relationship or not. Smiling when she saw Samantha's response, Lollie headed to the apartment to wait for Samantha's arrival.

Samantha pulled Lollie out of her car as soon as she parked next to her. Lollie went with it, and heat pooled in her belly as Samantha pressed her against the door of the car. Their lips were locked. Lollie's hand wrapped around Samantha's neck, and she moaned as Samantha tugged Lollie's lip between her teeth and pulled seductively.

"I hope you're wearing it."

Lollie chuckled. "No, not yet. I came right here."

Samantha growled. "Better get it on, my friend. I want to see you in it before I rip it off you."

With Samantha's mouth at her neck, Lollie tilted her head to the side and gave her more access. She loved that Samantha was so aggressive during their love making. She enjoyed it immensely when Samantha would wrap her fingers around her throat, cutting off her air supply all the while bringing her to an orgasm that made lights shine behind her closed eye lids.

"It's all for you," Lollie whispered, lowering her voice and making the tone husky to entice Samantha to keep going.

It worked. Samantha's hand slid up between her shirt and her body, her nails scraping into her skin. Shivers ran along Lollie's spine, and she pushed her hips out toward Samantha and away from the car. She closed her eyes and bit her lip as Samantha pressed her teeth into the soft spot just above her collar bone.

"Don't stop," Lollie whispered, knowing her words would spurn Samantha on. She typically wasn't one for public sex, but for some reason, anytime Samantha was involved, she didn't care. Lollie pressed her fingers into Samantha's hips and jerked her closer.

Samantha reached up and cupped Lollie's breast, squeezing. Lollie keened into Samantha's ear. "Let's go inside so I can show you this outfit I got."

"Good idea." Samantha promptly pulled away but grabbed on to Lollie's hand. She led the way upstairs to the apartment, unlocking the door and heading inside.

Lollie teasingly sauntered on ahead of Samantha and into the bathroom. She undressed completely and tugged on the black lace to cover her, scantily. She checked her hair and touched up her lipstick—well, Samantha's lipstick. Making sure everything was perfect, Lollie left the bathroom and went in search of her lover.

The living room was empty, and when she walked into the bedroom, she had to stop. Samantha lay on the bed, her wrists in cuffs on the headboard, her body completely bared to Lollie. Swallowing, Lollie walked tentatively over to the side of the bed and stared down at Samantha.

"What's all this?"

Samantha grinned. "Something for me and something for you. I thought it only fair."

"Hmm." Lollie bit her lower lip like she was contemplating. She ran one finger down Samantha's neck to her chest and over a nipple, stopping. "So do you like?"

Lollie twirled in a circle, wiggling her ass so Samantha could see. When she turned back, Samantha breathed hard, and her cheeks flushed. "Very much. Get on top of me."

Doing as commanded, Lollie straddled Samantha's legs. She leaned over and pressed her lips to Samantha's. "Why the cuffs?"

"You like it rough. So do I. Figured we could try this."

Pleasure burst in Lollie's chest. Samantha, always thinking of Lollie and her pleasure. That was what made them such a good team from the start. They anticipated what the other wanted. Pressing her lips to Samantha's pale skin and leaving red marks from her lipstick behind, Lollie kissed all over her body. Samantha writhed underneath her.

When she moved back up to Samantha's lips, she whispered, "Think any more on living together?"

Samantha jerked and stiffened. "I haven't. It's not something I'm interested in."

Lollie clenched her jaw as anger surged in her chest. She held it back enough. She didn't want this night to end too soon. This time, instead of pressing kisses to Samantha's body, she bit her. Not too hard, but hard enough to leave welts in the morning. Samantha hissed when Lollie bit down particularly hard at the top of her hip just on her side, but when Lollie moved her hand between Samantha's legs, she knew Samantha was enjoying their play time.

"Let me go grab something real quick." Lollie slipped from the bed and from the room. She headed into the kitchen and pulled open the silverware drawer. She'd already chosen that morning. The orange one. It was sharp, she'd made sure of that earlier in the day. But it was the odd knife out, the one that didn't match the rest of the set, which was very much like their relationship. She also set the timer on the stove for ninety minutes.

With the timer set, there was no going back. Her heart raced as Lollie headed into the bedroom and settled the knife toward the bottom of the bed. She kissed Samantha's lips and smiled against her. Lollie turned her body so her nose brushed the apex of Samantha's legs, and Samantha could reach her with her tongue through the open bottoms of her lingerie. She lowered her hips, and they moved together. Guilt almost ripped through her because they were so good at this, but if Samantha didn't want a relationship, then there was no other way. They were going to have to break up.

Blinking, Lollie moved her hips back and forth as they continued to pleasure each other. Samantha tugged her arms in the confines of the cuffs. The thought made Lollie snort. She'd made it far too easy. Her orgasm built as she thought about what she was going to do, her hands around Samantha's throat, the light as it would fade from her eyes, the pallor of her skin paling as her lips turned blue and would have that slight part to them.

Lollie moaned when Samantha's teeth brushed against her. She pushed back, liking the feel of it. The knife was within easy grasp. It would all happen so fast, Samantha would be none the wiser. Then she could go on her way, find someone new, and settle down with them. Her orgasm caught her by surprise, and Lollie stopped, curling her body in on itself as she rode out her pleasure.

Not one to leave her partner unsatisfied, she finished Samantha off before she moved, grabbing the knife and bringing it closer to Samantha's head. Samantha caught sight of it, and her chest jerked up and down as her breathing increased.

"What's that?" Samantha asked, nodding toward the metal weapon.

"A knife," Lollie answered, straight forward.

With her jaw set, she slid her hands up Samantha's chest, running her fingers over her breasts and her nipples, twisting them with enough pain to cause pleasure to ripple.

"Wh—what are you going to do with it?"

"Stab you."

"Lollie."

Chuckling, Lollie shook her head and shushed Samantha. "Don't worry, baby. It'll be okay."

With her hands around Samantha's neck, Lollie tightened her grip. Samantha jerked her knees up to try and throw Lollie off, but Lollie clenched her thighs together to keep Samantha in place, pleasure coursing through her body and to her core as Samantha's belly writhed against her. It gave her so much pleasure, more than anything else they had done. She rocked her hips back and forth as she kept her hands in place at Samantha's neck, but it was all over too soon.

Not satisfied, Lollie grunted and grabbed the knife, anger surging through her. She pursed her lips and jammed the knife into Samantha's chest once, twice, three then four times and finally a fifth and final blow. Blood spattered on her face, the warm liquid running down her cheek to her chin to drop onto Samantha's pale and unscathed belly.

Releasing a breath, Lollie pushed off Samantha's prone form and leaned against the wall, the knife held loosely between her fingers. She finished herself off since Samantha had failed to give her that good grace. After showering, she made herself some dinner and sat at the kitchen table to eat. She'd have to go somewhere new, find somewhere else to start over. St. Louis had been a bad idea. It was far too similar to Chicago. She needed somewhere new, somewhere completely different.

Opening up the iPad, she searched top places for people to move. Texas, Oregon, Arizona, Washington. There. Seattle. She'd been there once as a child, ages before. She had loved what she remembered of it. The streets were filled with people, friendly people. Booking herself a flight, Lollie finished her dinner and made plans for her next big move. It wouldn't be long until she found her new life and was able to truly start over.

## CHAPTER FOURTEEN

MORGAN HAD arrived early that morning, but she had to wait for the local PD to let her in before she could go to the crime scene. She'd walked the apartment complex twice before the detective arrived, well past nine in the morning. The murder had been discovered the night before, the car Morgan had been searching for parked by the apartment had only pissed her off even more.

When it had been run, an alert had popped up on her end, and she had immediately called Taylor and told him she was leaving in the morning. He readily agreed. She clenched her jaw and glared at the detective in charge. If the St. Louis Police Department had only taken her inquiries seriously, then perhaps they would have one less dead body on their hands.

Morgan stomped straight toward the detective's vehicle. Pax's rental SUV stopped her short, and the window rolled down. Pax gave her a grin, and Morgan sneered at him. "You better brighten up, buttercup, if you want any information from them. Going in there like that will get you nowhere."

"Shove it. You got the good stuff."

"Always, love." Pax handed her the cup of coffee out the window, and she breathed in the aroma before taking a sip and hissing. "It's hot."

"No shit," she muttered but took another sip anyway.

Pax drove ahead and parked next to the detective's vehicle. There were still uniformed officers on the property. Morgan walked to meet up with Pax, but he was already talking to the detective in charge. She raised her eyebrow at him and waited for introductions to be made.

He nodded at her. "This is my partner, Special Agent Stone. This is Detective Hadley."

"Pleasure to meet you." Morgan put her hand out for him to shake, but he stared at her and turned back to Pax. Inwardly groaning, Morgan listened and drank her coffee, absorbing anything he said. She worked it into her already-built profile.

When Hadley offered to let them in the apartment, he turned to her with a hand on his hip and a smirk on his lips. "It's a bloody mess in there, forewarning you."

"Why? Because you think that I'm a lowly woman who is going to faint at the sight of blood or because you just think I might be interested in the fact that this murder is a lot more violent than the others?"

Hadley's lips thinned.

"Yeah, that's what I thought." Morgan pushed her way around him and walked up the awkward cement steps to the building. She made it to the top floor before Pax and Hadley were even at the second floor. She was pissed, and the anger running through her veins was not going to do her well. She flashed her badge at the uniform and went inside after putting on her booties to cover her shoes, not wanting to wait one more minute for the asshole behind her.

No one was in the apartment but her. Taking in a deep breath, she caught the scent of flowers and bacon. Someone had cooked recently. Walking into the kitchen, Morgan found the dishes done and no sign that anyone had eaten there, much like the other crime scenes. Whoever was committing these murders was meticulous before they left about making sure the house or apartment was in complete order.

Morgan moved to the dining room. Nothing looked amiss there either. The chairs were tucked under the table, pushed in and out of the way. The living room had the throw blanket folded and tossed over the arm of the couch. Pax walked in, his breath slightly heavy from the climb up the stairs. She'd tease him about it later but really didn't want to open any opportunity for the asshat to talk more than necessary. "Body found in the bed?"

"Yeah, this way." Detective Hadley led the way into the back bedroom, past the bathroom. It was a small apartment. No more than five hundred square feet. It wasn't spotlessly clean, but it was tidy. Everything was in place, just as she had requested it, except for the body. They had already taken that to the morgue, she knew. She and Pax would make that stop next, but first she'd wanted to get into the mind of her murderer.

The bedroom was a completely different story. The bedsheets were bloody, but the vague outline of where the body had been was imprinted into the pattern of blood. Splatters of red littered the ceiling, the headboard, and two walls, like the killer had shifted position in the middle of stabbing the victim. Unlike Andrea's murder, this one was violent. If Morgan didn't know better, she'd say her killer was angry.

"She's getting more violent," Morgan commented to Pax, bypassing Hadley.

"She?" Hadley asked.

Morgan refused to answer and let Pax do the talking for her. If she didn't have a direct question to ask Hadley, she wasn't about to talk to him, and she might even be of mind to complain to his supervisor if she could find the energy and the time.

"Theory is our killer is a woman."

"Not theory. She is a woman. Your tests will come back, undoubtedly, that the victim had sex with a woman before she was killed. There has never been a sign of a male in the homes of our victims."

"Jesus," Hadley muttered.

Morgan spun on him with a grin on her face. "Want to make another snarky comment about women now or afraid one of us might kill you?"

Hadley blanched but wisely kept his trap shut. Morgan took her own photos on her phone, knowing she'd get copies of everything anyway but wanting access to it sooner rather than later. She looked through the stuff on the dresser, finding one of the small decorative boxes opened.

"Do we know what was in here?"

Hadley shook his head. "Our bet is nothing."

"Something was in here. Probably jewelry. It's missing. Make a note of that, Pax, would you?"

"She your boss?" Hadley whispered to Pax but loud enough Morgan heard him.

She shook her head as her back stiffened. Some people were just assholes. She knew Pax would have her back. She watched him in the reflection of the mirror over the dresser as Pax rolled his eyes and shook his head at Hadley.

"She is the behavior analyst, the smart one of the partnership, and she is the lead on the case, not me. I'm not her lackey, but we work together. Seriously, are all detectives in your departments such sexist pigs? If you want someone solving this case, you want her on it. Not me. Not you. Her."

Grinning, Morgan looked down at the floor so Hadley wouldn't see her. Pax always had her back, no matter what. Locking her lips, Morgan turned to the two men. "Which knife is missing?"

"No knife."

"Then where is it?"

Hadley gave her a look of bewilderment.

Morgan turned her head to the side and stared him down with a raised eyebrow. "If there is no knife missing, where is the knife that stabbed the victim? Or do you think our killer just ripped the nice clean lines into her heart with her bare fingers?"

Putting his hands up, Hadley stepped back. "Look, I think we got off on the wrong foot."

"About time you figured that out. The knife. Which one is missing?"

"There's no knife missing from what we can tell. There is one set in the kitchen, and it is all there."

"Our killer takes the knives with her, she always uses one from the residence of her victims. She took a knife. She clearly took jewelry, too. Are all of you inept or just you?"

Pax shot Morgan a look, but she ignored him. She wanted an answer, and she wanted to shut Hadley up for good, but she knew she was toeing the line to not having a willing partner in him. She almost didn't care. Almost.

"Look, I just got this case last night. You have clearly had more information for some time now. Why don't you tell me what you know so we can get an APB out for this killer."

"There's been one out," Morgan answered, fire in her tone. "For a rental car that is conveniently parked outside this exact apartment. I'll have that sent to the bureau here so we can have our team go through it instead of yours, since clearly you keep missing things."

Morgan stalked out of the room and into the living area. She needed a breather. Pax would finish up. She'd seen just about all she wanted in there, anyway. The body would tell her more. Morgan waited for Pax down at the car. He took another thirty minutes with Hadley, and when they got into the vehicle, he sent her a glare.

"You could have played nicer."

"He could have not been a dick."

Pax snorted. "True. To the morgue?"

"Yes, please. Drive on!"

After they spent an hour going over the preliminary report since the autopsy hadn't even been started, they went to the field office off Market Street and checked in with the agents who had been doing a bit more investigating than the local police department had. She was glad they'd taken over the case shortly after they'd been made aware of the murder, but still, working with Hadley in any capacity had been trying on her patience.

Morgan plopped down in an empty conference room and pulled up her laptop. She went through her emails, double-checked the credit reports and set up alerts for all of Samantha's information. As much as she hoped her killer was still in the area, she had a sinking feeling she'd already fled somewhere else. The violence in this crime over the others was unlike she had anticipated. Something about Samantha Gideon hit a nerve with their killer.

Morgan had the rental car towed and checked it over before letting the crime scene guys have a go at it. They'd pull fingerprints. She wanted more a feel for what her killer was thinking. She walked around the car three times before it hit her. If the rental was at the apartment, and the victim's vehicle was at the apartment, how on earth did her killer leave?

Spinning on her heel, Morgan called Pax on her cell. "Hey, set up a search for taxis and Ubers and whatever. She had to leave somehow, right? There's not exactly a bus route nearby there, so find out who had a pickup in that area sometime between last night and this morning."

"Got it. Also, we got a hit on Mr. Jimmy."

"You're kidding." Morgan rubbed her lips together as she walked toward the elevator.

"No. We gotta get back tonight. Turns out, he's in Chicago."

"Well, damn." Morgan let out a breath. "These guys here can finish this up easily enough, but I was hoping to stay for the autopsy at least."

"I know, but Mr. Jimmy—"

"Yeah, I get it." Her thoughts immediately turned to Dimitri. If they were able to take Mr. Jimmy into custody, the battle Dimitri would be fighting would just begin. She'd be seeing his name pop up for years to come. Morgan stepped into the elevator. "I'm coming up. I'll be there in a minute."

She hung up the phone, sliding it into her pocket and hit the button for the floor she wanted. If they had to get back, her time to work the murder was severely limited. Perhaps it hadn't been wise to take on another case just as their trafficking one picked up steam.

Finally at her floor, Morgan stepped out into the hallway and went down to the conference room she and Pax were holed up in. He was waiting for her, and she put her hands out in surprise as she walked in. "What did they find?"

"They're pretty sure Mr. Jimmy is Jonathon Lockland."

"Crap." Morgan paused. "You sure?"

"No. We have to verify some information first, but Dimitri's information and my kids' match up."

"I thought we were looking at someone in DC?"

"We were, but it didn't pan out. Lockland seems to be a better fit."

Morgan narrowed her eyes. "Let me see the profile again."

He handed it over. She skimmed it and took the second file he offered, which was a brief introduction to Jonathon Lockland, CEO of Lockland Divisions. It seemed to be a company that did...not a whole lot. His finances, however, told a completely different story.

"This could be him. I'd need to see an interview with him and have some more information before I can confirm if he matches the profile or not."

"We're working on it."

"The taxi search?"

"It's up and running, but Morgan..."

"What?"

"She did a couple searches on the victim's iPad. One of which was a search of top ten places to live."

Morgan plopped down into the chair by her computer, waiting for Pax to continue. She breathed shallowly as she clung on to her patience. "Well? You gonna share or not?"

"Seattle. They think she went to Seattle."

"I'm checking flight manifests."

"They're already running them."

"Well, I'll do them, too. It can't hurt."

"Morgan, don't you think, maybe, you're becoming a little obsessed with this case?"

"No." She turned her chair to face him. "It's new. It's different. It's rare to find a female serial killer. I much prefer murder to sex crimes, you know that."

"Yeah." He popped his head to the side and sat in his own chair. "That's true."

"Uh huh." Morgan looked at her computer, pulling out the annoying reading glasses she knew she needed in order to see better. Aging was not fun. Snorting at the thought, Morgan started her searches to run and notify her if anything matched up what she was looking for. She pulled Samantha's financials and bit her lip as she lost herself in the research that would eventually catch her a murderer.

Before she even had time to focus, she got a hit on one of Samantha's cards. "Pax, take a look at this."

Pax came around to lean over her shoulder, staring down at the screen in front of her. "Well, would you look at that."

"I'm going to Seattle."

"The field office there can take care of it."

"Pax, I'm the one who wrote the profile. This is my case. I want to go to Seattle."

He pursed his lips as he sat back in his chair. "You're going to have to convince Taylor. I can handle Mr. Jimmy easily enough without you, but you're going to have to talk to the boss."

Morgan grinned. She knew Taylor would let her go. She was one of his best agents, and certainly his best profiler. She had the pull to get him to let her go, especially if she promised to check in daily with him about her findings. Picking up her phone and standing up, she paced back and forth in the corner of the room as she called her boss, ready to make the argument.

"What you got for me, Stone?"

"I have a location."

"Where?"

"Seattle. Well, SeaTac. She's just outside the airport, getting coffee at Starbucks."

"The victim?"

Morgan sent a glance to Pax. "Our victim is Samantha Gideon. She was thirty-eight years old, a retail store manager. There is evidence of a sexual activity like the others. She was stabbed five times to the heart post-mortem. She was handcuffed to the bed before she was murdered. This crime was a lot more violent than the others. I believe, sir, that our killer is escalating her behaviors. The timeline is shortening between kills. Rather than months or weeks, she is down to days between. I fully expect another victim to surface in the next two weeks if we don't find her before then."

"Has there been a statement released about the victim there?"

"No. I've held the press off so far."

Silence permeated over the phone. Pax sent her a look with his hands out, mouthing "and?" as he waited for her response. Morgan shrugged and frowned at him, not quite sure what Taylor was thinking.

"You may go, if that's what you're not asking."

She grinned. "Thank you, sir! Pax will be back tonight to interview Mr. Jimmy in the morning."

Taylor grunted. "You make sure to keep apprised of the other case and don't go losing yourself in this one. You hear me, Stone?"

"Loud and clear, sir. I'll send you my flight information as soon as I've made it."

"You better." Taylor hung up.

Morgan fisted her hand and jerked it down with a shout of joy before she wiggled her hips and a happy dance. When she looked at Pax, he sat in his chair and shook his head side to side with his arms folded over his broad chest. "You are such a teacher's pet."

"Oh, you're just jealous."

He flicked his eyebrows up and down at her. Morgan laughed and went to her seat to make her flight arrangements. After she was done, she made a call to internal affairs at the St. Louis Police Department to lodge a formal complaint against Detective Hadley. Pax remained silent through that phone call but nodded his approval when she was done.

Both of them packed up their stuff and headed out of the building. They shared a ride to the airport, checked in for their flights and went opposite directions. Morgan stopped to get herself another dose of coffee before she settled down in her terminal to await her flight.

## CHAPTER FIFTEEN

SHE'D TALKED to Pax at every layover, and they'd updated each other on their cases. As soon as she got to SeaTac, she was ready for a break. Traveling that much in such a short period wore on her. She had a two hour time zone difference to contend with, so while it was only just past afternoon in Washington, her body thought it was far closer to dinner time.

It didn't take her long to collect her luggage, grab her rental, and head for her hotel. So far none of the cards they were tracking had popped back up in the area, but Morgan knew her killer would slip up again. It was only a matter of time. And she knew she was close.

After stashing her crap in her hotel room, Morgan walked out and across the street to get herself some coffee. She'd worked in the Seattle office at one point over a decade ago. She'd been decently green then, but Seattle had been closer to home and she'd wanted to stay nearby in case her family needed her. That had lasted all of two years before she jumped ship and ran even farther from her family—though, their drama always seemed to follow.

She felt like she was coming home. Pax had followed her to Houston a year later, and together they'd made the leap to try out Chicago when Mel had also expressed her dissatisfaction at living in Texas. Oddly enough, after her divorce in her marriage that had barely lasted a year because of the length it took for the divorce to happen, her ex had moved to Tacoma. They had kept in touch, since the marriage had been a drunken mistake they had attempted to make work before giving up and going back to being friends. She'd already contacted Barbie to let her know she'd be in town and inquire about a short meal before she dove straight into the case.

The coffee shop was three blocks down and two blocks over from her hotel, and she knew she'd find the best coffee in town there. It was a little hole in the wall place that had been her one saving grace when she'd had to trudge into work in the middle of the night or even in the middle of the day. She'd lived in the high rise two buildings down from it and had probably spent over half her paycheck there each month.

She grinned at Jaelynn who was still behind the counter. She looked older, wiser even. Her hair was still some fabulous color that she made sure to dye fresh every month, piercings littering her face, ears, chest, and forearms. Tattoos also beautifully inked across her once pale skin.

As soon as Morgan walked in and Jaelynn saw her, her face lit up and she ran around the corner of her counter and held her arms out, jumping into Morgan's waiting embrace. "Girl, what the hell you doing here?"

Morgan chuckled. "I've got a case, surprisingly enough."

"It has been too fucking long." Jaelynn stepped back and slapped Morgan hard on the shoulder.

Shyly, Morgan nodded. "It has. Thought I could get some work done here and away from the distractions of an empty hotel room."

"You didn't have to stay in a sterile place like that. You know my place is always open for you."

Morgan grinned. "I wasn't sure you were even still here."

"Like you couldn't look that up." Jaelynn sent her a sly look and wrinkled her nose. "Sit down and I'll get you a drink. Jeez, a little warning next time."

"I promise." Morgan glanced around. There was little changed about the coffee shop except the placement of the tables and chairs. Spying an outlet, Morgan claimed her spot and opened up her computer. She'd be spending most of her time running through plane manifests, video footage, and the preliminary autopsy reports on Samantha Gideon and Pepper Caldwell, her second murder victim she hadn't spent nearly enough time with.

She must have been there near an hour because Jaelynn had refilled her coffee twice and tsked at her even more for working too hard. Morgan had just sent her a grin and nodded. Sometimes she hated not being able to share what she was working on with friends or family, and other times, she was glad she didn't have to ruin their perfect assumption of what life was. No one wanted to see what she had seen or know what she knew.

When the petite brunette sat at the table next to her, Morgan couldn't help herself but glance over. Something about her was adorable. She was tiny, almost abnormally so, but she was lean and muscular and clearly took care of her physique, much like Morgan had to for work. Her eyes were a deep hazel-brown, and when she smiled in her direction, shivers ran through Morgan's chest.

They made eye contact a few times before Morgan's cup was refilled and Jaelynn took the new girl's order. Morgan focused in on her work, the case file littering her screen. She turned it so her new neighbor wouldn't see the photos of the crime scene and be offended. Rolling her eyes and thinking twice, Morgan opted to change to look over flight manifests again. It would be easier if someone accidentally caught whiff of what she was doing.

She was halfway through her fourth cup of coffee when the petite brunette next to her leaned over and smiled to get her attention. "I'm sorry, I'm new here, but I just can't get over your eyes."

"I...well, thank you," Morgan answered, a blush forming on her cheeks.

The woman was easily half her age or close to it, but she seemed genuine enough. Jaelynn caught Morgan's gaze and wiggled her eyebrows at her. Morgan resisted the urge to roll her eyes and shake her head. She was in Seattle for work and work alone. If she wanted a romp in the sheets, Jaelynn would no doubt accommodate if asked.

Not quite sure what else to say, Morgan turned back to her computer. She checked the time. She'd have to leave soon if she was going to make it south to Tacoma to meet up with Barbie for dinner, and she remembered how much Barbie hated when she was late. It had been a serious issue in not only their short marriage but their friendship.

"Do you come to this place often? I really like the aesthetic."

Turning to her neighbor, Morgan licked her lips. Starting up a conversation had not been where her mind was going, but she was willing to play the game. Perhaps if she practiced flirting, when she returned to Chicago she would actually be able to talk to Wexford in a manner that would achieve some semblance of interest in a relationship.

"I used to. I don't live around here anymore but thought I'd stop in to visit Jaelynn. She's an old friend of mine." Morgan nodded toward the counter. "Where are you coming from?"

"Oh, I just moved here from out east. Ready for some big and new changes in my life."

"Take the bull by the horns?"

"Yeah, you could say that." Her smiles were gracious and plenty.

Morgan closed the top of her laptop and leaned into the wooden chair she was perched on. "There are some great places around here to hang out. Perfect for starting fresh and new. A lot of people move to Seattle for that same reason."

"I certainly hope so. I just got out of a not-so-great relationship, and I need the fresh start."

"I hear you, sister."

Morgan shoved her computer in her bag and unplugged the cord from the wall, wrapping it around her hand before adding it to her pack. When she straightened up, the woman stared at her oddly with her head carded to one side. The curls in her hair brushed her shoulders but barely.

"Am I disturbing you?"

"No. I was just heading out. I have to meet my good friend for dinner. I haven't seen her in years."

"I bet you miss her."

"I do, sometimes. It's not often that we get together, but it's worth it every time."

"Friends and family are so important."

Morgan glanced at the watch on her right wrist and shook her head. "I'm sorry, but I really have to get going if I don't want to be late."

"It was nice chatting with you! I'd love to maybe get together again. I don't know if that's too forward for you. I'm not looking for anything. It's just...it's hard to move to a new place and not know anyone."

"It is." Glancing at Jaelynn, Morgan let out a breath. She could take the risk this once and see if it went anywhere. If anything, she at least had the fall out that she most likely wouldn't be back to Seattle in the next decade. "Here."

Grabbing the napkin off the brunette's table, Morgan scribbled her name and her personal cell number on it. She handed it over. "I have to work tomorrow, but I'm sure I could find some time to show you some of the cool niche places around town."

"I'd love that." She fingered the napkin. "Thank you. Morgan, that's such a pretty name."

"Thank you. I've really got to run."

Grabbing her bag, Morgan booked it out of the coffee shop after waving at Jaelynn. She speed walked her way to her hotel, got her rental, and shoved her bag into the trunk. Pulling out of the underground garage, she headed south for Tacoma and her ex. It would be an interesting reunion as it always was.

Morgan was late. She knew she was. When she pulled up outside the small pizza joint, she saw Barbie's slim figure through the big glass window. After parking, Morgan headed inside and ignored the rain that drizzled down on her head. As soon as she opened the door, Barbie grinned and enveloped her in a hug.

Morgan embraced her tightly. She rubbed her hand up and down Barbie's back and kissed her cheek. Glancing to the side, she saw a strange woman standing stiffly off to the side, staring the two of them down. When Barbie pulled back, she stepped away and gripped the stranger's hand.

"Sorry I'm late."

"When are you not late?" Barbie giggled. "Seriously, though, it's just good to see you."

"I have your table ready," the hostess interrupted them. The stranger led the way, followed by Barbie as Morgan picked up the rear.

"Oh! This is Sue," Barbie grinned over her shoulder at Morgan, who raised a single eyebrow at her. "She's my girlfriend."

"Ah," Morgan answered with a nod. That had been why the odd look. It wasn't every day someone brought their girlfriend to meet up with their ex-wife.

As soon as they were seated, Morgan looked around the room to get their surroundings. Barbie rolled her eyes, put a hand on Morgan's, and whispered, "Relax. Seriously."

Morgan grunted. "What have you two been up to?"

Barbie answered, Sue still remaining awkwardly silent. "Nothing unusual."

"What you working on?" Barbie asked, turning to Morgan. "You've always got some interesting case up your sleeve."

"I've got two cases, right now. Tug of war between them as they're both picking up steam at the same time. Pax is back continuing our other case. I'm out here working on a time sensitive one."

"Sensitive?" Barbie asked point blank, her eyes wide.

Morgan nodded and took a sip of the water in front of her, wishing it was coffee instead. "Been following this one halfway across the country."

"Crazy."

"Not so much. It happens."

They made their orders, Morgan remembering to add in the request for coffee, and turned back to the two love birds across from her. It was odd in one way to see her ex-wife in a committed relationship when she could barely even handle a one-night stand or one kiss with someone she'd had a crush on for years. Neither of them had ever truly been interested in anything long term, until now, apparently.

"What are you thinking?" Barbie asked, her gaze narrowing. "You've got that far-away gaze on your face."

"Nothing." Morgan wished the pizza were there already so she would have a distraction. "Just the case."

Her phone buzzing in her pocket distracted her. Morgan shifted her body so she could grab it. It was her personal cell, but she didn't recognize the number. Furrowing her brow, Morgan held up a finger to Barbie and Sue, answering the call.

"This is Morgan."

"Hey, hi. I'm sorry. I know it's probably too soon to call, but I couldn't stop thinking about our conversation earlier."

"Oh. Oh!" Morgan bit her lip. Barbie gave her a curious look, and she shook her head to brush her off. "Yeah."

"Would you have time tomorrow maybe to show me around a bit?"

"Umm...I think I could find some time after seven? Does that work for you?"

"It does."

"Okay, I'll give you a call then."

"Sounds like a plan."

Morgan's belly flopped, but before she hung up she pulled the phone back to her ear. "Oh! What's your name? I forgot to get it earlier."

"My name is Lollie."

"Nice to meet you, Lollie. I'll see you tomorrow." Hanging up, Morgan slid the phone into her pocket. Both Barbie and Sue stared at her with wide eyes. "What?"

"Did you just set up a date?" Barbie asked, curiosity lacing her tone.

"No. That wasn't a date."

"Sounds like a date," Sue added.

"It's not a date. I just met her at the coffee shop. She's new to town. I used to live here, figured I could show her around a bit."

"That sounds like a date."

Sighing, Morgan blushed. "It's not a date."

Barbie and Sue shared a look, and Morgan knew she'd lost whatever battle they were waging. "It's a date."

The rest of their night passed quickly, and before she knew it, Morgan was headed to Seattle to sleep. She'd have to check in with the office in the morning and set up her plans for how she was going to go about finding her suspect. Her thoughts turned briefly to Lollie as she settled under the covers in her bed. Maybe it was a date, but it wasn't such a bad thing if it was. She certainly deserved to enjoy her free time. And the Lord knew she hadn't been on a proper date in a long time. With a deep breath, Morgan turned on her side and smiled. Maybe she wasn't completely out of the dating game just yet.

## CHAPTER SIXTEEN

LOLLIE HEADED to the bar across the road from the coffee shop that sported a rainbow flag in its window. A search on her phone had told her it was the perfect place for her to meet other women and potentially find a soul mate. However, she couldn't stop thinking about the woman she'd met at the coffee shop earlier that day.

She'd been sweet, kind, and damn hot, and she didn't even know it. Morgan was certainly not her normal venture in terms of a relationship, but she could see how the differences in her might lead to a longer lasting relationship than the others. It was something she was willing to explore at the very least.

Stepping into the bar, Lollie glanced around. She felt slightly out of place, but it would do for what she was looking for. With her head held high, she glanced around at those who were in there with her. It was a weekday, so the crowd was light, but there were people dancing, others who were sitting at the bar top, and still more scattered around at the tables along the back wall.

Lollie felt at home. Everyone smiled, nodded, looked her up and down. These were her people. Relaxing, she ordered a drink and waited for the very cute bartender to make it. After a taste of her drink, Lollie was satisfied and headed for the back of the room. She sat by herself on a long bench and watched the men, women, and queer-folk on the dance floor as their hips jived to the beat and their feet moved.

When a woman sat next to her and grabbed her hand, Lollie grinned. This would be perfect for the night. One night of distraction before she truly began her seduction of the intriguing Morgan she had met earlier that day.

"How are you?" The woman's voice was low and right in Lollie's ear.

Leaning in, Lollie turned her chin down. "Excellent, and how are you, love?"

"About to be better."

Lollie wrinkled her nose as she smiled. It wouldn't take long for her to seduce this woman and find a place to stay for the night, but every time she tried to focus on her, her mind whirled to Morgan. Morgan might just be her perfect match. They weren't outright suited for each other. Morgan had been standoffish at first, but Lollie had pushed forward, and they'd found a way to chat amicably for a few moments before Morgan had rushed off.

She'd learned about Morgan's life, Lollie had shared about hers, so they were well on their way to becoming fast friends and lovers if Lollie had any say in the matter, which she did. Focusing on the woman next to her, Lollie pressed her lips to her cheek.

"I'm not looking for anything serious," Lollie said right into the woman's ear.

"Then you came to the right place, baby."

"Good." Not worrying about seduction, not worrying about making an impression or leaving a mark, Lollie pressed her lips to the woman's. If neither wanted a relationship, then sex they would have. They made out for near an hour on the bench. They got another drink, ground their hips together on the dance floor, and when Lollie was thoroughly worn out, hot and sweaty, they made their way back to the bench.

With a kiss to the woman's cheek, Lollie begged off with the claim she had to get some fresh air. She headed outside and fully intended to go in and take her date home for the night. As soon as she stepped out into the light drizzle of rain, she pulled the napkin from her pocket and called Morgan.

Their conversation was short, but Lollie could tell Morgan was just as intrigued by her. They set a date for the next day. Lollie would have to go shopping beforehand to make sure she had the perfect outfit, but she would have the time to do that during the day.

With one last breath, she went inside. Finding her date for the evening, Lollie sidled up next to her and pressed her breasts against the woman's arm. She didn't care about her. She cared about getting off, getting high—which had been an offer already on the table—and finding a roof for the night.

Their tongues danced again, and Lollie heated their embrace. She slipped her hand against the woman's thigh and brushed her fingers over her heated core. Oh yeah, they were both ready for their night together. With a laugh, Lollie pressed her mouth to the woman's ear.

"I'm about ready to take this to a bed, how about you?"

"Absolutely, love." With their fingers entwined, Lollie followed the woman's lead. They paid their respective tabs and left the bar far behind. It had been a long time since she'd focused on her pleasure and not on her hopes of a future. Tonight would be perfect as a last hoorah before she threw off her old life and started fresh with Morgan tomorrow.

She met up with Morgan at the coffee shop they'd been at the day before. It was decently close for Morgan, apparently, and Lollie knew where it was. When she walked up, she gasped. Morgan was finely dressed in a black pantsuit that was cut just for her body. Her curves were slight but beautiful as the tight material covered her. Her dark brown hair sat short against her head, and she'd spiked it up as was the fashion.

Her crystalline blue eyes stood out in a sharp contrast to her darker complexion. It made her seem mysterious. Lollie's stomach flipped. This woman was different than all the rest she had dated. With her heart in her throat, she walked up to Morgan and gave her a nervous smile, wanting to come off as insecure. She wanted Morgan to feel like the protector, the one she relied on, the one she went to with her problems. She discovered older women tended to like that.

"Hey there, stranger," Lollie said in way of a greeting, her voice still husky from the smoke she'd inhaled the night before.

"Back at you," Morgan answered with a grin. "This was perfect timing. I needed a break from thinking."

"Tough day at the office?" Lollie reached out and grabbed Morgan's fingers, finding physical contact always helped to draw people out of their shells.

Morgan glanced down at their hands, but she didn't pull away. "You could say that. Mostly just a long day of slogging through the not so fun work and finding not a lot that made it worth it."

"I'm sorry." Lifting one shoulder in a shrug, Morgan shifted her stance. Lollie stepped in closer. "Where are you going to show me?"

"I thought, since you said you'd never really been here before, that I would take you down to the market, show you the piers, and maybe we could grab a bite somewhere down there."

"Sounds good. Lead the way." Lollie held her hand out for Morgan to go ahead, but she kept her fingers twined with Morgan's. Together they walked hand-in-hand along the streets and down the steep hills until they came to Pike's Market.

It was a bustle of people and energy. Even though the evening was late, there were still people about. It was a nice night, one of the few where it wasn't drizzling or raining in the dead of winter, and it wasn't too cold. Lollie still shivered to make the point Morgan would have to stick closer to her. She didn't want her far enough away they would lose contact with each other.

Lollie wrapped her arm through Morgan's and shifted her head onto her shoulder to make sure Morgan knew she was interested in more than friendship and she would rely on her wherever Morgan led them. They went in and out of a few shops, Morgan talking randomly about things she had bought at some of them.

They came out at the bottom of the market and along the piers. Morgan pointed her hand down the way. "There's a seafood restaurant that way that's pretty good if you're into that kind of cuisine. I've been there a time or two."

"I'd love to try it out."

"Good."

Before they could take another step, Lollie pulled Morgan to a stop. Her gaze flicked from Morgan's eyes to her lips, and by the third time she did it, Morgan leaned forward like she'd hoped. Matching the angle, Lollie pressed their mouths together in a sweet and tender kiss.

Morgan pressed a hand behind Lollie's head and held them together. Lollie didn't deepen the embrace, sensing Morgan was very unlike Samantha in that she took her time and was hesitant in the beginning of a relationship. Holding still, Lollie smiled when they broke their embrace.

"That was nice," Lollie whispered, fingering Morgan's lapel.

"It was. Come on." Turning, Morgan wrapped an arm over Lollie's shoulder and hunched against the cool breeze picking up off the Puget Sound and walked toward the restaurant.

They ate well, laughing throughout the meal. Lollie didn't make any further advances as she wanted Morgan to make the next move. It wasn't until they were back at the coffee shop where they met that Morgan tugged Lollie in and kissed her again. Lollie folded her arms around Morgan's neck, tilting so Morgan would have to lean over her and deepen their kiss.

She drew in a sharp breath, moaning lightly and dashing her tongue out against Morgan's light-pink lipstick. When Morgan sighed and her shoulders relaxed, she knew she had her. Morgan's lips parted, and together their tongues danced.

Lollie stayed as still as she could, reveling in the feel of Morgan against her. It was so different than all her other dates. Before everything was fast and heated. Morgan was slow, calculated in every decision and move she made. Lollie enjoyed it. She knew whatever Morgan did, it was because she'd thoroughly thought it through. So when Morgan's hand skirted against her back to her hip and then up to her breast, her heart raced.

This moment was so distinct compared to any other relationship she had been in. Maybe Morgan was the one. She'd wanted to be married and well on her way to kids by the time she was thirty. Maybe all she'd had to do was get to Seattle and find this lovely woman she held in her arms.

Lollie nipped at Morgan's neck lightly when they broke apart and giggled. Then she pressed their foreheads together and closed her eyes, breathing in the fresh sea air from the Sound as it blew in their direction. "I had a lovely evening."

"I did, too," Morgan answered.

Lollie remained plastered against Morgan. She didn't want to move. She wanted this moment to last forever. It was damn near perfect. Once again, she slid forward and moved her lips against Morgan's. Morgan responded in kind. Lollie threaded her fingers through Morgan's short hair, reveling in the feel of the rough spikes against the palm of her hand.

They stayed that way for some time until Morgan's phone in her pocket buzzed. On the third ring, Morgan pulled back and sent Lollie a look of apology. She glanced at the caller ID and then shook her head. "I have to get this. It's work. I'm so sorry."

Lollie swallowed but nodded in understanding. She didn't want Morgan to think she was overbearing too early in their relationship. She wanted her to think they both had the freedom to continue their work and do as they pleased.

"What do you have?" Morgan said into her phone.

Curious, Lollie turned toward the road with her arms over her chest as she watched the traffic pass by. She listened in on Morgan's half of the conversation, wishing she could hear whoever was on the other side. Maybe it was a woman, a woman Morgan had a crush on, and maybe they were planning a secret meet up after Morgan and Lollie went different ways. Shaking her head, Lollie pushed the thought from her head. While plausible, it was unlikely. Morgan seemed entranced by Lollie. There wasn't likely another woman in the way.

"Really? Well, shit."

Lollie looked over at Morgan and raised a brow. Morgan shook her head at her and walked a couple steps away, lowering her voice.

"I'll get on it in the morning. Not much I can do about it now that it's broke."

Lollie's heart rapped hard in her chest.

"Yeah. Thanks for the call. Yup. Talk to you tomorrow." Morgan hung up and came back to Lollie with an apology on her lips and in her eyes. "So sorry, but it's a good thing I took that call. It was super important."

"What happened?"

"Just some idiot who didn't listen to me."

Lollie gave a wan smile. "That happens a lot when you're the boss."

"Hmm. Yeah, it does." Morgan bit her lip. "I do have to get going, though. I have a super early morning now with some clean up to do. I had a lovely evening."

"Sure you don't want to extend it?" Lollie asked, hopeful as she reached for Morgan's hand again.

Morgan gripped her fingers tightly and squeezed once before letting go.

"As much as I would like to, I would seriously regret it in the morning."

"Tomorrow then? It's so lonely here not knowing anyone."

Letting out a sigh, Morgan glanced at the phone still in her hand. "It's going to depend on how much clean up I have to actually do. I'll call you around lunch time and let you know, okay?"

"Sure." Disappointment slipped into Lollie's stomach, and she let it linger. She wanted to make this work, wanted Morgan to be the one, so she would play the role she needed to for now. Moving up on her toes, she pressed her lips to Morgan's in a chaste kiss. "I'll look forward to your call, then."

"Tomorrow. I'll call. I promise." Morgan sent her a lopsided grin, kissed her loudly, and then turned, leaving Lollie alone on the street.

Lollie stayed put for at least another five minutes before she headed the opposite direction. If she wasn't going to be staying the night with Morgan like she had hoped, she was going to have to find another home for the evening. It shouldn't be too hard. The bar she'd visited the night before seemed like a good place to start again. Headed in that direction, Lollie made plans for how she was going to take the next step with Morgan.

## CHAPTER SEVENTEEN

SAMANTHA'S MURDER had broken on the news the night before. Pax warned her it was coming, but still, Morgan's heart clenched as it hit. It wouldn't be long before her suspect stopped using Samantha's cards like she had the previous victims, and she would lose track of her again.

With that in mind, as soon as Morgan walked into her makeshift office, she doubled down on her efforts. It didn't take too long for the credit reports to come in, and in the last two days Samantha's card had been used several times. Twice at a local bar Morgan had been to once or twice in her years in Seattle.

"Hmm..." She leaned in her chair and stared at her computer screen. The bar was known to cater to the rainbow community, and it wouldn't be hard to figure out if anyone ran a simple Internet search. Two nights in a row, however, did not fit the profile of her killer.

In all the records of the stolen cards, her killer never frequented the same place twice. She always seemed to be looking for the next best thing, the new thing, whatever would hold her attention for the next period of time she hadn't tried or experienced before. So for her killer to go to the same place twice was an interesting conundrum.

At least Morgan knew she was in the right city. Her heart fluttered as she ruminated. She was in the same place as the woman who had murdered at least five times and was no doubt searching for a sixth kill. Rubbing her lips together, Morgan wondered if she even saw it as killing or if there was some other twisted way she explained it all. If she could even admit it after the fact.

Remembering at the last minute, Morgan requested an update from her tech people on the tracing of the searches run on their victim names.

The last she'd checked with them, they didn't have anything, and she was sure if they did find something, they would call her, but she couldn't help herself from checking in one more time.

She fingered her phone, debating once more if she should call Fiona Wexford or not. She'd never returned her calls earlier, and after her date the night before and her planned date coming up, Morgan wasn't sure she wanted to. Clearly there was no interest other than professional, which it would be nice to discuss the case with someone else—at least, what she could discuss with Wexford that wouldn't cross the bounds of confidential.

Shoving the phone in her pocket, Morgan leaned forward over her computer again. She'd gather up the rest of the credit records and head out to collect statements and footage if there was any. Last she remembered of the bar there was no footage to help protect the clientele but that didn't mean they hadn't added any in the last ten years.

Morgan stopped by the office of her long time friend, Geraldine, whom she'd worked with decades ago when they were both at the Seattle office. She knocked on the door with her knuckle and grinned when her old friend held up a finger and finished her phone call. Morgan leaned against the doorframe, crossing one leg over the other and her arms over her chest as she waited.

Geraldine was probably close to retirement by that point. She'd been Morgan's mentor for years, even after she'd moved to Houston, Geraldine had been there for her. Zoning out and thinking about her case, she almost missed it when Geraldine waved her into the office.

"I was wondering how long you would hole yourself up in there before you ventured in here."

"Not long enough I suppose." Morgan grinned. She slid into the chair opposite Geraldine's desk and folded her ankle over her knee. "I have an interesting case."

"I've gathered."

"Want to do some wandering today?"

Geraldine glanced at her computer, her phone, and then her watch. "I can join until lunch. After that, I have to be back for a meeting."

Morgan's nose scrunched as her lips upturned. "Perfect. We're going to a gay bar."

Geraldine's face lost its smile, and she shook her head slowly. "Are you kidding?"

"Nope." Slapping her hand on her knee, Morgan stood up. "But you already agreed, so let's go. I'm driving."

"You better not kill me."

Chuckling, Morgan headed for the door with a much lighter step. She missed spending time with her friend, and she probably should have called her sooner, or even at all, to get her opinion on the case. Geraldine grabbed her wallet and gun before shutting her door. Together they walked down the hall. When Morgan hit the button for the elevator, Geraldine looked her up and down.

"Looking good, kid. Find anyone out in the windy city?"

"Oh, you know me, the wind blows me this way and then it blows me that way."

"So that's a no."

"That's a no." Morgan laughed. "I did get married, though, didn't I tell you that?"

"No!" With wide brown eyes, Geraldine turned on her.

"It lasted like a year. We were drunk and in Vegas on vacation. It was stupid. Tried to see if it would work out and gave up."

"Stone, you've got a heart of gold and a brain of muck."

"You know it!" Stepping into the elevator, Morgan pressed the button for the parking garage. "My killer is doing something different."

"What's that?"

"She went to the same place twice."

"Interesting. Why?"

"Don't know. Maybe her plans got messed up. Maybe she's trying to expand. Or most likely, she didn't find what she was looking for."

"What makes you say that?"

Morgan shook her head. "Gut, mostly. Every time she's been to a new city, she only makes a few charges on cards before it stops. Then usually within a week or three we find a body. I presume she uses the cards until she finds someone else who will buy her stuff and give her a room, and then she doesn't need the cards anymore."

Nodding, Geraldine licked her lips. "Makes sense, I guess."

"But she went to this bar twice, which I'm still not fully understanding why. There have been no reports of dead lesbians out there, so...I don't know. It's leaving me confused."

"You'll figure it out."

"Maybe."

It didn't take them long to get to the bar. It was early in the morning, and Morgan hoped someone was there to let her in. She pounded her fist on the locked door, but there was no answer. Grunting, she stepped away and looked around to see if there were any cameras on buildings nearby she could look at. There seemed to be one right outside the main door to the bar, which was a bonus.

"They've got cameras it seems," Morgan commented.

"Yes, but no one home."

"Can I help you?"

Morgan spun on her toes toward the voice. "I'm Special Agent Stone. This is Special Agent Morrison. We're with the FBI. We were just going to ask the owner or someone who works here regularly a few questions."

"I'm the owner."

"Good." Morgan softened her expression. She knew Geraldine would give her point on the investigation since it was her case. "Could we talk inside?"

"Yeah." Shifting, the owner shoved keys into the door. After turning off the alarm and hitting lights, the three of them walked inside. "I'm Hailey Kraus, by the way. I've owned this place for a couple years."

"I used to come here every once in a while like a decade ago. A lot has changed." Morgan spun in a circle, looking around. "We're looking for a woman who has come in here the last two nights. Was hoping you could help us find her."

"Sure, what's she look like?"

Morgan shifted a glance to Geraldine and blew out a breath. "We don't exactly know. Was there anyone new in here the last few days? She'd likely be picking up another woman. We know she's relatively small in size and is left handed, young, in her late twenties or early thirties."

Hailey leaned against the bar and bit her lip as she thought. She shook her head. "Not ringing a bell. We have a lot of people in and out of here every night."

"Perhaps you can look up the receipts and that'll jog your memory. The name on the card was Samantha Gideon."

"Sure." Hailey walked around to her computer and booted it up.

"What did this Samantha do?"

Morgan rubbed her lips together and once again glanced around the bar. "She's a person of interest in a case. We would like to speak with her and see if she knows some information about a case we're working on."

Hailey nodded. "She doesn't target our folk, does she?"

Morgan shifted a sharp look to Geraldine. Holding her tongue and clenching a fist, Morgan side-stepped the question. "She's just a person of interest."

"Here it is." Hailey turned the screen so Morgan could lean over the counter and see it. "Looks like she ordered a couple rum and cokes, but that's it. Pretty standard order, so it doesn't really ring a bell for me, but one of my bartenders could have served her, too."

"Do you happen to have any cameras?"

"No. My clientele doesn't particularly care for them. The one outside is for show. There's no actual camera in it."

Clenching her teeth, Morgan shifted her weight onto one foot and handed over a card. "If she comes back, will you give us a call?"

"Yeah. I can do that."

"Thanks."

As soon as Geraldine and Morgan were outside, Morgan let out a sigh.

She had hoped that would give her more information. Her hopes were dashed except for the fact she knew she was finally in the same place as her killer. Geraldine walked to the shop next door.

It didn't take them long to gather up video footage from the neighboring businesses. Morgan would likely spend most of the next day going through them unless there was another major development or another hit on the card somewhere. She wanted to go to the one other place Samantha's card had been used, but she'd have to drop Geraldine back at the office before she did that, and maybe get herself some lunch. Her growling stomach told her it was about time to eat.

With a goodbye to Geraldine at the door, Morgan pulled out onto the road and headed downtown for the last place Samantha's card had been used. It was a very small clothing shop. It matched similar to what she would use the other cards. She'd purchase food—always eating out—sometimes alcohol, and clothing. Other than that, she charged nothing.

Shaking her head, Morgan walked into the small shop. The air was musty, but it was warm and welcoming. Morgan immediately looked for cameras and saw none. Clenching her jaw, she headed for the back where the register was. Her perp certainly knew where to go that didn't have cameras to keep track of her. It was a theme she'd been discovering as she'd gone to each city tracing her killer.

"Can I help you?" The petite woman behind the desk smiled.

Morgan flashed her badge. "I'm Special Agent Stone with the FBI. I'm following up on a case, and there was a stolen credit card used here yesterday."

"Oh no! That's awful."

Giving a grim nod, Morgan plowed forward with her spiel. "I was wondering if you could help me in locating the thief."

"Sure, anything."

"The name on the card was Samantha Gideon."

"Let me look it up."

After a few minutes of silence, the woman pulled up the receipt. "Looks like she purchased a dress, some pants and a couple shirts."

"Can I get a copy of that?"

"Sure."

"Do you have any cameras in the store?"

The woman shook her head. "No, sorry. We keep meaning to get them installed. I have them in the back, but we haven't had the time or the funds yet. Everything moves slower with smaller stores."

"I understand that." Morgan let out a breath and took the proffered receipt. "Were you the one who was here when she came in and purchased these items?"

"No. I wasn't. I was off yesterday. I can get you the number for my partner. She was the one who was here."

"Your partner?" Morgan raised an eyebrow, trying to discern if she meant partner as in business or pleasure. When the woman's cheeks tinged pink, Morgan knew it was the latter. It added an interesting layer into her investigation. "Is your store known for serving the LGBT community?"

The woman shrugged. "It's not a secret we're lesbians, but it's certainly not something we tend to promote, either."

Nodding, Morgan held up the receipt and then handed over a card with her contact information on it. "Thank you for this. If you think of anything else, please give me a call, or if she comes back in."

"Will do."

After leaving, Morgan spent the next two hours gathering even more footage from neighboring businesses that did have video surveillance. Loaded up with more digital footage, Morgan went to the office after picking up some food and coffee to go. She'd no doubt be bent over a computer for the rest of her day.

## CHAPTER EIGHTEEN

MORGAN HAD gone back to her hotel room and changed before her date. She hadn't exactly brought clothes with her that she would typically wear on a date, but she certainly didn't want to be in her standard get-up for work. She wanted to make the distinction in her head that this was fun time and not work time. Swallowing, she pulled on a pair of clean tan slacks and a white button down shirt which she left unbuttoned at the top.

Nerves raged in her belly. The last night she had spent on a date with Lollie had ended well enough. She was sure Lollie had wanted an invite back to her room, but Morgan was not typically the first date kind of girl. Second dates were always debatable, and it had been quite some time since she'd had a second date.

Lollie had texted her a couple times throughout the day, and Morgan had responded in kind, letting her know she was equally excited about their planned evening. Lollie had requested Morgan plan the night again since she knew the area better. Determined to find out more about her date that evening than she had the last two times they'd met, Morgan put on a coat of light pink lipstick, brushed up the mascara she made herself wear and put in earrings.

With a deep breath, Morgan left her gun in the safe and headed out. Tonight was not for work. It was for pleasure. She needed to relax. Pax had been telling her that for years. Her own mother had been telling her, not that she listened to her mother often, but sometimes she was right. Smoothing her hands down her sides to her legs, Morgan headed out and down to the front desk.

She met Lollie at the Uptown Grill. As soon as she walked up, she felt her knees go weak. Lollie looked gorgeous. She wore a sleek green dress that flared at her waist and flowed around above her knees. Her hair was done up and twisted around in a bun at the back of her head.

"Wow," Morgan whispered. Clearing her throat, she tried again. "Wow. You look amazing."

"You look stunning, too." Lollie stepped forward and wrapped her arm through Morgan's and rested her head on Morgan's shoulder, much like they had been the night before.

Taking a risk, Morgan wrapped their fingers together as they walked the rest of the way inside. After they were seated at their table with drinks ordered, Morgan's anxiety picked back up. She wasn't sure what to say, what to do, where to go.

"What do you do for fun?" Lollie asked.

Morgan let out a breath. "I, uhh, I work a lot and weird hours. So fun isn't something I generally get to do."

Lollie rubbed her lips together. "That's a shame."

"Sometimes. I am mainly caught up in family drama. I'm the oldest of nine kids, so they all call me when their lives go awry and want me to fix their mistakes."

"Nine is a lot."

"Yeah. I don't know what my parents were thinking."

"Do you want kids?"

"Uhh...maybe? I'm a bit old for starting a family." Morgan took a sip of her beer and let the cold liquid slide down her throat to her belly. She needed it to bolster herself. Talk of kids was definitely not second date material. It was more like contemplating marriage material, and she certainly was not at that stage in this relationship yet, or ever.

"You're not old." Lollie grinned. "And no one is ever too old to start a family."

Morgan snorted. "Well, I appreciate the sentiment even if it's not reality. You want kids?"

"Oh yes. Just two."

Morgan was thankful when the waiter came over to take their order and distracted them from the conversation at hand. Morgan really needed to steer them away from that type of conversation and down another path. She wanted to learn about Lollie, not about what Lollie wanted from her.

She thought of Fiona and what they would talk about on their first date, if Fiona would ever agree to one. Clenching her jaw, Morgan tried to shift the thought from her head. Thinking about Fiona while on a date with another woman made guilt and shame flare in her belly. It was not a pleasant feeling. Fiona wouldn't even call her back, so she was pretty sure there was no chance of them ever having a date. She'd probably ruined that by kissing her in the middle of a bloody crime scene.

"What are you thinking? You seem so far away." Lollie's voice carried over the din of the room.

Morgan jerked. "Nothing. Just something to do with work, a phone call I need to make. Where did you grow up?"

"Out east."

"Out east where?"

Lollie took a slow drink of her wine. "Kind of all over. I moved a lot."

"Army brat?"

"Yeah. My dad was career army, so we moved every few years. My mom didn't like it at all, but that was life."

"Ever live out west then?"

"No."

"I grew up outside of San Francisco, so this is very close to home for me. I moved to get as far away from it as I could, but it just seems to follow me no matter where I go."

Lollie giggled and wrinkled her nose. "Maybe you secretly like it."

"Maybe I do. It keeps me entertained at the least."

Lollie reached over and grabbed Morgan's hand. The rest of their meal sped by, and by the time they were leaving, Morgan was relaxed, slightly buzzed, and ready to take a leap of faith. When they got to her car, Morgan leaned in and kissed Lollie. Lollie freely returned the embrace, smiling against Morgan's lips.

"Want to go back to my place?" Morgan whispered into Lollie's ear.

Lollie nodded. "I think I would love that."

"I should forewarn you, I'm staying in a hotel right now, so it's really just my room."

"Oh." Lollie stepped away. "You don't live here?"

"No, I'm here for work."

"Hmm." Lollie licked her lips, hesitation marking her gaze. "Let's go then."

Morgan didn't wait. As soon as they were in her room, she pushed Lollie into the door and pressed their mouths together. Her hand skimmed down Lollie's front, barely touching her breasts, until she landed on Lollie's hip. Their tongues tangled together, and Lollie held Morgan close with a hand at the back of her neck.

Morgan's body heated. She pushed herself into Lollie, melding them together as best she could. Lollie moaned sweetly and nipped Morgan's lower lip. She pulled back and reached between them, undoing Morgan's shirt one button at a time. It was slow and sensual.

Lollie grinned as she pushed the blouse from Morgan's shoulders. Morgan moved her arms to let the material fall away and to the ground. Lollie raked her gaze up and down Morgan's chest, causing goosebumps to raise on Morgan's skin.

"You're so beautiful," Lollie whispered, reaching out and fingering the plain bra Morgan wore.

"Likewise. But you're going to have to tell me how to get that thing off you because it looks complicated."

Lollie laughed, her voice echoing in the room. She turned around and put her hands flat on the door like she was getting ready for a pat down. Morgan's stomach clenched, but she saw the thin zipper decently well hidden in the fabric of the dress. She tugged it down, surprised when she found Lollie wore no bra and no underwear. Her mouth dried instantly, her heart in her throat, and her stomach twisting in excitement.

"You're certainly ready for tonight." Morgan pressed a kiss to Lollie's shoulder and dropped the dress to the ground.

Lollie ducked her chin, her cheeks reddening with pleasure. "I had hoped we would end up here."

"You and me both." Morgan's lips moved to Lollie's other shoulder. With one last kiss to the center of Lollie's neck, Morgan reached up and tugged the clip and pins from Lollie's hair, letting her soft brown curls fall around her shoulders. "Stunning, and so soft."

Lollie hummed in the back of her throat, but she stayed put while Morgan skimmed her fingers over her newly-exposed skin, the center of her spine, the curve of her ass, the slope of her waist. Morgan was entranced and consumed as she lost herself in the petite woman in front of her.

"Will you let me touch you?" Morgan whispered.

Lollie shivered. "You are touching me."

Morgan chuckled low in her throat. "No. Will you let me take you?"

"Yes." Lollie hissed as Morgan's still clothed hips pressed into her back.

With a deep breath, Morgan wrapped her hands around Lollie's front and over her stomach. She dipped her fingers lower in circles. She scraped her nails gently up Lollie's thighs. When Lollie let out a sweet breath, Morgan dipped her fingers between Lollie's legs. She was wet, hot, and ready for her. Morgan used her thumb to swirl slow gentle circles, mimicking the ones she had traced on Lollie's belly. Her other hand continued to trail over Lollie's body, distracting and enticing. She pulled at a nipple, then the other.

Lollie groaned, and Morgan knew she was headed in the right direction. When Lollie's hips bucked, Morgan pushed into her more to hold her into place. Bending, Morgan nipped at Lollie's neck, sucking to leave a mark on her skin, a reminder in the morning of everything they were about to do. Pleasure swirled in her belly and moved lower.

Rocking her hips, Lollie grunted as Morgan brought her closer to her release. With her lips pressed to Lollie's ear, Morgan ordered, "Tell me when you're about to come."

"Yes."

"Lollie?"

"Yes. I'm...I'm close. Don't stop."

"Wouldn't dream of it." Morgan dashed her tongue out just under Lollie's ear and nipped her way down the cord of muscle to her shoulder. She gripped Lollie's hip to hold her still as Lollie's body jerked, and she let out a rush of air. Her chest heaved with breath as her forehead rested against the metal door.

Laughing, Lollie shifted and turned around. With her shoulders against the door, she dragged Morgan toward her so their chests were pressed together and their lips connected. Morgan cupped Lollie's breast, squeezing, as they tangled their tongues in another long and deep embrace.

When they broke apart, Lollie laughed again. "You certainly know what you're doing."

"Sometimes experience comes in handy."

"Always. But the question remains, can the old dog handle some new tricks?"

"Oh? What kind of tricks?"

"You'll see." Lollie grabbed Morgan's fingers and led her down the short hallway and toward the bed. She stepped out of her heels and turned around, climbing onto the bed and walking backward on her knees.

Morgan shucked her pants, her panties, and her bra before she joined Lollie. She was intrigued to find out what Lollie had up her sleeve. Once they were in the center, Lollie asked Morgan to lay down. Complying, Morgan grabbed a pillow and shoved it under her head, lying on her back.

Lollie towered over her in all her beauty. She touched herself, dipping her fingers between her legs and running her sticky wet fingers over her breasts and tweaking her own nipples. Entranced by every move Lollie made, Morgan clenched her fists, wanting to touch but letting Lollie lead.

Dipping her head down, Lollie captured Morgan's lips and reached out to her hands, bringing them to Lollie's hips. She straddled one of Morgan's thighs and alternated between scraping her nails against Morgan's sensitive skin and feather light touches. Morgan's eyes drifted shut as she focused solely on the sensations Lollie caused as she worked her magic.

When Lollie's core slid against her thigh, Morgan knew where this was going. Lollie ground her hips again and again while Morgan was distracted by Lollie's hands. It wasn't long before Lollie trailed her fingers down and slid one finger and then two inside Morgan. Morgan clenched her jaw, arching her back, and drawing in a deep breath.

Every time Lollie's hips jerked forward, her hand mimicked the motion and a shot of pleasure burst inside Morgan. Again and again they moved together, rising together. It wasn't long until Morgan found herself on the precipice of her own orgasm. Lollie's movements sped up, and as Morgan fell over the edge, she knew Lollie wouldn't be too far behind her. Together they let their bodies calm.

Lollie pressed against Morgan's side, gently rubbing her hand back and forth against Morgan's arm as their bodies cooled and relaxed. She leaned in and pressed a kiss to Morgan's cheek. "New trick good?"

Morgan chuckled. "Yeah, but not a new trick."

"Oh really?"

"Really, really."

They stayed that way for a while, and Morgan wondered if Lollie had fallen asleep on her, but when she felt Lollie shift, she knew she was still awake. Awkwardly moving, Morgan pulled down the covers and slipped underneath, holding the edge open for Lollie to follow.

Lollie turned on her side, and Morgan pressed her front to Lollie's back, spooning her body. She pressed a tender kiss to Lollie's neck and breathed in her scent, memorizing it. "I have to wake up pretty early."

"Okay," Lollie answered with a yawn. "I'll leave when you leave."

With one more kiss, Morgan closed her eyes and let herself fall asleep.

## CHAPTER NINETEEN

LOLLIE WOKE first. The sky was still dark outside, and Morgan was wrapped around her middle. Shifting in the slightest, Lollie settled into the comfortable bed and sighed. She had not expected Morgan to be staying in a hotel. Nothing in their conversations suggested she didn't live in the area, or at least within the state. Which, Lollie supposed, Morgan could still live within the state, but certainly she didn't live in Seattle.

Lollie closed her eyes. Their night had been sweet, wonderful. She felt loved even though they'd just met, and it was clear Morgan held back. She could see how they would be good together, how they had a strong and deep connection that would bring them closer as time wore on and as they got to know each other better. Morgan not living in Seattle proper could easily be a problem.

With her lip pulled between her teeth, Lollie debated what to do. She could work on finding someone new, someone who could take care of her needs. Her date the night before hadn't been a bad choice, although their connection surely wasn't as strong as it was with Morgan.

Maybe Morgan would move to Seattle to be with Lollie. Their connection could easily be strong enough for that, or maybe Lollie could move to where Morgan lived, wherever that was. She hadn't even thought to ask after her surprise of finding out Morgan was staying in a hotel.

Lollie shifted in the bed, turning over so she faced Morgan. She was beautiful in her sleep. She looked younger, relaxed, sweet, and innocent. The hard exterior that she'd had the first time Lollie had met her was completely melted away. Taking one finger, Lollie trailed it along the curve of Morgan's cheek. She was sure Morgan's alarm would be going off soon. It was nearing five-thirty.

With her thumb, she traced the soft skin at Morgan's lips, then she leaned forward and pressed a gentle kiss to them. Whatever happened with her and Morgan, she liked her. They were good together. Their flirting brought new thrills and the sex was decent. She would stick with Morgan for now, for however long she ended up staying in the Seattle area, and they would figure it out from there. If either of them were to move, Lollie would need the time to convince Morgan it was a good idea. When Morgan's lips turned upward into a sly grin, Lollie couldn't help from smiling.

"You're up early," Morgan whispered.

"I don't tend to sleep much." Lollie leaned in again and pressed her lips once more to Morgan's. This time, she elicited a response. Morgan was slow to wake up but warm against Lollie's skin as their embrace deepened. The sleep and weariness of the night faded to the edges as Lollie moved to entice Morgan into another round of lovemaking.

Morgan jerked back as her phone alarm sounded into the room. She spun around and grabbed it off the night stand, turning it off. When she twisted to Lollie, Lollie was ready and waiting. Lollie pressed kisses to Morgan's chest and her breasts and then her belly. She was about to kiss the inside of Morgan's thigh when her stupid phone went off again.

Lollie glanced up in time to see Morgan look at the caller ID. Morgan took a deep breath and sent an apologizing gaze down to Lollie. "I'm so sorry. I have to take this. It's from the Chicago office so the time zone is different."

Lollie moved away from Morgan in the slightest, letting her answer without distractions. Morgan's voice wasn't quite clear as she answered with one more look down to Lollie.

"Fiona, what can I do for you this morning?"

Lollie could barely make out the other woman's voice on the other end of the line. She mostly heard mumbling and muttering. Giving in to temptation, she pressed a kiss to Morgan's inner thigh.

"No, I'm in Seattle. Yeah, it's early here. It's fine. Really, what did you need?"

Scraping her teeth down Morgan's skin, she looked up to see what Morgan's reaction would be. Morgan stared directly down at her, heat in her eyes. Morgan didn't make a move to stop her or sway her in the other direction, so Lollie continued. She didn't want Morgan to be thinking about another woman—coworker or otherwise—she wanted Morgan's sole attention on her.

"I'd like to talk to you about it, too, but now's not the greatest time. Do you think I could call you back in an hour? Yeah. Okay. Talk to you soon."

Morgan hung up and dropped her phone onto the night stand. Lollie rested her chin on Morgan's hip and smirked.

"That was interesting."

"What was?" Lollie asked.

"You." Morgan rolled her eyes, gripped Lollie's hair, and shifted so her legs were spread wider, and the invitation was clear.

Lollie licked her lips, and this time didn't tease as she dove straight between Morgan's legs. She made it quick, knowing Morgan would not be remiss to be late to work and they could certainly pick up where they left off later. When Morgan moved to reciprocate, Lollie shook her head, kissed her cheek, and sent her to the bathroom to get ready for her day.

While Morgan was in the shower, Lollie picked up her dress off the floor by the door and slid it over her legs and hips. Tugging the zipper up, she slipped on her shoes and sat on the bed to wait for Morgan to be ready. It wasn't long before Morgan popped out of the bathroom with a towel wrapped around her middle.

"I'm going to have to work late tonight. Disadvantage to not being at the home office means I have longer hours."

"I'd still like to see you." Lollie rested onto the rumpled bed, her hands behind her, and she sent Morgan a seductive look. "I can wait until you're done with work."

Morgan nodded. "I'll call you."

Lollie watched as Morgan came closer, her skin pink from the shower and damp as water droplets fell from her short hair down her chest and into the white towel. Her heart raced. Morgan leaned down and kissed her, deepening their embrace but still keeping fairly separate.

"I do want to see you tonight, I promise," Morgan whispered. "I'll just have to find the time."

"Can hardly wait."

"Now get. I've got to get ready." Morgan chuckled.

Lollie got off the bed slowly and headed for the door, sending a smoldering look over her shoulder. She'd have to find a way to entertain herself for the rest of the day while Morgan worked. She could buy herself a new outfit or perhaps even some lingerie. Wearing nothing the night before had obviously been the right decision, so perhaps she would attempt that again.

With the door shut behind her, Lollie made her way to the front desk unabashed in her walk of shame. It felt glorious. The connection she had with Morgan was strong and impenetrable. She would move with Morgan if Morgan wasn't willing to move with her. She couldn't deny or resist the call to the perfect woman. She could see their future together, the time they would spend together, their life. Smiling and blushing, Lollie headed out to entertain herself for the day.

Lollie had everything prepared for when Morgan was done with work. It was already past seven before she heard a single word from her about when they could potentially meet up for dinner. By the time Morgan texted she was ready it was half past eight. Lollie let out a breath. She'd planned everything perfectly, and she wanted it to go off without a hitch.

She was going to go all in with Morgan that night. She ditched her car down by the piers, knowing she wouldn't be back for it, and walked into the entrance at Morgan's hotel. Deciding it was too late for a dinner date, she was going to skip straight to the dessert. Lollie rapped her knuckles on Morgan's door, smiling to herself when she heard Morgan rustling around inside.

When Morgan opened the door, Lollie grinned. "Couldn't wait."

"Couldn't wait for what?" Morgan asked, stepping aside to let Lollie in as she finished buttoning her pants.

Lollie stilled her hands. "For you."

Sliding Morgan's hands away from the button of her pants, Lollie stepped in closer. Morgan stepped back. They walked until Morgan's back was plastered against the full sized mirror. Lollie walked two fingers up Morgan's belly, over the swell of her plump breasts, up her neck, and to her lips. She brushed her fingers against Morgan's mouth.

"We can order some food when we're hungry."

Chuckling, Morgan relaxed against the mirror. "I have a feeling you're actually very hungry."

"Hmm, yes, I suppose I am." Lollie tried to tamp down the urge she had welling within her to be rough. Morgan might like it, but she wasn't sure. In that aspect, she and Samantha had been a near perfect match. If only everything else had worked out. Frowning, she focused on the lovely woman in front of her. "Strip."

"Uh...what?" Morgan's lips parted in surprise.

Lollie raised an eyebrow and took a step back. "Strip. And make it good."

Grinning, Morgan started with her shirt. Pulling it up and over her head, she dropped it to the floor, next to her. Without another word, Morgan shoved her thumbs into the waistband of her slacks and shimmied them down. She didn't stop moving her hips when the fabric was gone. Lollie had clearly interrupted her from dressing because she didn't have shoes on and her bare toes peeked out from under the material until Morgan stepped out of her pants.

"That's it," Lollie whispered. "Make it sexier."

Morgan bit her lower lip and leaned back against the mirror. The barely there reflection Lollie could see added to the ambiance she was trying to create. She wanted Morgan to be thrown off a bit, off her game, and curious as to what Lollie had up her sleeve next.

Morgan slid the straps of her bra down her arms before she reached behind and unhooked it, letting it fall to the ground to join her shirt.

Instead of reaching for her panties, Morgan arched her back and played with her breasts. Heat hit Lollie's belly, lust driving her to want to touch, but she held herself back. She wanted to know how far and where Morgan would take this.

Leaning against the wall opposite Morgan, Lollie mimicked Morgan's teasing through her own clothes. Each time Morgan tweaked her own nipple, Lollie would touch hers. When their eyes connected, Lollie moaned. Morgan eventually slid her hands down to her hips, pushing off her underwear. She didn't bother stepping out of it as she reached between her legs and parted herself so Lollie could see everything.

Lollie grunted and took in a sharp breath. While Samantha may have matched her in one way, Morgan's unabashed sexuality drew her in deeper. She was confident in everything she did, sure that she would bring herself and Lollie the most amount of pleasure. That assertiveness was Lollie's undoing. She knew they'd be perfect together.

Giving in, Lollie stepped forward and pressed her mouth to Morgan's, not touching her anywhere else as Morgan continued to work her own body. Lollie pressed her palms flat against the mirror to hold her body as she leaned in to deepen their embrace.

When Morgan's body convulsed, Lollie reached out and soothed her fingers up and down Morgan's arms and back. She pulled her into a comforting hug and pressed gentle kisses into her hair, behind her ear, and waited as Morgan calmed down. When Morgan's body was no longer completely lax against her, Lollie whispered, "That was better than I expected."

"I thought so, too," Morgan answered and turned her head so they could kiss again. "I think it's your turn."

Lollie grinned. Morgan would be perfect for her. Licking up Morgan's neck, she led her to the bed that was neatly made and untouched by either of them. Lollie sat on the edge of the mattress and beckoned Morgan over with one finger.

"Let me have my way with you."

Chuckling, Morgan bit her lip. "I suppose since we only have a few more days, we can indulge as much as we want."

Lollie pouted. "You're leaving soon."

"Maybe. It depends how work goes, but I do have to go home at some point."

"Where is home?"

"Chicago."

Lollie stiffened. She lowered her gaze so Morgan couldn't look in her eyes, and she hoped her surprise came off as sadness. It must have because Morgan stepped forward and curled her fingers and hair around Lollie's ear.

"You knew this was temporary."

"I did. I had hoped it wouldn't be. Chicago is so far."

Morgan lifted Lollie's chin up with a finger. "We still have tonight."

"We do."

"And tomorrow night."

"That too." Lollie turned her surprise into a smile, knowing she had Morgan right where she wanted. They could have tonight. She'd wake up first in the morning, she'd make love to Morgan one more time, and then she'd go find someone who was willing to make this more permanent. There was no way she was going back to Chicago, not after Andrea and Katie. Neither of them would want to see her again.

"Lollie." Morgan broke her reverie. "What's going on in that head of yours?"

"Nothing. Come here." Lollie tugged Morgan closer.

"No, really, tell me."

Lollie shook her head, leaning against the bed. "I feel this intense connection to you. I don't know how to explain it. I wouldn't call it love...yet anyway. But it feels good to be with you."

Morgan climbed onto the bed next to Lollie and laid down on her side, propping her head up on her fist. "Connection is good."

Turning to look at Morgan, Lollie furrowed her brow. "You don't feel it?"

"I do. I just...I never thought this would go beyond a night or two."

"Well, that's the difference between us. I'm always looking for the perfect match."

Morgan made a small smile. "I admire your hope. I think I'm too old and have been around the block one too many times to have that kind of outlook any longer."

"Nonsense." Lollie turned so she could straddle Morgan. She grabbed her hands after turning Morgan onto her back and held them above her head. "You're not too old. Never too old."

Morgan rolled her eyes and rocked her hips. "If you think so. However, I do think you are over dressed for this little excursion of ours."

Lollie bent down so her breath brushed against Morgan's ear when she spoke. "I do suppose you are right."

Shuddering, Morgan turned her head to kiss Lollie's cheek. "Then get naked."

"Is that an order?"

"I suppose it is."

Lollie put her heart and soul into the rest of the night and making Morgan feel as much pleasure as she possibly could. There was the small niggling hope in the back of her mind Morgan would take back everything she had said and they would stay together. Morgan was perfect for her; she had no doubt of it.

## CHAPTER TWENTY

MORGAN'S ALARM went off before the sun was up again. She had been lucky to get at least three hours of sleep after Lollie had kept her up most of the night. The petite woman still slept soundly next to her in the bed. Morgan opened her eyes and stared at her. She looked so innocent in the light from the window and dark of the room, in the stillness of sleep.

Morgan didn't dare touch her for fear of waking her up, but she so wanted to. Whatever was between them, no matter how short lived or long lived it was, it had been a wonderful break from Morgan's norm. Lollie had brought her a small touch of brightness in the very dark and dangerous world that she lived in.

Staying put on the mattress and watching Lollie take deep breaths as she continued to sleep, Morgan took in the slowness of time. Sometimes her work showed her the seediest side of the world, the darkest side, the side no one wanted to think or talk about. Like the kids thrown into sex work in order to survive. The violent murders of women who had unexpectedly brought a date home one night.

Whatever she'd found in Seattle now that she was back for a brief time had been more than she'd found there in the years she'd lived in the busy city. Morgan rubbed a hand through her hair, knowing she was going to have to get up and moving shortly.

When she finally dragged herself out of the bed as quietly as she could, Morgan made her way into the bathroom. She shut the door before turning the light on, not wanting to wake Lollie if she didn't have to. Checking her phone, she saw the messages Amya had sent her the last two days that she had refused to answer. Deciding then was as good a time as any, she picked up her phone and dialed.

Amya was as much a morning person as she was. It didn't take long for her sister's soft and sweet voice to fill the other end of the line. Morgan kept her volume down as she smiled into the phone. "Morning."

"Why are you calling me so early?" Amya pouted.

"I'm working a busy case. If you want me to call you, now is when I have time to call you."

Rustling echoed on the other end of the line, and she figured Amya was moving some place away from Grace, who was no doubt still sleeping hard as a rock. "What case are you working?"

"You know I can't tell you that."

"I know...it just...you worry me sometimes."

"I worry you?"

"Yeah. I mean, you can never talk about anything. You bottle it all up. I know you take the brunt of the family drama. Who do you have to talk to and let it all out?"

Morgan rubbed her lips together and stared at her reflection in the mirror. Amya wasn't wrong. She'd relied on Pax for the better part of a decade for that, but even he didn't know everything going on in her life. "Well, maybe it'll please you then to know I've had a date the last two nights."

"What!?"

Chuckling, Morgan spun and turned the shower on. "Yes, and it's been wonderfully good even if it won't last."

"Won't last?"

"Well, yeah, duh. I live in Chicago, and she lives here."

"You could always transfer back."

Morgan scoffed. "I love Chicago. I finally have all four seasons, Amya. I can't give that up."

"I know. Just hopeful, I guess."

"You're always the hopeful one. Always the one who looks toward the future. You've got a future, Amya. You have a wonderful future with Grace. I'm...I'm not sure I'll ever have that or that I want it. I enjoy my freedom and being single. I don't need someone else to make my life better. It's pretty damn good as it."

"That's why I love you."

"I love you, too, baby sis. I gotta get ready for work. Long day, hoping to finally have some success."

"I'll pray for it."

"Uh...yeah. You do that. I'm just...going to work hard and focus harder. Love you."

"Love you, too."

Hanging up, Morgan set her phone on the counter and stepped under the hot spray of the shower. It felt glorious. As much as she loved her free time with Lollie, she definitely needed a night of actual sleep so she could think clearly at work. Taylor would only give her so much time in Seattle before he would insist the Seattle office take over the case until her perp moved to a new city again. Morgan didn't want that to happen.

She finished her shower and wrapped a towel around her after running it through her hair to dry it off. When she headed into the bedroom area, Lollie was awake and touching herself seductively on the bed. Morgan's chest warmed, and her heart jumped. She was so tempting.

"Want to come join?" Lollie's voice carried over to her.

Morgan bit her lip. On one hand, she definitely wanted to join; on the other, she knew her time was growing short before she'd have to be off to work. Giving in, Morgan dropped her towel and crawled onto the bed. "Just a quick one."

"Absolutely."

Morgan pressed her mouth to Lollie's, and Lollie flipped them so she was on top. Morgan knew it was her preferred position at that point with how often they ended up in it. Morgan ran her hands up and down Lollie's sides and tugged her down for a kiss. With their mouths pressed together, Morgan focused on how she wanted to get this done efficiently.

Lollie had other plans. Her fingers trailed up Morgan's chest, into her wet hair, and down to her neck. Her thumb and forefinger from each had circled her neck. Morgan's back stiffened and goosebumps rose on her arms. She looked up into Lollie's eyes. While strangulation was not something she hadn't experienced before, it was not a particular sex act she enjoyed, and to do it without talking first was beyond her.

Reaching up, Morgan brushed her fingers over Lollie's cheek and implored her. "I don't really like that."

Lollie ignored her, her grasp tightening. Morgan swallowed and breathed in, knowing if Lollie got much tighter she wouldn't be able to speak or breathe. Preparing for what she may have to do, Morgan clenched her jaw.

"Lollie. Stop."

Smirking, Lollie shook her head and leaned down to whisper. "No. You're going to leave me, and I can't have that."

Without another warning, Lollie's fingers tightened against Morgan's neck. Morgan squirmed as fear ratcheted up in her stomach to her heart, making it even harder to breathe. She gasped. Digging her fingernails into Lollie's wrists, Morgan tried to twist her body and knock her off, but Lollie clenched her thighs down.

As Morgan looked up, the cold stare down at her was shocking. It was so unlike the Lollie she had come to know. Grunting, Morgan let go of Lollie's wrist and shoved her forearm between Lollie's, bracing her palm just above Lollie's wrist. She pushed her hand down and her elbow up, forcing

Lollie's arms to buckle and her grasp to loosen.

Lollie let go, and Morgan took her chance. She shoved her palm up straight into Lollie's nose and threw her off the bed. Standing, Morgan went straight for where she knew her weapon was—the safe in the closet. Her bare feet padded on the floor, her heart racing as she turned her back on her attacker, but she had no other choice.

Flinging the door to the closet open, Morgan reached in and up on her tiptoes. The slam against her head knocked her all the way inside the closet. When she turned around, Lollie breathed heavily over her with wide eyes, lamp on the floor, and knife in her left hand.

"Shit," Morgan muttered.

Kicking out with her foot, she caught Lollie's knee and sent her backward. Morgan reached forward and grabbed Lollie's wrist with the knife in her hand and bent it sharply, pivoting it down so that the angle forced her to let go of the weapon or else she would break her wrist, which Morgan was tempted to do anyway.

Before Morgan had a chance to grab the knife, Lollie socked her in the side of her head with a closed fist. Grunting and trying to see past the white stars littering her vision, Morgan leaned against the door frame to the closet. Her eyes locked on the safe. It was open. Reaching up, she grabbed her gun and spun around, aiming it at Lollie.

With her jaw clenched, Morgan dared Lollie to take one more step toward her. "Don't bring a knife to a gun fight, bitch."

Lollie's chest heaved. Morgan stayed put, her line of fire exact on Lollie's head. She was close enough there was no way she would miss. Lollie lowered to the ground slowly, and Morgan wondered if she was about to give up. Without warning, she gripped the lamp and threw it at Morgan. Screaming, she raced out of the room, the door slamming shut behind her.

Morgan let out a breath. She shut and locked the door, grabbing her phone that still sat on the counter in the bathroom. Immediately, she called the local police department to report a naked lunatic on the run out of her hotel who had just tried to murder her during the heat of the moment.

When she hung up with them, she grabbed the robe from the back of the door. With shaking hands, she swung it around her body and tied it tightly in front of her. She had another phone call to make, well more than one, but one she really didn't want to make. It would start her life into a living hell, but it wouldn't be long until they found out anyway.

Opening her phone, Morgan dialed the first number she could think of. The sun peeked over the horizon, her room lightening up. Morgan's heart still hadn't stopped pounding as she sat in the chair at the desk with the phone pressed to her ear. Local PD would be there soon enough, asking a million and one questions, and the FBI needed to be shortly behind them.

"This better be good, Stone." Geraldine's voice filtered through the line, gruff from sleep.

Morgan rubbed her lips together, not quite sure what to say or how to put it. Tears slipped down her cheeks as she bolstered herself.

"Morgan?"

"She...I need you to come to my room. She was here."

"She? Who is she?"

"Lollie."

"I'm confused."

Morgan knew from Geraldine's tone she had her full attention at this point, and that she wasn't doing a good job explaining what was going on. "Lollie is the killer."

"Your killer?"

Morgan nodded, but then she remembered last minute Geraldine couldn't see her. "Yeah. Pretty sure."

"What's your room number?"

"Six-thirty-nine. I already called Seattle PD."

"What? Why? What happened?"

"Just...just get here. Please."

"I'm coming. I'm coming right now."

Morgan hung up the phone and blinked back even more tears. Geraldine would be there. Taylor and Pax would likely find out in the next thirty to sixty minutes, and maybe Pax would even show up in the next day or two. Morgan sniffled and brushed at her face to wipe the tears away. When she moved her hand down, she noted the blood.

"What the hell?"

She stared at her hand and the slice mark cutting straight across it. Blood dripped from it onto the white robe. Morgan looked at the floor, noting the trail she had left behind.

"Fuck," she said on a breath.

She wasn't sure she could stand enough to get a towel, but just as she was about to attempt it, there was a loud knock at the door and call out of Seattle Police Department. Morgan pushed herself up, knowing she looked a fright but not caring in the least. They knocked again, but she couldn't make her voice work.

Morgan was startled when the alarm on the night stand blared into the room, loudly beeping at her. She breathed heavily and ignored it. She got to the door and unlocked it. They stared down at her, and she about broke. The next twenty minutes was a whirlwind of descriptions and recollections of what had happened. They had her weapon in their possession, and it made Morgan feel barer than she had the entire time she'd fought Lollie off. She heard Geraldine before she saw her.

Her voice was strong and powerful as she forced her way through the throng of uniforms and into the room. One look at Morgan and Geraldine twisted back around to the Sergeant in charge and barked at him. "Where the hell is the medic?"

"They're coming."

"Get them here now." Geraldine grabbed a towel from the bathroom and wrapped it around Morgan's hand tightly. "Where else did she get you?"

"She knocked me on the head with the lamp."

"Let me see." Geraldine moved Morgan's head down so she could look over her. "You're going to need stitches. A lot of them."

"Fuck."

"Yeah." Turning once again to the Sergeant, Geraldine glared. "Medic. Now."

He put his hands up in the air and spoke into his radio. Morgan shook her head and looked up at Geraldine, not sure what to say or what to do. Geraldine bent down and looked Morgan straight in the face.

"You don't say a fucking word. Got it. You say nothing."

"I—"

"No. There will be an investigation. You will be on leave. We will figure this out. Until then, you don't say anything that isn't useful. Got it?"

Morgan nodded, her head spinning. It wasn't long before a medic arrived and knelt down before her where Geraldine had once been. They took the towel off and replaced it with gauze and tape. Then held something to the back of her head.

She was ushered onto a stretcher, and Geraldine grabbed her hand before they pushed her out of the room. "Want me to call someone?"

"No." Morgan set her face. "No one finds out about this at all."

"Morgan, you're pretty beat up."

"No."

"All right. I'll meet you at the hospital. Garces is coming up here to deal with the uniforms." Geraldine squeezed Morgan's hand. "You'll be fine. You just let the doctors do their thing, okay?"

"Yeah, okay."

Morgan let out a breath and let the paramedics take her to the elevator on the stretcher. She would have preferred to walk out of the hotel with a bit of dignity, but at the same time, she wasn't sure she had it in her to even take the steps needed to get out of the room itself. Closing her eyes, Morgan relaxed at let the systems in place do what needed done.

## CHAPTER TWENTY-ONE

MORGAN WAS stuck in the hospital overnight for observation, not that she really wanted to go back to the damn hotel room anyway. Every time she thought of returning, her heart would race and her blood pressure would rise—the stupid machine she was still hooked to told her every time. Doing some deep breathing exercises, she closed her eyes and tried to distract herself with the television in the corner.

It wasn't working. When Geraldine showed up with Morgan's suitcase in her hand, Morgan could have hugged her. She would have if she'd been allowed out of the damn bed without assistance because of her concussion. "I thought you might like some of these."

"Thank you!" Morgan rested. "They give you my gun back?"

"No. Not yet."

Something in the way Geraldine said it made her think that wasn't the entire truth, but she let it slide. She hadn't fired her gun, as much as she'd been tempted to and wanted to, so she wasn't going to lose possession of it for very long.

Geraldine sat on the edge of the bed. "How you feeling?"

"Been better. I've got this wicked headache." Morgan grinned and raised her hand. "And I don't know what happened here, but man, it stings. Seriously, I'm not doing too bad. Sore, that's it."

"Good. They said they'll release you tomorrow. Where do you want to go?"

Morgan shrugged. The only thing she knew was not back to that hotel room and probably not back to that hotel. Maybe she'd eventually go there, but not in the near future.

"I'd say you held your own pretty damn good."

"Sure. You can say that if you believe it. Any idea where she got off to?"

"No. They lost her before they found her. Cameras show her running out of the building through the side door emergency exit, after that, she went south and vanished."

"Great."

"There's a protective detail outside."

"Oh, I'm aware." Morgan glared at the door. "It's unnecessary."

"Really? Don't fight me on that one."

Morgan closed her eyes. "I doubt she'll come back and finish me off. I'm out of her hair, she's gone, there's no reason for her to come back."

"No reason?"

"I should probably finish her profile now that I have some major insight into how her brain works."

Geraldine's hand was on her thigh, and Morgan jumped but calmed herself as quickly as she could. She knew Geraldine had noticed it, but she couldn't help herself. It had been the world's longest day, and she wasn't even allowed to sleep for most of it.

"You'll come home with me. At least until we get you back to Chicago."

"They're sending me home?"

"You know they will as soon as they're done taking statements and when you're still on leave. You'll need to be cleared before you can come back to duty."

"Great. My sister-in-law went through something similar, if I remember."

"Oh yeah?"

"Yeah. I'll deal with it. But your place sounds lovely. Scott still your main man?"

"You know it."

They fell into a gentle silence. Morgan's brain already spinning to complete out her profile of Lollie, especially now that she had a name and a face to go with the killer. Morgan reached out and grabbed Geraldine's hand to get her attention.

"Let me finish the profile at least."

"That's it, though. Then you're off the case."

"For now."

"We'll see," Geraldine answered. "You get some rest. You need it."

Morgan chuckled. "Like anyone can rest in a hospital."

"True, but just ignore the nurses. They like it." Geraldine took a deep breath. "You're sure she didn't know you were the agent on her case?"

"I highly doubt it. I'm not sure if she's even figured it out now. I never mentioned where I work or that I was even in law enforcement. Sometimes it's a big turn off. You know the drill. So I sidestepped that conversation every time. She seemed utterly surprised I had a gun."

Geraldine nodded. "Well, if she doesn't know, that is a bonus."

"Won't be hard to find out if she's good with Google, which we know she is."

"True. Last name?"

"I didn't tell her, but it doesn't mean she didn't snoop."

"You realize, Morgan, that you are one of the luckiest fucking women on the planet right now."

"Yeah. Yeah, I do."

The mood turned somber, and it wasn't much longer until Geraldine left and Morgan attempted to get some sleep. She easily saw the uniform outside her door every time he shifted his stance. She felt more like a prisoner than someone who was protected, but Geraldine had been right. There was a slim chance Lollie would come back to finish the job, though she doubted it would happen at all. She strictly followed her plan, and since Morgan had thrown that plan completely awry, she would be looking for calm and order again.

She knew Geraldine was already looking into Lollie more now that they had her phone and her purse. It hadn't had much information in the wallet minus all the stolen cards she still had on her, but at least they had the phone. It would hopefully prove to be somewhat useful.

Until Morgan was cleared to return to duty, she would be on the outs with knowing about the case until Geraldine or Pax kept her in the loop. It wasn't a place she was longing to be in. This was her case. It was the thing she had been obsessing over for the last three weeks, and it wasn't something she was going to give up easily. Gripping the notepad and pen she had next to the bed, Morgan wrote out a full and complete profile for Lollie, her serial killer looking for love in all the wrong places.

When she walked into the Seattle Bureau for the first time since being released from the hospital, Morgan swore everyone stared at her. She didn't look too bad. There were still marks around her neck from where Lollie had tried to strangle her. She wasn't allowed to wash her hair because of the twelve staples on the crown of her head, and she had to wear a glove over her hand any time it went near water because of the twenty-seven stitches in it.

She would no doubt have two more scars to add in to her list, but only one of them would be visible. Looking down at the ground, Morgan focused on where she was headed and went straight for Garces' office. She'd already briefed him twice, but this was to be her full length interview about the incident in her hotel room. Her union rep was going to be on the phone the entire time, but Morgan was ready to tell all. She had done nothing wrong, except maybe miss some major signs Lollie had put up, but even then, she was pretty sure it would have been normal for someone to miss them.

The conference room was near silent when she entered. She sat down and made herself as comfortable as possible and open to the conversation. She did not in any way want to come off as defensive. With her foot tapping against the floor, Morgan waited for it all to begin.

"Why don't you tell us, in your own words, what happened since you arrived in Seattle?" Garces' started, his dark brown eyes locked on Morgan's face. His look was grim, but he didn't seem to be overly concerned. Perhaps Geraldine had filled him in some.

"Sure." Morgan took a deep breath. "The first day I got here, I went to do some work at my favorite coffee place I frequented when I lived here. I met a woman there, Lollie, and we talked briefly before I left to meet up with my ex for dinner. I had given Lollie my personal phone number since she was new to town and I used to live here."

"And then what happened?"

"She called me that night. We set up a date for the next day. We went on that date. It went well."

"Where did you go?"

Morgan swallowed. "We walked the market and went down to the pier to one of the seafood restaurants there."

"And did Lollie join you in your hotel room that night?"

"No." Morgan let out a breath. It was officially on her record that she'd slept with a woman. There was no way around it. In Seattle that didn't make a difference. Had she still worked in Houston, she would have likely requested an immediate transfer to somewhere else. Chicago...it was hit or miss. "Lollie didn't come back to my room until my third night here."

"All right, so tell us what happened yesterday."

"Yesterday, we were supposed to meet for dinner, but I was late leaving the office, as you know. I was working the case. Lollie came up to my room, and we didn't leave. We had sex. Fell asleep. My alarm went off in the morning, so I got up, called my sister, took a shower, and went to get ready for work. Lollie then attacked me."

"What instigated her attack?"

Morgan's jaw clenched. She shot Garces a glare and shook her head. "Nothing."

"You didn't argue?"

"No."

"You didn't tell her you were an FBI agent?"

"No."

"You didn't kick her out of the room?"

"No. Nothing happened to instigate her attack."

"Something must have." He crossed his arms over his broad chest and stared her down.

Morgan was unfazed by his attempt at intimidation. She knew she was right. She had done nothing, at least nothing in a normal person's brain, that would tick Lollie off. Letting out a breath, Morgan leaned forward. "She's a psychopath. She doesn't think like you or I think. So no, I didn't say or do anything that would anger a normal person. Lollie, however, is not normal. She fights for shelter and food and love. When she feels those are in jeopardy, she strikes. She knew I was staying in a hotel. I had mentioned the night before that I lived in Chicago and wasn't going to be in Seattle for much longer. I made it very clear this was not a long term relationship. That's what set her off, but she waited. She waited for when she had the upper hand, she waited for when I wouldn't be paying attention, and she waited to get out of it what she wanted."

"And what did she want?"

"Love."

"But how did she get love if she killed you?"

"Love to her is attention. She gets attention if I am dead, or any of her lovers. She sees them in the media, on the news, she hears the rumors and the whispers within the community. She gets the attention if we fight back. She wants her name out there. She's not afraid of being caught. She leaves DNA samples, finger prints, everything all around every single one of her crime scenes. She doesn't care if she's caught."

Morgan's heart rapped hard in her chest, beat after beat. She vaguely heard her phone buzzing in her pocket, but she ignored it. No call was going to distract her from this moment. If she didn't get it across to them the pathology of this woman, no one would be able to catch her.

"So why did she run if she wants to be caught?"

Chuckling, Morgan shook her head. "She wasn't expecting me."

"What do you mean?"

"She wasn't expecting a cop. I have training. I've taken defensive tactics every year since I joined the force and even before then in college and in high school. I'm fit because I work out and I keep up with my fitness evaluations. Not to mention, I had a gun. No other victim has had a gun. She didn't expect me one to fight back but two to know how to fight back and win."

Garces nodded. "Where'd she get the knife?"

"Not one clue. She must have brought it with her. I suspect it came from Samantha Gideon's house, that it's the same knife she used on her."

"We'll look into that."

Morgan heard her phone go off again. "Good. Are we done here?"

"For now. We'll need you to stick around for a few more days, but then you'll need to report to Taylor and return home. You'll be on leave until you pass your evaluations and until this investigation is resolved, although I don't foresee any problems in that happening. You didn't discharge your weapon; it was clearly self-defense. The biggest issue is that you slept with a suspect."

"Well, I didn't know she was a suspect at the time. Trust me, I wish I had. Everything would have turned out differently."

Garces grunted and shuffled his paperwork. Morgan's phone went off a third time. This time she did grab it and look at the name that flashed across her screen. Her mother. Ignoring the call, she looked back at Garces.

"May I use a conference room for a call?"

"Be my guest."

Morgan left the room and headed down the familiar hallway to another small conference room she knew was rarely used. It was the least updated with technology, so no one wanted to be in there if they could avoid it. Pax had checked in on her every morning and every night since he'd learned about what happened, and Pax had been the one to call Barbie, who had been up to visit twice already and was planning on taking the next day off work to stay with Morgan. Morgan had already yelled at Pax for that one.

Geraldine had informed Morgan every step of the way through the rest of their investigation. They had every cop available looking for Lollie, but she had pretty much vanished. To be fair they had all of her technology and a good chunk of money, so she would have to start from scratch.

Morgan shut the door to the conference room after flicking on the light. The other two calls hadn't been from her mother. When she scrolled through her missed calls, she saw Fiona Wexford in stark red. With her heart in her throat, Morgan dialed the number and lifted the phone to her ear.

"Morgan! I just heard, are you okay?"

"How did you hear?"

"Grapevine."

Morgan narrowed her eyes, truly curious how the grapevine of FBI intel ended up at Chicago PD in under seventy-two hours. "I'm fine."

"Good." Fiona let out a breath. "But really, how are you?"

"Sore. I've got like a constant headache from where she slammed a lamp across the back of my head." Morgan sat down in one of the comfortable rolling chairs and watched the window next to the door to see who would walk by and find her. "But we've got more information now than we did before."

"That's good. Not the brightest way to go about getting it." Fiona let out a wry chuckle.

Morgan licked her lips. "What exactly did you hear through the grapevine?"

A door closing sounded through the phone, and Morgan knew Fiona had found somewhere private to talk. "Just that you'd been attacked by the woman strongly suspected in my murder cases."

"You still working those? Didn't I take them over for you?"

"Sure, you did." The smile was evident in her tone. "How did you find her?"

"By pure accident and coincidence. Call it a mutual love—or obsession, if you prefer—of coffee."

"Coffee?"

"Yeah. Long story, but I found her. Her name is Lauren Jasper—she goes by Lollie. She's young, twenty-eight. She's definitely lived out east, but I suspect the story she shared with me is most likely a lie. I doubt she'll ever come back to Chicago. She balked at the idea of it."

"The idea of what?"

"Uh...also a long story." Morgan closed her eyes, really not wanting to explain the whole story to Wexford at the moment, or ever, if she were honest. She'd much rather keep the fact that she slept with a murderer of at least five women under the radar as best she could. "I'll be headed back to Chicago in a few days once I finish up some interviews and paperwork here."

"Good. I'd...would I be able to meet up with you, maybe?"

Morgan's heart was in her throat. She had been waiting for this moment, but so much had happened in between their kiss and now. Rubbing the bridge of her nose, Morgan shook her head. "For professional reasons or for personal reasons?"

There was a distinct pause before Fiona answered. "Personal. I want to make sure you're okay."

"I'm fine. I promise. Just...well, I will be fine when I get these damn staples out of my head and I can wash my hair again. Then I'll be hunky-dory and well on my way to fine."

"Morgan..."

"I'm fine, Fiona. I'll see you around." Morgan hung up. No matter how much she had wanted to start a relationship with Fiona before, she could in no way contemplate it now. She needed time to process everything that had happened, find her happy place, and maybe even stand to be in her apartment alone before she dared invite someone to her bed again. God, she'd probably need ten years' worth of therapy to get over this one.

Grunting, Morgan shoved to her feet and headed for the elevator. She was ready for some rest, for some calm, and for some updates from Geraldine. She felt so out of the loop that she couldn't even see it. If it weren't for Geraldine, she would be utterly lost.

## CHAPTER TWENTY-TWO

LOLLIE HAD managed to snag a suitcase from the hotel before she'd slipped out of the emergency exit and into the damp morning air. Her heart pounded hard as she stared at the building, her jaw set, and her eyes hard. That had been unexpected to say the least.

With the clothes wrapped around her body, even though they didn't fit perfectly, Lollie had to make some decisions. Morgan had a gun, and she knew how to use it and well. Her aim had been confident. Lollie stopped walking as the sun blazed over the horizon. She licked her lips and leaned against the brick wall of an older run down building. She needed to breathe and to think.

She knew if she wasn't careful, someone would find her. She could either go back and find Morgan and end their relationship once and for all, or she could move on. She wasn't sure which she wanted. She'd never left a relationship so unfinished before, well, except her first, and in that case, she had gone back to find her lover in the arms of another. It had spurred an even bigger argument between them when Lollie had confronted her then ultimately ended their relationship.

Either way, she was going to need to lay low for a bit, figure out what the cops knew, what they didn't know, and what lies Morgan told them. Letting out a breath, Lollie stepped away from the building and sauntered toward her rental car. She could break into it easily enough and be on her way. She'd get her back up cash and wallet, grateful the one she'd left with Morgan had very little information in it, although it did have her most recent phone, one she really liked.

Pursing her lips, she stepped out into the street lights that were popping off as the sun shone brightly into the area. Perhaps she would leave Morgan alone. They hadn't been soulmates. Lollie wanted their connection to be deeper than it was.

With a sigh, Lollie broke into her rental and sat in the driver's seat. She'd learned this trick when she was ten. It had advanced over time, and she was far quicker at it now than she'd been eighteen years before, but it had been useful. Her brother had taught her in one of the many fits of kindness he had bestowed in her direction.

Leaning down, Lollie hot-wired the car and the engine roared to life. It would be a bit of a drive, but she could readily get her back up cash which would get her wherever she needed to go. She'd have to get her stash of knives anyway. While she lived for the thrill of a new relationship, she also wanted to be safe, and truly she wanted to settle down with someone. She wouldn't be able to do that in Seattle with constantly worrying and looking over her shoulder.

It was a mess. It really was. She had screwed up royally, and the only way to fix it was to run or to go finish what she'd attempted to end. Sitting in the empty parking lot with her car running, Lollie was at a loss. For the first time in years, she didn't know what to do or what decision was the right one. She'd always known, always been forward thinking and working toward her plans and her dreams of a family. The whole white-picket fence dream her parents had taught her from a young age was her role in life. She wanted that. They had wanted that for her.

Putting the car into drive, Lollie stepped on the gas. She went aimlessly through the streets and into the next town over after stopping at her storage locker and getting her cash and knives. She went south and then she went east and back north. She ended up on Interstate 90, and in the middle of Snoqualmie Pass. It wasn't until she was coming down on the other side of it, the roads slick with ice and wet from rain that she knew she was leaving.

Morgan could go back to Chicago and live out her life. She wouldn't bother with her, though she was pissed about the knife and she wanted it back. She could very easily get it eventually, but for now, her priority was finding the love of her life, the woman with whom she could and would start a family. Someone who knew what Lollie needed and wanted and was able to meet those without hesitation.

Eventually the mountains faded into rolling hills and flatter plains. There was snow that covered them, but the highway was clear. Lollie would make a pitstop in Spokane then keep going until she hit the next major city. There she would stake her claim, her new beginning, her clean slate.

With Morgan still heavily weighing on her mind, Lollie drove the entire day until she got to Spokane. Her first stop was for shoes and some clothes that fit, and frankly, looked better than whatever she'd found in that suitcase. She had standards, and she wanted to maintain them.

Heading downtown, Lollie walked into the first shop and slipped on a pair of flip-flops, pulling the tag and shoving it into her pocket. She wandered around for a few more minutes, pretending like she was looking at certain items, and she left with nary a thought of stealing.

She went to the next store, picked out a tight pair of designer jeans and a cute shirt that cut at an angle across her chest, wrapping around her neck. She also pulled the tags and walked right out of the store, not bothering to look back. Slipping into her rental, she went get a new car at the airport out west of town.

Lollie made her last purchase of the day on a whim. Crawling into her new rental car, she slid behind the wheel and ripped open the plastic covering the phone with one of the knives she had stashed in her bag. With the plastic open and off, she pulled out the phone and plugged it in to charge as she drove. Lollie headed straight out of town and continued east on Interstate 90. She drove another three hours before stopping for the night in Missoula, Montana.

Pulling into the beautiful lodge-style hotel off the highway, she paid for a room in cash and slipped into her room. Her phone was charged, and as she laid down in the comfortable bed with the warm blankets, she dialed the number she had memorized. She had been wrong before. Morgan had been the most perfect woman she had found yet.

They fit together sexually; they had laughed and enjoyed each other's time when they'd dined together. Morgan was the match she had been waiting for. She'd just have to convince her of it. With the phone pressed to her ear, Lollie listened with her breaths coming in short and fast.

"This is Morgan, leave a message, and I'll get back to you."

Lollie hung up. She tossed the phone to the end of the bed and relaxed into the pillows with her arms crossed over her chest. Whether it was because it was a new number or what had happened earlier that morning, Morgan hadn't answered. Lollie bit her lip, wondering if Morgan was laying in the bed in her room and thinking about her.

No matter how hard she had tried during the eight hour drive that day, she could not get Morgan out of her head. And she had tried. She'd recalled every woman she had been with in the past year, wondering and debating their relationship, the good stuff and the bad stuff, and at long last, remembering why they had broken up in the end. Justine had a girlfriend on the side and hadn't shared that information with Lollie until they were caught in the act. Pepper had screamed too much during sex. Katie hadn't wanted to commit. Andrea had been too flirtatious with other women. Samantha had wanted nothing more than a good fuck. But Morgan...Morgan was different.

Together they had found a connection, a hope for the future. They balanced each other out. Morgan had implied as much in the reason she gave for wanting to go on a date with Lollie in the first place. Lollie had sensed Morgan's comfort and willingness from the outset. Together they had a burning desire for the other.

She had been wrong to try and end the relationship when she did. Morgan may not have wanted to move to Seattle, but Lollie hadn't really explained to her why they couldn't go back to Chicago. Perhaps if she had done that, then their relationship would have ended differently.

She waited two more days before she called Morgan's cellphone again. She'd spent the time exploring her new home and learning the lay of the land. It was a gorgeous and interesting city, a mesh of the conservative and the liberal. The locals referred to the town as Zoo-town, and it was easily that.

They were in the full swing of winter, snow covered the Rocky Mountains she could see from her hotel room window, and the valley she was in was barren, which was quite unexpected. The phone rang and rang and rang, and Lollie knew Morgan wouldn't answer, so when her sweet voice filled the line, she was surprised.

"Hello?"

Her heart clenched. This was what she had been waiting for. All the women she'd tried to pick up in the last few days had paled in comparison to Morgan. She'd called, but she hadn't thought about what to say.

"Hello?" Morgan repeated.

"Morgan." Just her name slipped from her lips. Morgan gasped, sending a shiver running up Lollie's spine. She licked her lips and closed her eyes, her body warming as pleasure surged. She wanted to touch herself, to remember what it felt like to have Morgan's body against her own.

"Lollie?"

"Yes," Lollie answered. "I wasn't going to call you, but...I couldn't help myself."

Morgan's breathing shifted. It was noticeable even through the line of a phone. Lollie imagined she might be touching herself as well, and so she reached down between her legs and rubbed at herself through the fabric of her jeans.

"Why are you calling?" Morgan asked, her voice sweet and innocent.

Lollie had loved that dichotomy. Morgan had seemed in the end so much softer than she'd come off from the beginning, but that raging fire underneath had been obvious when Lollie had looked at her. "I needed to hear your voice."

"For what?"

Lollie let out a breath and moved her hand under her clothes. "I think I love you."

Silence rained down on the other end of the line. For a brief moment,

Lollie worried she had lost the connection, literally and figuratively, and waited to see if Morgan would answer her at all. When she said nothing, Lollie swallowed.

"I got to go, but I'll call soon." Hanging up, she tossed the phone next to her and continued to brush her fingers rapidly in a back and forth pattern against herself. She closed her eyes and imagined Morgan's lithe body against hers in the many ways they had fucked in the past week. Morgan's gentle noises, her writhing, her confidence. Shuddering, Lollie let her body fall over the edge into oblivion.

With a hand to her head, Lollie bit her lip. She couldn't do this. Morgan would tell the cops where she was at. She had to get her off her mind. Letting out a sigh, Lollie fixed her pants, grabbed the keys to her rental, and stormed out of her room. She got into her car and went in search of a date. She needed the distraction, needed to know there were women other than Morgan out there for her. She needed to feel alive again, whole again, and the only way to do that was to find a date.

A mission on her mind, Lollie spun her wheels against the pavement as she sped out of the hotel parking lot and down to the local coffee shop she had come to know and love in the few days she had been there. They had everything she needed; she was sure of it.

## CHAPTER TWENTY-THREE

PAX PICKED her up at the airport. She hadn't wanted him to, but he had insisted she not take the train with her injuries. It had been near a week since she'd last seen Lollie, and the itching at the back of her head was obnoxious enough that sitting for hours in a flying tube had set every nerve ending on fire.

He shifted a side glance to her more than once, and by the time they were only three blocks from the airport, Morgan had had enough. "What's the problem, Pax?"

"No problem." He stiffened and turned to the front windshield.

Morgan rolled her eyes and leaned into the car seat, trying to get as comfortable as she could. "Seriously, what do you keep staring at me for?"

He looked at her once more and shrugged. "I've seen you hurt in the line of duty before, Morgan, but this...this is something else."

"Well, this wasn't the line of duty, to be fair."

And that was it. That was what had been bothering Morgan the entire time. This wasn't the line of duty. This was a relationship gone sour, albeit a relationship with a psychopath, but it had been entirely done on her personal time. She couldn't blame the job for sticking her in a position where she was at risk. She had willingly taken steps to put herself in that vulnerable state. She'd been naked, without her weapon, totally unaware that she was sleeping with a serial murderer.

"Yeah, I guess."

"What do you mean you guess?" Morgan turned her head and glared at him. She was about fed up with people walking on eggshells around her. She was still on leave, pending her investigation, she was sent home to wait it out and have yet another interview about how everything went down, and to finally meet with the psychologist who would hopefully release her from this hellhole so she could get back to work.

"I've seen you hurt. I've seen you working a case until all hours of the night and having to force you to go home and get some sleep, but this is different."

"Is it different because you now have final proof and confirmation that I sleep with girls?" Her patience was gone. It had been used up in Seattle, and Pax should have known better than to step into this wide-ass pothole the size of Texas.

Pax, wisely, chose not to comment, but Morgan knew she'd called him out on his bullshit. He had never wanted to admit she didn't swing the normal way. He was comfortable enough when she dated men, cis-men or at least trans-men who came off as cis enough he could ignore the fact they were trans. He'd invite them over for double dates with him and Mel. But any other relationship, Morgan had kept it out of his line of sight, including her sham of a marriage, and Pax had never looked any deeper. This had put them squarely in the boat of having to look.

Sighing, Morgan closed her eyes as he drove her home, her head aching and itching, her hand sore from moving it so much while running through airports. She was exhausted and needed a good night's sleep, something she knew she would never get in her lonely little apartment.

"Where are you on the case?" Morgan finally asked, wanting answers to the questions running through her brain.

Pax shrugged. "You know I can't talk to you about it."

"Jesus, like that ever stopped you before. I'm not going to do stupid and fly off to wherever the hell she is. I just want to know if you've even found her."

"No."

"No as in you haven't found her or no as in you're not going to tell me?"

"The former."

Morgan huffed. "Figures. Bitch is good at flying under the radar."

Pax let out a breath. "Where did you meet her, anyway?"

"Coffee shop, just like Samantha and Katie." Morgan clenched her teeth. That had to be it. They had talked about their obsession with coffee, Morgan beating Lollie out by a mile with how much she drank a day, but it had been a simple point of connection between the two of them. She blinked back her tears and turned to face Pax. "You don't think differently of me, do you?"

"No, Morgan, you're the same bullheaded asshole and brilliant profiler you always were. You just made a mistake."

She snorted. "I've made a lot of mistakes in my life. Sleeping with my suspect—albeit completely unaware she was my suspect—probably takes the cake."

"It might. But like you said, you had no idea who she was or what she was capable of."

"Neither did all the other women she strangled and stabbed."

"You're lucky, Morgan." He turned to look at her. "You are really damn lucky."

"Bitch shouldn't have brought a knife to a gun fight." Grinning, Morgan let out a wry chuckle in the back of her throat. "She was certainly not expecting that one. I wonder if she's even figured out who I am. If she hasn't, we could use that to our advantage."

"You're talking about putting yourself back out there for her?"

Morgan shrugged. "It might be a way to entice her out. If she hasn't killed me yet, she might still want to."

He narrowed his eyes at her before looking back at the road. "What aren't you telling me, Stone?"

"Nothing." Morgan settled into the seat, not ready to spill the last of the information she had gathered about Lollie, not ready to share the phone calls just yet, though she knew as soon as she stepped into the office for her final interview, they may come up. Lollie had called her twice since everything had happened. Their conversation the second time had been short. Morgan hadn't shared with a soul.

She'd wanted to trace the number, trace the call, but she couldn't without alerting someone to the fact Lollie was still contacting her. She hadn't expected it. Honestly, she had thought after Lollie had failed that she wouldn't dare get in touch with her again. Pax pulled up outside her apartment and parked. Morgan stared up at it, foreboding. She was going to be alone for the first time since Lollie had tried to kill her.

At least she was in a different state and in a place she knew very well, her home, a place she felt safe. Still, the idea of being on her own scared her more than the potential of another phone call from Lollie. She cleared her throat and pushed to open the door with her bandaged hand.

"Thanks, Pax. I'll see you Monday."

"Monday?"

"I have to be interviewed."

"Still?"

"Don't ask me about it. Taylor is insisting."

Pax grunted. He got out of the car as she did, pulled her small suitcase from the trunk, and set it up so she could wheel it in. "You want me to go up with you?"

"No," Morgan answered. She absolutely did not want him in her space. With one more look at the high-rise, Morgan headed for the door with determination set in her shoulders and fear pounding in her heart.

The apartment was still an utter mess the way she had left it a week and a half ago when she'd followed Lollie to St. Louis. Clothes were strewn everywhere, dirty and clean mixed in, dishes piled in the sink, and the coffee pot with a layer of dried brew in the bottom.

Morgan let out a breath. At least she could entertain herself with cleaning to distract herself from the bigger issue raging through her mind. If she just knew where Lollie was, she could sleep better. Unless she was in Chicago, which then she probably wouldn't be sleeping, but Lollie would be stupid to come to Chicago. Between two murder victims and one attempted murder victim, she would be picked up as soon as she entered the border—or at least that was what Morgan kept telling herself.

She dumped the clothes she'd brought with her into the stackable washer and dryer in the closet on the edge of her kitchen. With the laundry basket shoved into the center of the room, Morgan walked barefoot around her apartment and picked everything up. It had been too long for her to remember what was dirty, so she would just wash it all. A ritual cleaning of sorts.

The floor cleared, Morgan headed for the sink. She piled dishes onto the counter so the sink itself was free to wash. Turning on the water, she looked down at her right hand and cursed. She still wasn't supposed to get it went, and frankly, soaking it with soapy water for an hour while she washed didn't sound ideal in any way, shape, or form.

She turned the water off and plopped down onto her couch, staring at the turned off television. She didn't know what to do with herself. At least while she'd been in Seattle, Geraldine and Barbie had been there to distract her and keep her updated. Here she was alone.

When her phone rang, it startled her. Morgan stared down at it, her heart racing as she flipped it over to see who was calling. She prayed before looking that it wasn't Lollie. She wasn't sure if she could handle it or not that night. When she saw Wexford's name, she let out a breath.

Picking up the device, Morgan answered and put it to her ear. "Wexford," she stated simply.

"Morgan, are you back in Chicago yet?"

So this was a personal call. Any time Fiona talked to her and called her by her first name, Morgan knew it was personal, but if she called her Special Agent Stone that meant professional. Settling into her couch and letting the large and well-used cushions swallow her up, Morgan closed her eyes. "Got back a couple hours ago."

"How are you doing?"

"I wish people would stop asking me that."

Fiona chuckled. "Right, I bet. But really, how are you doing? I want an actual answer."

Fiona's voice was smooth and sweet, but she held an authority in her tone Morgan was remiss to deny. "Not so good. I can't do my dishes."

"You what?"

"It's stupid, I know. I was cleaning up my place, and I can't do dishes because of the stupid stitches in my hand. I need to go buy gloves or something, which means no coffee in the morning."

"Uh oh. That could be dangerous in and of itself."

"Right?" Morgan found herself smiling as she listened to Fiona. They didn't know each other well, but anyone who knew anything about Morgan other than her status at the FBI knew she was obsessed with coffee in an unhealthy sort of fashion. "Whatever will I do come morning?"

"Do you want me to come over and help?"

Morgan's heart clenched. "No."

"I wouldn't mind. I just finished my own load of dishes, just call it an extension of what I was already doing."

"I couldn't ask you to do that."

"I really don't mind."

Morgan rubbed her lips back and forth. Dishes aside, the company would be preferred to being alone. "Okay."

"Text me your address. I'll head over in a minute or two."

"Okay."

Fiona hung up with another promise of being there soon. Morgan texted her address and waited. She glanced around the apartment wondering what she was supposed to do. Her cleaning spree before the phone call had solved what she would normally do anytime someone invited themselves over, so she was stuck sitting on her couch and waiting.

She texted an update to Barbie, letting her know she was home safe and sound. The response she got made her smile. She set her phone down on the arm of her couch and closed her eyes as she tried to ignore the itching at the back of her head. Her hair was a greasy mess by that point, and not only was it starting to bother her in a constantly annoying kind of way, but she knew she had at least another three or four days before the doctor would even let her think about washing it.

The knock on her door startled her out of her reverie. Morgan scuttled up and looked out the peephole to see a freshly and comfortably dressed Fiona Wexford standing on the other side. Morgan pressed her forehead to the metal door briefly before she stepped back and plastered a smile on her face, opening the door.

"Hey," Morgan started.

"Back at you." Fiona gave her a small smile and stepped into Morgan's home. "Didn't think you'd be back so quickly."

"Why's that?" Morgan shut and locked the door firmly.

"Figured they wouldn't let you travel or leave or whatever. I don't really know the inner workings of the FBI."

"Ah." Morgan rubbed her lips together. "I'm still on paid leave pending investigation, if that's what you're asking. They just sent me home to wait out the rest of it."

Fiona nodded. She held up her hand with a stout white paper cup in it. "I thought I'd bring you a little something since, you know, you can't make it here."

"Oh thank the Lord. You're an angel." Morgan took the coffee and popped the lid off it to let it cool a bit before she sipped. "This is perfect."

Fiona reached out and grabbed Morgan's free hand, her right hand, the one still wrapped with gauze. She brushed her thumb over it and pulled her lip between her teeth. "You didn't tell me about this."

Morgan shrugged, pulled her hand away, and sipped at her coffee. "Didn't think to."

Fiona's look was pity and sympathy mixed in one. She reached back out and circled her fingers around Morgan's wrist, tugging slightly to get Morgan's full attention. "It's okay not to be the strongest person in the room all the time. You know that, right?"

Tears threatened Morgan's eyes. She buried her nose in her coffee and took a long whiff of its overpowering scent. She ignored Fiona's statement, because as much as she was right, Morgan didn't want her to be. "This is good stuff. Where'd you get it?"

"My apartment."

"No shit, you made it?"

"Yeah. Come on. You can tell me all about Seattle—if you want—while I do dishes."

"I don't."

Fiona stopped short as she'd been about to take a step toward the kitchen. "Don't what?"

"Want to talk about Seattle."

"Then we'll talk about something else." Fiona pressed forward, stepping around Morgan and into the kitchen.

With the water running in the sink and Fiona clattering dishes, Morgan leaned against the counter and sipped at her coffee. She watched Fiona carefully. Something was different about her, about the way she was acting. Never before had Morgan seen her so relaxed, so in her element, so human and not detective. It seemed Fiona had found the elusive balance Morgan had never really wanted to find.

"Did you grow up here?" Morgan asked, wanting to start some sort on conversation to take her mind off the fact she couldn't keep her eyes off

Fiona.

Fiona nodded. "Born and raised. I did go to college in DC, though. That was an expensive four years to come back and be a cop."

Morgan snorted. "I get it. My masters was more expensive than my undergrad, but still not sure it was all worth it."

"You have a masters?"

Morgan nodded. "In psychology and in law. I did a double-whammy, because you know, first born always the over achiever."

"You have siblings, then?"

Morgan grunted. "Eight."

"You're shitting me."

"No. I'm not. There are nine of us." Setting her coffee down, Morgan took out a towel from the bottom drawer next to the sink and dried the dishes Fiona had cleaned. "How about you? Siblings?"

"Just one."

Something on the edge of Fiona's tone that had Morgan's shoulders tensing. When she risked a glance at Fiona's face, it was hard set. There was certainly a story there, but she didn't feel close enough to try and pry it out of her. They finished dishes and settled in on the couch. Morgan struggled to keep her eyes open even with the added caffeine to her system. It wasn't long before she felt a hand on her foot, and when she popped her eyes open, Fiona stared directly at her.

"What?" Morgan asked, grouchy and grumbly.

"I think you should go to bed."

"Don't wanna."

"Morgan, come on." Fiona gripped Morgan's wrists and dragged her up to stand.

Together they walked slowly toward the small bedroom in the back of the apartment. Fiona watched Morgan as she slipped under the covers of the unkempt bed, the light from the living room filtering through into the dark of the bedroom, backlighting Fiona so it made it hard for Morgan to see her face. They stared each other down. The pit of Morgan's belly twisted, but she couldn't tell if it was a good or bad sensation. Breathing deeply, Morgan stayed completely still and wondered what Fiona was thinking.

"Do you want me to stay?" Fiona's sweet voice barely filtered over to her.

Morgan's mouth dried instantly. That was why she hadn't wanted to go to sleep. That was why she'd pushed herself to stay awake for hours beyond when she should have. But she wasn't sure she had the courage to ask for the help. Fiona must have sensed her turmoil, because she shifted her feet and pointed out the door.

"I'll just crash on the couch."

Morgan let out a heavy breath. "No. Stay here. I promise. No funny business. I just—I—"

"I get it." Fiona slipped her shoes off and walked around the bed after turning the light off for the hallway and leaving the light on in the living room. She slipped under the covers on the other side bed, turning on her side. Morgan flipped to face her.

It was the first time she fully relaxed in days. Staring into Fiona's eyes in the middle of the night, knowing nothing was going to happen, knowing she was only there for comfort and peace. It was perfect. Before she knew it, Morgan was slipping into a restful sleep.

## CHAPTER TWENTY-FOUR

WHEN SHE woke up, Fiona was still asleep. Her hand ached from being clenched into a tight ball. The sun still wasn't up, as was her norm for waking so early. Morgan suspected Fiona was not the same. She wanted to move, get out of the bed, maybe sneak in a shower even though she wasn't supposed to, but she certainly didn't want to wake Fiona. It was a work day, and no doubt she'd have to get up soon enough, trudge back home to get clean clothes, and head in to the office.

"You're staring," Fiona muttered.

Morgan rubbed her lips together, surprised Fiona was awake. Her heart lodged itself in her throat, and she wasn't sure what to say. Fiona groaned and stretched, rolling from her side onto her back and stretching her hands up and toes down. Her shirt rode up on her belly, exposing sweet, glorious, and no-doubt hot-to-the-touch skin. Morgan swallowed.

When she looked back up, Fiona stared at her with a knowing gaze. "Do you always wake up this early?"

"Every morning," Morgan confessed. "You don't?"

Fiona snorted. "Not quite this early, but early enough."

Neither of them made to move. Morgan wanted so badly to reach over and brush her fingertips along Fiona's belly, curious as to what it would feel like. When she caught Fiona staring at her again, she flicked her gaze back to Fiona's face and dared herself to keep her eyes there.

Fiona let out a sigh and turned back onto her side, resting her head on her hand. "I'm sorry."

"About what?" Morgan's voice was harsh when she spoke, but she couldn't help it. She wasn't mad at Fiona, she was mad at herself, and she was certainly lost to what Fiona would be sorry for.

"I'm sorry I didn't call you back sooner."

"Why? It wouldn't have made any difference. I was in Seattle. You were here. I was with a lunatic. You, obviously, were not."

Fiona's lips thinned. "What do you mean with?"

"Doesn't matter. You have nothing to be sorry for. I was calling to see if you had any more insight into our killer. I think I found out enough for the both of us. I'm rather glad you weren't with me."

"I wish..."

"No, you don't. Just drop it."

Morgan spun on her other side and sat on the edge of the bed. Whatever they were talking about, it was far too intimate for her likes. She had to get out of the situation, put some distance between the two of them. Morgan went to the bathroom and splashed freezing cold water on her face. She dried her skin, and when she faced the door, Fiona stood in the doorway, leaning against the frame with her arms over her chest.

"I'm in a relationship," she confessed.

Biting her lip, Morgan shook her head and clenched her jaw. Of course, Fiona was seeing someone, of course, she probably should have asked before kissing her at a crime scene and all but begging her to come stay the night at her place—not that she had any designs on the evening, but still. Nodding, Morgan stayed put.

"We've been...I don't know how to explain it."

"Then don't. Unless you're in an open relationship, there's nothing else to talk about." Anger flared in the pit of her belly, and had she not been so hurt by her own stupidity, she would have realized before she spoke that her anger would come off as an attack.

Fiona didn't budge from her spot, completely blocking the escape. Morgan could push past her if she wanted, but she didn't want to touch Fiona, didn't want to make any type of physical connection. Morgan's breathing came in short rasps. She had not expected this type of conversation either. She was pretty sure they had put to bed any kind of potential relationship the last time they'd chatted in person, and with her last disastrous attempt at anything relationship wise, Morgan certainly didn't want to step anywhere near a relationship with a twenty-foot pole.

Fiona moved forward and reached for Morgan's hand, but Morgan jerked out of Fiona's reach. She sent Fiona a look, telling her to back off to which Fiona complied. "My relationship is complicated."

"I don't do cheating."

Fiona nodded. "I understand."

"And to be quite honest, the last thing on my mind right now is a relationship of any kind. I need...I need to get my life on track, be back at work, get these damn staples out of my head and stitches out of my hand, and maybe some legit therapy before I even think about a relationship."

Fiona's brow furrowed, and she cocked her head to the side in curiosity. Morgan ignored her. She really didn't want to get in to how she met Lollie and why they were in a hotel room together, naked, or why Lollie wanted to kill her. Clearly Fiona didn't have the whole picture, whoever had told her what was going on had not spoiled that surprise, and Morgan would much rather leave it alone.

"I think you should leave. I need to get ready for my interview, anyway."

"Okay." Fiona licked her lips. "Okay, but I want you to know you can call me tonight if you need me to come over again. I will come, Morgan, okay?"

"Fine. But I won't be calling."

Fiona took one step closer, this time grabbing Morgan's wrist in a tight grip. She leaned in, her voice firm for the first time since Morgan had met her. "Don't be a stubborn fool just because you think it'll make you stronger. It's okay to ask for help."

When she stepped away, Morgan knew what everyone else saw in her. Fiona wasn't just a smart and damn good detective, she had the hard side that came with the job, the jaded edge all law enforcement knew far too well. She wasn't innocent. She had seen things she wanted to forget, done things she wanted to forget, just like Morgan.

With a breath, Morgan nodded and brought her free and injured hand up to slide it against Fiona's cheek. She was right, her skin was soft, smooth, and hot from sleep. Looking into Fiona's eyes, Morgan nodded. "Yeah. I know. I may not want to admit it, but I know. And thank you for coming last night. I...I needed it more than I could probably ever admit."

"Any time." Fiona turned her cheek into Morgan's palm and let out a very slow breath as she closed her eyes.

Morgan stepped away and around Fiona, going to her room to get her clothes out for the day and try to remember to change out the laundry before she left. Before she knew it, she heard the click of her front door, and Fiona was gone without another word. When she headed out to her living room to make sure she was alone, she smiled at the coffee maker bubbling as it brewed its life-giving elixir.

Her interview with Taylor had gone well. She didn't have any more information to share that he didn't already know, and she wisely kept the fact Lollie had called her twice afterward to herself. Lollie still hadn't called even three days after the interview when Morgan was officially cleared after speaking with a psychologist. She was finally back at work.

Surprisingly enough, Taylor let her stay on Lollie's case, although Pax would have to do everything with her from there on out. Officially, their serial killer was their top priority while the human trafficking case took the backseat. There were still agents working the other case, but she and Pax were in charge of Lollie's case.

Morgan sat at her computer, with her ever present blue-toned coffee mug next to her. It was still full with one teaspoon of sugar in it, steaming when she turned on her computer and waited for Pax to arrive and get to work himself. She was so happy to be back in the office, back in the routine of life, back to what she wanted—normal.

She hadn't called Fiona again. That had been a rat trap she certainly did not want to step into. She did not mess with other people who were already taken, no matter what arrangements they had unless it was in a completely open relationship that was confirmed and well thought through. Whatever relationship Fiona was in was her business, but Morgan would have none of it.

With a week behind her, she'd finally been allowed to shower, and it had been glorious. Pax had made a comment about her smell the other night when he and Mel had dropped her by some dinner. Mel had elbowed him hard in the gut, but he ignored her. Morgan was glad to be clean and in fresh clothes and at her desk.

Running searches on the information they had wasn't hard. Figuring out a way to find a phone number by a different means than they already had was another issue entirely. As much as Morgan wanted to run the cell phone number, she knew questions would be asked if she did, questions she certainly did not want to answer. If she did, she'd be thrown off the case in two-seconds flat without a second thought.

Pax set his briefcase down on the table top and plopped into his chair. "You coming?"

"Coming to what?" Morgan asked, not glancing up at him.

"Our vow renewal."

"You actually planned that thing?" Sending him a sidelong look, Morgan shook her head.

Pax shrugged. "Yeah."

"When is it?"

"Next month."

"I guess. Do I have to wear a dress?"

"Wear whatever the hell you want. It's not a big formal thing."

"Okay. Just tell me when and where and I'll go. Do the kids know?"

"God no. They can't keep a secret worth shit."

"You have a good Christmas?"

"As good as expected."

"Santa bring you something big?"

He frowned at her. "No, but the kids have a whole new room devoted to the shit they got."

Chuckling, Morgan turned to her computer. "I'm running the cards we found on her along with the names of her victims, but I doubt we'll find anything. Lollie is smart."

"Smart and fast if you didn't get her."

"I didn't shoot," Morgan chastised. "If I'd shot her, she'd still be on the ground, but she had a knife and I had a gun."

"I would have shot her."

"You weren't there."

"I didn't screw her, either."

"Pax!" Morgan spun and glared at him. "That was uncalled for."

He shrugged.

Morgan shook her head. "No. No, I'm not doing this. You don't get to be an asshole about this. If you have a problem with the fact I slept with a woman—"

"I don't care about that. You slept with a suspect."

"I didn't know she was a suspect. If I had known, I wouldn't have done it. I thought I was having a nice little fling while I was out in Seattle for a week, away from home, something to burn off some energy and steam, maybe get back in the game."

"Get back in the game?" He jerked his head and shook it at her. "You thinking about dating someone, Stone?"

Morgan let out a breath. "Not now."

Focusing on her computer, she effectively ended the conversation. Immediately, she stopped and looked at him. "Pax, look at this."

He leaned over her desk, his eyes squinting at the screen. "Shit."

"Yeah."

Morgan scrolled down the crime scene report to the photographs. Sure enough, there was a woman lying on the ground, blanket on top of her, but blood everywhere. The walls were covered, the carpet covered, the bed she was laying next to covered. "She's mad."

"Maybe, but either way, we've got to get there. Where is it?"

"Missoula, Montana."

"Yeehaw," Pax muttered.

Morgan scrunched her nose. She'd been to Montana before, once, with a boyfriend more than a decade ago. They'd thought it'd be a good idea to visit the national parks. It had not been a good idea. Morgan had ended up working because some idiot thought it was a good idea to shove their newly-married wife off the side of one of the cliffs, and federal ground meant federal investigation, and since her supervisor had known she was already out there, she got called back from work. Needless to say, there was more than one breakup involved.

"Gonna talk to Taylor?" Morgan asked Pax.

"Yeah. You gonna go?"

"Don't know if he'll let me. The last time I left..."

"Yeah, yeah."

Pax and Morgan walked into Taylor's office, Morgan's chest tight with tension. She forced her shoulders to roll and relax, but it was still hard to breathe. Morgan let Pax do the talking.

"There's another murder."

"Already?"

Pax nodded. Morgan watched their boss. "Missoula. We're pretty sure it's connected but can't be positive until the autopsy report comes back."

"Follow it," Taylor ordered.

"Like to Missoula?" Pax asked, his eyes going wide.

"Yes. It sounds like she's escalating."

Pax nodded and turned. Morgan remained rooted on the spot, looking from Pax to Taylor. She wasn't sure if she was allowed to go yet. She was still on semi-restricted duty with the staples and whatnot, but this was her case, and she wanted to bring Lollie in. When Taylor raised his chin to her, he lifted one brow in a question.

"Am I going to?" Morgan asked, her voice coming off a lot more intimidated than she really was.

"Did I say you were staying behind?"

"No?"

"Then get."

Morgan grinned and turned on her toes, heading out of the room. She was back. It was perfect. She and Pax would go to Missoula, and she would find Lollie. If she got there, maybe they could get Lollie's number off their newest victim's phone then they'd be able to track it. The only downside was Lollie had called Morgan's personal cell, and that would no doubt come up as soon as they ran a trace. Pushing the worry from her brain, Morgan headed to make their next plans for investigation.

Pax was already on the phone making their flight reservations. Morgan pulled out her personal cell and stared down at it. Taking a risk, she pulled up Fiona's number and simply typed, "Headed out of town. Got a new lead. It's fresh. Thanks again for the other night." She hit send, pocketed the phone, and packed up her desk. They were leaving soon, and she didn't want to waste another minute.

## CHAPTER TWENTY-FIVE

WITH HER last fling out of the way, Lollie took the car, switched plates, and drove straight out of town. She didn't even bother to look back. Something about Missoula gave her the creeps, so she wanted out as soon as possible. She drove south and east again, following the highway until she felt like she was far enough away she could stop for the night.

Bozeman was unlike Missoula in its majesty. These mountains were completely covered in snow, and there were piles of it along the sides of the streets. Lollie pulled into the mall on the outskirts of town. It was run down, but perfect for finding someone else she could meet. Lollie was always looking for places to meet people. She loved talking to new people, getting to know them, making intimate connections.

She grabbed some coffee and a fluffy salted pretzel and sat down on a metal chair in the center of the mall. The phone in her pocket called to her, and she pulled it out. She wasn't one to play games on a device or scroll through social media. In fact, she didn't even have social media. It had never interested her. But suddenly curious, she wanted to know more about her mysterious Morgan. It seemed like a contradiction for a woman of her personality to have a gun in her room, and to know how to use it, and Morgan had known.

She realized she really didn't know anything about Morgan. She hadn't learned her last name, or where she lived other than Chicago, or her friend's name. She was at a loss of where to even begin a search. Frustrated, Lollie grabbed her coffee after finishing her pretzel and wandered through the mall. She stopped in a small jewelry store and looked through the different earrings and necklaces.

The woman behind the counter was cute. It was a chain store, nothing fancy, but the woman looked competent enough. Lollie sauntered over and smiled. "I was wondering if you had anything with sapphires in them. I absolutely love sapphires."

"We do, was there something more specifically you were looking for? Rings, necklaces, earrings?"

"Do you have a matching set?"

"We have a couple. Let me get them for you to look at."

Lollie waited while the slim brunette moved away from her. Her ass was plump, and her curves stood out sharply as she walked. Her waist was very small. Lollie licked her lips as she came back. This time, Lollie read the woman's name tag. Nadia. Smirking, Lollie lowered her gaze down to the jewelry Nadia presented her.

"Oh, this is beautiful."

"It's one of my favorites," Nadia whispered like it was a secret.

"I can see why. It'd match your eyes." Lollie fingered it gently. "May I try it on?"

"Certainly."

Nadia pulled the jewelry from the box and handed it over so Lollie could put it on. Lollie clasped the necklace around her and then held up one of the earrings. She grinned at Nadia. "I think it's perfect. I just moved here last week, and I'm starting this new job in the next few days. I'm a nervous wreck, so I thought I'd splurge on myself to make me feel a little better."

"This piece is perfect for you, I think. It brings out the highlights in your hair."

Lollie's stomach warmed. "I'll take it. Say, do you know where there's a good place to buy some clothes around here? I need something a bit more professional. It's my first real job, where I'm actually in charge of something."

"That's exciting. You can check the stores down that way. There's a few of them that probably have what you're looking for."

"Thanks! You've been so helpful." Lollie fingered the credit card and bit her lip. She knew she could be found by it, but she couldn't help herself. She needed the connection, needed to make the purchase to get Nadia's attention. The rest of their interaction was cold, and Lollie shook herself of it. She could find someone else, someone warmer who was more into her.

It didn't take her long before she wandered into another small store, very much the opposite of what Nadia's had been. This one had all things leather, t-shirts with slogans painted across the front, all kinds of rings for piercings, and little odds and ends. The lighting in there was subdued, and the woman at the counter was the complete opposite of Nadia. Her hair was dyed black with a splash of red and purple on the tips. It was cut so it spiked up sideways on her head, and when Lollie made eye contact with her, she knew she had her mark.

Lollie strolled right up to the counter. "Not to be too forward, but do you know where there are any good gay bars in this town? I just moved here, and I need to find my people."

She snorted. "I'm Mandy, by the way, and yes, I know where the good gay bars are. What'd you move here for?"

"Work. But I literally don't know anyone here. It sucks. I need friends. So, here goes, I'm Lollie, and I just moved here from Seattle." Lollie added in a pout. She knew she looked out of place in the shop, but she couldn't help it. She was drawn to Mandy and her tight pleather pants, nose ring, and dark, almost-black eyes.

"I think I could help you with that."

It didn't take much enticing. Her shift was ending anyway, and Lollie waited around until it was over. Lollie walked with Mandy away from the store, but Mandy stopped with a grin on her face. She was much younger than Lollie would normally go for, but something in her gaze spoke volumes of wisdom. Mandy grabbed Lollie's hand and leaned in to her ear.

"Do you really want to go to a bar or are you just looking for a quickie and thought that'd be a good place to find one?"

Lollie grinned and leaned away from Mandy so they could stare each other in the face. "A bit of both, honestly."

"I like an honest woman."

"Then I am here to serve." Lollie curtsied a little.

Mandy growled. "I also like a femme."

"Sounds like a match then."

"Come here."

Mandy dragged Lollie by her wrist in the opposite direction they had been going. She pushed open the door to the restroom. Bathroom sex she had done before, and it had not been the best experience in the world. When Mandy pushed open the handicap stall and shoved Lollie against the wall, Lollie knew she was going to like it this time. Mandy had that edge to her, the speed, the roughness Samantha had, but the dark quality she had always longed for in a mate.

"You first," Mandy whispered harshly into Lollie's ear. "Then me."

"Okay."

Mandy was already undoing the button on Lollie's jeans, shoving them a little bit down her hips. She kissed Lollie's neck, nipping and biting her way up and down to the tops of her breasts before moving up again. Never once did she press a kiss to Lollie's mouth. Her hand slithered between Lollie's legs, and Lollie helped move her pants down even farther to give Mandy easier access.

Her body heated with pleasure. Just like with her last girlfriend, though, every time she closed her eyes, she pictured Morgan at the helm of making her feel pleasure, not whoever stood in front of her. Lollie ignored Mandy and focused on Morgan. She'd dreamed of her, masturbated to memories of her, thought about what they'd do next time they met. Before she knew it, she was hitting her high and falling over her orgasm.

Mandy licked her fingers and undid the zipper of her pleather pants, shoved them down to her ankles. She leaned against the wall to the stall, opened her knees and stared at Lollie. "It's my turn."

With a deep breath, Lollie slid down to her knees and pressed her mouth to Mandy's center. Her scent was so different than Morgan's. Where Mandy was spicy, Morgan had been sweet. Where Mandy was rough, Morgan had been caring. There had always been a sense of danger with Morgan, but it was subtle. With Mandy, it was overt. They were having sex in a public bathroom.

Mandy gripped her head hard, tugging, and Lollie shoved her tongue inside Mandy's body. She'd make her come, and she'd seduce her again and again and again just to get Morgan out of her head. She had to. She had to stop obsessing over the woman who very well could have been the one, but who had tried to kill her. And Mandy had to last longer than her last girlfriend, because that had been the shortest relationship Lollie had ever had.

When Mandy came, she wasn't quiet. Her voice echoed in the tiled bathroom like a gun that had gone off. Lollie gritted her teeth and wiped her mouth with the back of her hand as she stood up. She wanted to kiss Mandy, wanted to know how different it would be to kissing Morgan. She pressed her hand against Mandy's neck, keeping her still as she covered her mouth with her own. Their tongues slipped together, Mandy's knees buckled, and Lollie held her up. Mandy tightened her fingers sharply around Lollie's wrist. Lollie let her go with a grin.

"That was good." Mandy pecked Lollie's lips once and fixed her pants.

Lollie mimed her, fixing her own jeans. Once they looked decent enough but still tousled and aroused, Mandy opened the door to the stall and walked out. "Let's go do it again."

"Sure. Give me your address, and I'll meet you at your place."

Mandy bit her lip as she thought but then nodded. They split up when they made it outside. Lollie walked to her car with Mandy's address in her phone. She turned on her GPS as soon as she got to the car, but since she had her phone in hand, she had to make the call. Morgan had been on her mind too much.

Dialing, she let it ring. Morgan picked up on the third one. She didn't say a word. Lollie listened to her breathing, a calm coming over her. Lollie looked around the half-filled parking lot of the mall. She rested her head, not quite sure what to say.

"You there?" she asked.

"Yes," Morgan answered, her voice wavering. "I'm here."

"Where are you?"

There was a pause. Hesitation. "M—my apartment."

"Chicago."

"Yes."

Lollie glanced down at her nails, wishing she was in the same room as Morgan, wishing they could see each other face to face, that she could see what Morgan was thinking. She answered with the first thing that came to her mind. "I really liked Chicago."

"Why do you keep calling?" Morgan asked, her voice a little stronger than before.

Letting out a breath, Lollie closed her eyes. "I can't stop thinking about you."

"Since you tried to kill me?"

"Since we broke up. I was with a woman today, and the entire time, I couldn't stop thinking about you. Your taste, your smell, the little noise you make every time you come."

Morgan snorted. "That's precious."

"What?" Anger surged in Lollie's chest.

"You can't stop thinking about the one who got away. You missed your chance to kill me, so now you can't stop thinking about me, have become obsessed with me. I've got news for you. I don't think about you. Ever."

"Don't make me mad," Lollie warned. "I do bad things when I'm mad."

"You do bad things when you're happy. I don't think you know what it is you feel. You're neurotic. You're manipulative. You have no idea what is right and what is wrong."

"Yes, I do!" Lollie practically shouted into the phone. Her jaw clenched. "I do know what's right and what's wrong."

"Then tell me, Lollie. Did we really break up from a relationship? Or is that all in your head?"

"We broke up."

Morgan let out a breath. "No. We didn't break up. We weren't in a relationship to begin with. We were having sex, good sex, but that was it. Nothing more."

"Is there another woman?"

"What?"

"Is there another woman? Are you seeing someone else? Is it that woman who called you so early in the morning? You fucking her?"

"What would make you ask that?"

"Why else would you leave me?"

"I didn't leave you. Lollie, I did not leave you. There was nothing to leave. Look, we can go round and round in this conversation if we want, but we'll never come to the same conclusion."

"You're right." Lollie pursed her lips. "It's time for me to move on."

"Wait...what does that mean?"

"It means I've found someone else."

"Lollie—"

"I'll see you never." Lollie hung up the phone and tossed it into the seat next to her. Fuming, she took a deep breath and pulled out of the parking spot. She headed straight for Mandy's address. If Morgan wanted nothing to do with her, then she would focus on someone who did have attention turned toward her. Someone who cared about her, loved her even. If Morgan was going to have such a cold heart, then she would find someone else who did love her and whom she could love back.

## CHAPTER TWENTY-SIX

HANGING UP the phone, Morgan's heart rate pounded. She was beyond glad Pax wasn't with her, that she was in the room they'd been given by the Missoula Police Department to work in for the brief time they were going to be there all by herself. No one had heard that conversation, and yet, Morgan wasn't sure she could keep it hidden much longer. Bile roiled in her belly, and she wanted to let it all out.

They'd been there for a day already, had been through the crime scene, seen the blood spatter everywhere. Just like before, a knife was missing from the set in the kitchen. She'd been stabbed seven times, which certainly was a break from the pattern but not completely, more like a modification. Morgan had wondered for a moment if she was saving the six for her, for whenever they met again, and Morgan knew they would meet again.

Pax came into the room, and she jumped when he opened the door. "Jesus, Morgan, scared much?"

"Shove it," she muttered. "What do you have?"

"Well, they found Chris' phone and tracked down the numbers before we got here. They found one that was to a prepaid phone, and they've been tracking it. It just made a call."

The bile swirled like a hurricane. Morgan swallowed. "Oh?"

"Yeah, she was on the call long enough to trace her. She's in Bozeman. That's three and a half hours south of here. We can make it in decent time. Weather is going to turn tomorrow with a storm coming in, and they said we'll have a harder time driving it if we wait."

Morgan's palms were sweaty. Her face clammy, and her ears buzzed obnoxiously. She had no idea what she would do when they figured it out, and they would figure it out. It was only a matter of time. They were so close to catching her. If only it could be held off for a few more hours or even a day if she were lucky. She knew she was toying with her job, walking the line of losing her badge, but she had to be the one to catch her. She wasn't lying, but she was strongly omitting the truth, which in a way wasn't much different.

"Morgan?"

She snapped her attention back to Pax.

"You okay?"

"Uh...yeah. I'm fine. Just...you know." She waved up and down her body. "Still recovering."

He nodded. Morgan let out a breath that he took her excuse as valid. They gathered up their things and headed for their rental car. Pax convinced Morgan to drive, citing that she had more experience in the snow, which was a complete farce, but she didn't mind. She enjoyed having the control of the vehicle.

They were about halfway there when Morgan broached the topic of how to lure their killer out. If she really was in Bozeman, and they had that knowledge, then they could try and keep her from killing anyone else and instead focus her energy on Morgan herself. It was an insane idea, but it was one that might work, especially if Pax was there as backup.

"We could put out a media release."

Pax turned from looking at the file in his lap and narrowed his gaze at her. "You want to put out a media release? That sounds very unlike you, Stone. What's up?"

"It's just a thought. What if she's already found someone and is basically waiting it out to kill them. She skipped from five stabs to seven. I'm the one in the middle, so I must be six. She might be obsessed, and if we do a media release, if I do a media release, it might refocus her attention on to me and save someone."

Pax grunted and shook his head. "Noble but stupid."

"Come on, you can see the logic in it."

"I can. It's still stupid."

Morgan would have to convince him. If she could save a life, then she could end this. It was her fault Lollie was loose anyway and that even one more person had to die on her watch. She couldn't, she wouldn't, let it happen again.

"Think about it, really. It's not that insane of an idea."

Pax let out a breath and closed the file in his lap, staring out the front windshield. Morgan kept her speed even, driving through the mountain pass as they made their way toward Bozeman. The Missoula detectives were going to let them know if there were any more calls from the phone, but they were stuck in the middle of nowhere with no cell service, so they could be missing vital information.

"I won't do it without Taylor's approval."

Morgan rolled her eyes. "He was already pushing for a media release. I didn't want to scare the whole world of lesbians into thinking someone was after them."

Pax chuckled. "Yeah, that'd be bad."

"But we don't have to be that specific. I can get on local news, we don't have to make it national yet. If I do it, she'll see me, she'll figure out for sure who I am, and then she'll come find me."

"Are you sure of that?"

"As sure as I can be."

Pax didn't say anything for a good five minutes, and Morgan knew him well enough to know he was actually considering her thought process. If she could get Lollie back on the phone, she'd be able to steer her in a different direction hopefully. It felt like a shot in the dark, but Lollie's psyche wasn't fragile, and there was some weird connection she seemed to have with Morgan. If she was truly looking for love, she'd thought she found it. Morgan was willing to play the enticer to get the killer.

"You know, Stone, here's my hesitation."

"What?" She switched lanes to pass a lumber truck.

Pax turned to look at her, and while she would have liked to make eye contact with him, she wasn't moving her gaze from the road. "You, my friend, are lucky to be alive, whether you are willing to admit that fact or not."

It was like he stabbed her in the heart. Tears stung at her eyes, and Morgan knew she wasn't going to be able to hold them back. When she risked a glance in his direction as she slid back into the right hand lane, a tear streaked down her cheek and fell into her lap. He was right. She was very lucky to be alive, and she had no answer for him, no come back, no way to rebut what he said.

"I don't want to lose you." His voice was close to a whisper.

Sometimes Morgan forgot just how close they were, just how long it had been since they'd met all those years ago at the academy. She had been with him longer than he'd been married. She'd been there for every big moment in his life, meeting Mel, asking her out, engagement, his first assignment, his first arrest, marriage, the twins, his first nationally known case. She was his partner through it all. If he were in the same position as she was, she knew she would feel the same. He was her brother, her best friend, through and through. She couldn't live life without him.

"You won't," Morgan stated simply. "You'll be there. You won't lose me."

He nodded. "I'll talk to Taylor."

It was a whirlwind, but by the time they got to Bozeman, Morgan had a spot on the five o'clock news. She sat in the chair, fiddling her thumbs and staring at Pax in the back corner through the bright lights. This was a hail mary, but one they knew they had to take. Enough women had died already.

With a deep breath, Morgan listened as the anchor prattled on about whatever news story she was on. The next thing she knew, the story had changed to hers.

"In other news, the Federal Bureau of Investigation is in town on a man hunt. They are searching for a twenty-eight-year-old woman, who is wanted on suspicion of murder. We have Special Agent Morgan Stone, who is heading up the case, right here to tell us a little more about how we can help them."

The camera was on her. She'd done this dozens of times before, given a brief, she knew what she had to say. She and Pax had gone through it at least twenty times as soon as they got approval. No lesbians. Yes murder. No specifics. Yes armed and dangerous.

With a deep breath, Morgan nodded at the anchor and reiterated her planned press release. "Thank you. We are needing help in finding Lauren Jasper—she also goes by Lollie—who is suspected of murder. As you said, she is a younger woman in her late-twenties to early-thirties, she is about five foot six with brown hair and brown eyes. She speaks very well for her age. We do consider her armed and dangerous at this time. This suspect is very dangerous, so if you see her, please do not approach. Please call the tip line at the number on the screen or call 9-1-1 immediately and officers will come to your location."

The anchor took back over. "This investigation is being conducted in conjunction with the Bozeman Police Department. If you have any information on Lauren Jasper, or Lollie as she goes by, please call our tip line at the number on the screen."

As soon as Morgan was done and off the camera, Pax came around and touched her shoulder lightly in a show of support. She had just outed herself to Lollie. Morgan knew it would only be a matter of time before Lollie called her again and they either found her or she killed someone else. They would have to work fast in order for it to not be the latter.

Pax and Morgan headed to their hotel after grabbing a bite to eat. Morgan slipped into her room and sat on the edge of the bed. She was so tense she didn't know what to do with it. She had anticipated since it was her decision she would be able to handle it, but it seemed as though the moment the decision was made and approved by Taylor himself, she wasn't ready. She couldn't do it. But she had.

The phone was next to her, and when it buzzed, she jerked in fear. She waited three rings before flipping it over to see Fiona's name gracing the screen instead of the random number Lollie had. Letting out a breath, Morgan answered, "Hey."

"You left town?"

"Yeah. They cleared me for light duty, and we got this lead, so I guess I'm back at full duty."

"Where are you?"

Morgan pursed her lips and stared at the closed blinds to her window on the third floor. "I can't tell you that, but it won't be that hard to figure out in a few hours."

"Oh really?" Fiona's voice turned excited at that.

Leaning into the pillows on her bed, Morgan closed her eyes. She hadn't expected Fiona to call her ever again nonetheless only a few days after they'd last talked. "What'd you call for?"

"I wanted to check in on you. My little birdie is gone, and I can't keep tabs on you."

"Who is your little birdie you keep mentioning?"

"That's for me to know and you to figure out."

Morgan grunted. "I suppose that's how you found out about Seattle?"

"Affirmative."

"That's classified information."

"Told in friendship and nothing else. There was concern for your well-being."

"But why tell you? That's what I don't get."

"You will eventually. I'd like to talk to you about it. I know the other night was not the right time, but I do want to talk to you about it."

Morgan sighed. "Not tonight."

"No. In person."

"Okay." Morgan closed her eyes. "I have to get going. I am waiting on a phone call."

"All right. You're sure you're doing okay?"

"Yes. I'm fine. Ready to be home and be done with this case."

"Sounds like you're on the right track."

"I suppose. I'll call you when I get back."

"Please do."

Morgan hung up as Pax knocked on her door. She got up, let him in, and laid back down on the bed with her eyes closed. He sat at the desk and pulled out paperwork to go through. She should probably join him, but she was exhausted. It had been a hell of a month.

"She call yet?"

"No."

"Who were you on the phone with?"

Morgan narrowed her eyes and stared at him over her feet. "How'd you know I was on the phone?"

"Heard you talking through the door."

"Creep."

"Who's the girlfriend?"

Morgan groaned. "Not a girlfriend."

"Who is it?"

"Wexford."

"The Chicago homicide detective?"

"Yeah. She's having an issue giving up the case I took from her, so she keeps calling for updates, of which I do not give her."

He gave her an odd look, a judging look. Morgan rolled her eyes and ignored him. If he was going to be an ass about everything, she could be an ass back, but she wasn't quite sure what he was thinking. For the first time in a long while, Morgan felt something had come between them in an unexpected and awkward way.

Pax shoved a file over toward her. Morgan opened one eye to stare down at it. With a roll of her eyes, she picked it up to flip through it. They both stopped short when her phone buzzed. Morgan froze. Pax looked from her to the phone and back again.

"Answer it. Speaker."

Morgan picked up her cell. Sure enough, it was Lollie's number. Swallowing, she did the one thing she'd asked for. She answered the call.

## CHAPTER TWENTY-SEVEN

MORGAN SENT a glance to Pax, her entire body tensing as the phone rang again. With a deep breath, knowing this time she had backup, Morgan slid the virtual button and answered Lollie's call.

"H—hello?" she said, wanting to make it seem like she was nervous for Lollie's sake and like she didn't know who was calling for Pax's sake.

"You work for the FBI?"

Morgan rubbed her lips together and sent Pax a look. "I do."

"Fuck!" Lollie shouted. "What the fuck, Morgan? How the fuck did you not tell me that?"

Drawing in a short breath, Morgan shook her head. "Probably for the same reason you didn't tell me you had killed at least five women, now six. I don't like to share about my work."

"I didn't kill those women."

Morgan sent Pax a narrowed glare and shook her head. They had a lot of proof and evidence to say otherwise, not to mention the attempt on Morgan's life. "Then what did you do?"

"We broke up."

"You're delusional."

"I am not!" Lollie yelled again, her voice echoing in the small hotel room. "All of them. We broke up. I left. I found a new girlfriend. We just broke up."

"Okay, okay. You broke up." Morgan changed her tone. She had to keep Lollie on the line as long as possible. Pax had already contacted their office to have them trace the call to Morgan's cell. She just had to keep her on the line so they could find her and avoid another murder. "You're not delusional. It just didn't work out with us."

"I wanted it to." Lollie sounded like she was about to cry.

Morgan had to think of another way to keep her distracted, to keep her on the phone. "Where are you now?"

Lollie snorted. "I bet you already know. You're tracing my call. You've been following me for weeks now. I bet that's what Seattle was all about."

"No. That's not what Seattle was. I...I didn't know who you were in Seattle."

"Don't lie to me," Lollie warned. "Don't you dare lie."

"I'm not lying." Morgan's voice turned soft, and she sent Pax a sad look with the lifting of one shoulder before she dropped it. "I'm not. I had no idea who you were in Seattle. I thought you were this fun cute girl I met at a coffee shop. I liked you even."

"But you didn't love me."

Morgan let out a short breath. She had to tap into her emotions, she had to play this off well otherwise Lollie would be able to see through it. She couldn't jump the gun again. "I didn't, but that doesn't mean I couldn't love you. We were just getting to know each other."

Morgan knew the agents back home would be recording the call, they would be able to hear everything she said. She had to keep Lollie on the line, but she had to also play by the rules and not reveal more than she was willing to share. Pax knew what happened, but the random special agent tapping her phone didn't.

"Don't you want to get to know me better?" Morgan asked when Lollie didn't answer.

"Yeah, yeah, I do. I thought you were the one. I thought I loved you."

Morgan twisted it again. Maybe, if she was lucky, she would not only get Lollie's location, but she would get her to come to them. "Yeah, that could very well be, but we've got to spend some time together to find out."

"You have to stop."

"Stop what?" Morgan asked, confused by the sudden turn. It was then Morgan heard the woman's voice in the background asking who Lollie was talking to. She shot a worried glance to Pax, and he was immediately out of his seat with the phone to his ear and walking out into the hallway. "Lollie, who is with you?"

"No one of your concern. If you had just left me alone, none of this would have happened."

"None of what? Lollie, what's going on? Talk to me."

"You have to stop looking for me. If you don't stop, there's only going to be more heartache and pain. Leave me alone. I don't want you anymore."

"Lollie. Who is with you?"

"My new girlfriend. She's better than you. She's perfect. She loves me."

"Who? Who is she?"

"Her name is Mandy." Lollie's voice had an air of arrogance in to. "Mandy, come here, sweetie. I want you to say hi to someone."

It took a minute, but the phone was jumbled, and a new voice slid over it. "Hi! It's nice to meet one of Lollie's friends."

"Mandy—"

"Don't." Lollie was back. "Don't even try it, Morgan. I'll talk to you soon enough, I'm sure."

Lollie hung up. Morgan stared down at her phone, her heart pounding so hard she struggled to draw in breath. Pax still wasn't back. They had to find her. Jumping off the bed, Morgan flung open the door to her room and searched for Pax. He was down at the end of the hall still on the phone. She waved him down, and he came in her direction.

"Did you get it?" she asked, not caring he was clearly still talking to someone.

He shook his head at her and mouthed "not yet" before speaking back into the phone. Morgan bounced in her shoes, really needing him to end the call. She had to tell him what Lollie had said. Their conversation had not ended well, and Morgan feared she had pushed Lollie to do the one thing she had tried to avoid.

Finally, she couldn't wait anymore. She flagged her hand in front of Pax to get his attention. He told whoever was on the phone with him to hold on and shoved it down into his with a raised eyebrow.

"She's got a woman with her. Mandy. And she was mad, Pax. We've got a problem. They need to work faster."

"They're working as fast as they can."

Morgan shook her head. "I've got a bad feeling about this."

He nodded at her and moved down the hall on the phone. Morgan went into her room and sat on the edge of her bed again, waiting for what he came back with. She wanted to find Lollie, but she felt like she had nothing to go on. Grabbing her work phone, she called the local police department to check on the tip line and see if they had anything substantial yet. She was just hanging up when Pax came in with a sigh.

"They're still tracing it."

"What the hell? It shouldn't be that long."

"I know. I don't know what's wrong."

"Pax, she's going to kill Mandy. I know it. If we don't get there like ten minutes ago, she's going to be dead, and it will be our fault."

Shaking his head, Pax grabbed Morgan by the shoulders to still her. "It won't be our fault. We didn't murder her. We didn't make that decision."

"Yeah, but we weren't fast enough to stop her either."

Their phones rang at the same time. Morgan answered hers with a brusque, "This is Agent Stone."

"We have a lead."

"What is it?" She glanced at Pax and saw him writing information down as she listened to the detective on the other end of the line, hoping the tip was a good one. She grabbed the pen by the hotel phone and the notepad there, writing down everything he said.

"We got a call about thirty minutes ago from a woman who claims her friend went home last night with someone who fits your description. They met at the mall where her friend works. She even sent a picture."

"Text it to me." Morgan's heart was in her throat. They were so close. They could do this. They could stop another murder. "What's her friend's address? Send uniforms. We'll be there shortly."

She wrote it down, and before Pax was even done on his call, she was hanging up and running out of the room. He followed her, hot on her tail. When she got to the car, Pax slipped into the passenger side. He finished his call and showed her the address. Morgan nodded. It was one and the same.

Stepping on the gas as Pax used the GPS to direct them, Morgan sped through the streets. She didn't care. She had to get there in time. It took ten minutes for them to arrive. When they pulled up to the house, there were two police vehicles parked on the edges of the street. Morgan drove slowly, not wanting to alert Lollie they were there. The uniforms followed her.

Pax grabbed her wrist as she parked and sent her a worried look. "You can do this?"

"No other choice."

She leaned in the back, pulled out her vest and slapped it on her chest. Pax had already wrestled his on during the drive. Morgan gripped her weapon tightly in her left hand and pushed out of her car into the cold winter air. Her shoes crunched in the snow, the sound loud in her ears, her breath hot in puffs of fog. Silently, she nodded at Pax to let him know she was completely ready for whatever was about to happen.

They walked up to the door, the uniforms fanning out behind them as provided backup. Morgan went to the door and pounded her fist on it. "FBI. Open the door!"

There was no response. Her heart raced. Pax pounded this time, his larger fist making a bigger sound. Morgan's voice boomed. "FBI! Open the door and come out with your hands up!"

Silence was their only answer. Morgan knew what Pax was thinking. He wanted to go in. Morgan was thinking she didn't want to see what they would no doubt find. She nodded at Pax. Once more and they would go in. Her voice echoed in the street as more officers arrived as backup. Her fingers were cold at the trigger on her gun, but she kept her hand steady.

Pax reached down when there was still no answer and tried the doorknob. It turned freely. He swung the door open, his hands in front of him as he aimed inside the house, his eyes wide. Morgan went in right after him, moving in the opposite direction to make sure the room was clear.

They went room to room until they came upon the bedroom. Morgan had seen the streaks of blood on the walls, fingerprints and handprints littering the white paint.

The bedroom was a bloodbath. The uniforms finished clearing the house. No one was there. No Lollie, just the very dead and very bloody but clothed body tossed haphazardly in the middle of the bedroom floor and the alarm on the stove going off incessantly. Morgan could only assume the deceased was Mandy.

"Fuck," she muttered and turned toward the door. Pax was back on the phone, and Morgan holstered her weapon. Two uniforms stopped by the door and stared in. She shook her head at them. "Go search the area, see if you can find her. Figure out if Mandy here had a car she took or if she's still in a rental. Put out an APB for the vehicle, please."

They nodded and left. Morgan squatted down by Mandy's head and sighed. This had not been Lollie's norm. This was done completely out of the ordinary, completely out of her general desire for killing. This was done because she was pissed. There were eight stab wounds to Mandy's chest, but there were also stab wounds to her legs and her stomach. Her neck was sliced, which explained all the blood. Lollie might have strangled her, but there was no way to tell without an autopsy, and sex had definitely not been part of this kill.

Morgan licked her lips and let out a sigh as Pax came into the room. She shook her head at him. "We took too long."

"She was probably dead as soon as Lollie hung up the phone. We're not that far behind."

"But how many more have to die, Pax? How many more? I'm tired of finding dead women left on my doorstep and being three steps behind Lollie."

"I think we're only half a step behind her now." He held up the phone in his hand. "Found this in the kitchen. She left it."

"Great, one less way to track her."

He shrugged. Morgan wanted to reach out and close Mandy's eyes, but she resisted. She couldn't touch the body before the right people got there and did their thing. Slipping gloves out of her pocket, Morgan stood up. A uniform handed her booties to protect her shoes from blood and to protect the house from her. She slid them on and wandered around.

She turned off the oven alarm to silence its inane beeping. It didn't take her long to find Mandy's wallet. She flipped through it. Amanda Caprese, age, thirty-two. She was much younger than Lollie's norm as well. Morgan must have pushed her to try something new, to step out of her routine and comfort zone. That meant her profile was no longer necessarily the best way to find Lollie.

When her phone rang, she saw the local number and answered it.

"Special Agent Stone."

"Did you find her?"

Morgan's heart clenched. She spun in a circle, her gaze looking widely for Pax. When she saw him, she waved him over with a finger over her lips. Putting the phone on speaker, Morgan stared down at the number.

"Did we find who, Lollie?"

"My last girlfriend."

Morgan licked her lips. "I did. I did find her. She seems to not be in a great state after you left."

Pax took down the number and made a call. She knew he was having the number traced.

"You didn't have to do that, Lollie. You could have just left."

"She knew. What else could I do? She'd find you, and you'd take her from me."

"Lollie. I don't even know what to say to you anymore."

"Don't say anything. Just stop looking for me."

"You know I can't." Morgan stared at the kitchen window, bouncing in her shoes. "You know I have to keep searching for you. I have to find you."

"Then find me. But know this, Morgan, if you find me, I will make sure we have a proper break up. I need the closure."

When Morgan turned around, Pax was in the doorway, staring at her. She swallowed. "I'll see you soon, Lollie."

"It wasn't long enough," Pax said after listening to his phone for another minute. "If the phone is still on, we may have some luck, but that depends where she's going."

"She was in a car, that's for sure. She has Mandy's phone."

"We'll get her, Stone. You have to be patient."

She glared. "You know how I feel about being patient, and you know how I feel about this case."

Stalking out of the kitchen, she went back to the murder scene to re-evaluate her profile. Lollie was feeling backed into a corner, chased, and it was making her more violent, less careful. It was less about the hunt for love, and it was turning into revenge. Blowing out a breath, Morgan headed outside to get some air. She needed a moment to think, to center herself.

## CHAPTER TWENTY-EIGHT

LOLLIE HAD thrown the phone out on the highway after taking the battery out and smashing it. She ditched her car in Billings and stole another one. Then she switched plates with a third vehicle in Sheridan, Wyoming. She drove through the night, following all the speed limits and taking deep breaths of meditation.

She had been far too angry the last few days. It was the one emotion that seemed to be able to grab her and take her on a ride. Mandy was done. That hadn't been a good start anyway, but it was fun while it lasted. Morgan, however, she was still hung up on her. No matter how hard Lollie tried to push Morgan from her mind and from her heart, she couldn't.

Morgan was everything that every other woman she had met was not. She was strong, generous, and loving even when they were arguing. And they were in a doozy of a fight now. She turned off the highway on the north side of Casper. It had been six hours of driving not including her random stops to switch vehicles. With a sigh, she drove around town until she found downtown and parked on the side of the street.

She stretched her back, closed her eyes, and debated what she was going to do. Morgan was an FBI agent. How she had not figured that out before was shocking. They hadn't talked much about their lives in general. There were a few things here and there about stuff when they were growing up, but most of their time together—especially toward the end of their relationship—had been physical.

It made sense, though. Morgan had followed her from Chicago, where she'd likely been assigned the case. She'd probably been in St. Louis at some point and because she'd used Samantha's card in Seattle, Morgan had known to go there. She'd said she was there for work but hadn't elaborated what that work was. Rubbing the bridge of her nose, Lollie looked out her window at the streets filling with people. There must be some event or something going on.

Getting out of her car, Lollie threw on the jacket she'd taken from Mandy's house and hunched down against the cold air. It was New Year's Eve, so surely that's what everyone was getting ready to celebrate. They were all walking toward one central point. Lollie wandered along, curious as to what everyone was doing and where they were going.

Lollie made her way, stopping when she saw the bright lights of a glorious coffee shop. She hadn't had any that day, and it beckoned to her. Leaving the throng of people, Lollie stepped into the warm coffee shop and shuddered as the heat hit her cheeks. It smelled glorious inside. She walked up to the counter, waited in the line, and looked around the cafe.

There were tables and chairs strewn about, people of all sorts sitting and drinking coffee. Cowboys, hippies, artists, college students. Lollie settled in. It was nice to see the diversity in a place where she didn't think she would find it. Maybe this could be where she found love, found someone other than Morgan. She'd have to change herself. She'd have to become someone other than Lollie Jasper.

Her plan formed in her head. She would have to find someone who looked like her. It wouldn't be that hard. She wasn't anyone special. She wasn't someone who stood out in a crowd, that was for sure. As soon as she stepped up to the counter, Lollie smiled at the barista and made her order. It didn't take long for her drink to be ready, and she sat down in the back of the room, sipping at the steaming liquid. It was heavenly on such a cold evening.

It was still early enough that she could find someone who would take her in, who would be perfect for assuming an identity. She kept her gaze on those around her, looking, analyzing, perfecting, and judging those who walked by, who stopped for a drink.

There were a couple women she made eye contact with and smiled at them to test and see if they would be interested. She didn't find the instant connection with any of them that she was looking for. Certainly none who matched Morgan's caliber. She was about to leave, when a new barista came in, rushing in the door and swinging her apron over her waist.

She must be late. Rubbing her lips together, Lollie took the last sip of her coffee and watched carefully as the young, petite woman clocked in and stood behind the counter. She could work. Petite brunette. She had short hair, unlike Lollie, but that wouldn't be too bad. Lollie could cut her hair and grow it back out. She had to get a closer look.

She dropped her paper cup in the trash and went to into the line for another one. It wasn't long until she was at the front. The woman smiled at her. "What can I get for you today?"

Lollie smiled back, softening her features to try and come off as over-friendly and bubbly. "I'd love another coffee. The last one I had was amazing, and I need the pick me up."

"Rough day?"

"Rough week."

"I get that." The woman chuckled. "What'd you have?"

Lollie ordered the same drink again, all the while flirting with the barista. She was cute. Even if she didn't end up in a relationship with her, she would be useful. Lollie sat at the table she was previously at and waited. She ordered another coffee and a muffin after an hour. Every time it was slow, she'd make her way over to the barista and chat her up or she would watch as the barista came to her to talk.

When it was no doubt close to closing time, Lollie finished her food and drink. She stood up and wandered to the counter, leaning over it as she waited for her little barista to pop up.

"So you said there's a big shindig downtown tonight?"

"Yeah, First Night. It's the only reason we're still open, honestly. More business. Normally, we close around six."

"Well, I'm glad you're still open. You're closing soon, though, right?"

"In fifteen minutes, and I'll be out of here in thirty."

"Want to maybe show me around this First Night thing? It sounds intriguing, but I think some company would be nice."

She grinned, her green eyes crinkling in the corners. "Sure. You'll just have to wait until I'm done here."

"No problem. What's your name, by the way? You don't have a name tag on."

"Dawn."

Lollie reached her hand over to shake Dawn's. "I'm Lollie. I just moved here from Seattle."

"We get a lot of us moving in here. I moved from Spokane ages ago. I love it here. Wouldn't move back."

"Glad to hear that. I'll just wait outside for you."

Lollie walked out of the building, standing on the edge of the sidewalk. Once again, the cold bit at her cheeks. She took in a deep breath, fingering the phone she had stolen. Her thoughts once again turned to Morgan, and she wondered if she'd followed her to Casper. They just couldn't seem to get enough of each other. After that night, Lollie was going to be someone new, someone Morgan would never be able to find again. This was her last chance if she wanted to try and be with her.

Biting her nail, Lollie glanced at Dawn. She was cute, she was fun, clearly a little exotic, but perfect for what she wanted and needed. Morgan, however, was perfect in every sense of the word for her. Pulling her phone up, she dialed the number she had memorized.

Morgan's sweet voice filled her ear, and Lollie smiled. "Lollie."

"Morgan."

"Where are you?" Morgan asked.

"Around," Lollie answered. As much as she wanted Morgan there, to have Morgan come when she wasn't ready would be a disaster. She needed the extra time. "You'll find me, I'm sure."

"What are you doing?"

"Standing outside. It's pretty snowy here."

"It's the middle of winter."

Lollie snorted. "Yeah. I miss you."

There was hesitation from Morgan. Lollie wasn't sure why, but she could hear it in her voice as she spoke. "You could have stayed."

Lollie bit the inside of her cheek. "I couldn't. You know I couldn't. Mandy wouldn't have it. She would get jealous."

"Lollie, what are you thinking about right now?"

"You."

Morgan sighed. "Is that why you keep calling? You said once you thought you loved me."

"I think I do. I can't get you out of my head. Every time I fucked Mandy, I was thinking about fucking you." The words leaving her lips sent shudders down her spine. Lollie turned to look at Dawn again. Her heart warmed. Her plan was going to work, it had to. "Does that make you hot?"

"I...I don't know how to answer that."

"Honestly." Lollie scraped her shoes against the cement, moving the hardened snow.

"No."

"That's a pity. Every time I think about you, I get wet."

"Lollie, why are you calling me?"

"I want you to come find me. I'm in Casper. It's a cute quaint little town in the middle of nowhere."

"I know where it is."

Lollie nodded and took a deep breath. "It's First Night. That's a New Year's Eve thing here. Lots of people walking around, lots of women. They won't keep me from you. They may be a good distraction for now, but when you get here, love, I'm all yours."

"What are you going to do?" Morgan's voice had a scent of fear to it that made Lollie's heart bubble with joy.

"I'm going to go home with the pretty brunette from this coffee joint. She's adorable. The exact opposite of you. You're strong and confident. She doesn't even know what she's in for."

"Lollie. Don't. I'll come. I'll go wherever you want me to go. Don't take her home."

"Too late." Lollie hung up and popped her head inside the building as Dawn shut the lights off. "You about ready?"

"Absolutely! I didn't think I was going to get to go to First Night this year. I'm glad you want to go. It's always better with company."

"Always." Lollie held out her elbow for Dawn to take after she was done locking the door to the shop.

There were cops here and there. Lollie skimmed right around them, steering Dawn in another direction. They checked out some small sellers of art, some different bands, some food trucks. Lollie willingly paid for Dawn's portion of their eating with the cash she had left on her. She was running out, but as soon as her plan happened, she would be free to do whatever she wanted.

They stayed until midnight, which was only another hour from when the coffee shop had closed. They stood in the center courtyard of the courthouse while everyone counted down. As they yelled "Happy New Year!" Lollie turned and pressed her mouth to Dawn's, carding her fingers through her short cropped hair.

They made out under the falling snow in the center of the courtyard. If Lollie hadn't had other plans in mind, it would have been a perfect way to start a new relationship. But Dawn wasn't Morgan, and Morgan was coming. She pulled Dawn's lip between her teeth, grinning when she let it pop out of her mouth.

Dawn put her head on Lollie's shoulder as they stood together. It wasn't much longer until the crowds dissipated. Dawn stayed right by Lollie's side. Together they walked toward the coffee shop, and Lollie couldn't help herself as they stood outside and kissed Dawn again. Dawn being willing to explore them together in this way would make Lollie's plan that much easier. All she had to do was end their relationship and take her identity. It was perfect.

If Morgan wasn't looking for her because she was someone else, then they could be together again. They could have the life Morgan promised her, the one Lollie wanted to have. They could get married, have kids, and be together intimately each and every day. They could grow old together.

Grinning down at the woman in her arms, the one who looked similar enough to herself, Lollie made her move. "Want to maybe take this inside somewhere?"

"Yeah," Dawn whispered, her voice squeaking as excitement hit her. "My place is just around the corner, actually."

"Let's get warm then."

Lollie once again held out her elbow for Dawn to lace her arm through. They walked together, Dawn leading their direction. Once inside, Lollie put her plan to action.

## CHAPTER TWENTY-NINE

MORGAN AND Pax were in the car pretty much as soon as Lollie had said Casper. Pax drove while Morgan bounced her foot up and down and up and down, waiting impatiently to get there faster. She'd been on the phone near constantly while Pax focused on driving through the snow. Her heart was in her throat as she once again hung up with the local police department in Casper.

"They have no calls about her."

"None at all?" Pax asked.

"None. I'm betting the local media release didn't reach down this far, but no one has called with a sighting so far. The locals have a description and a photo, but it's New Year's so they're pretty busy with everything else going on."

"I imagine," Pax muttered.

Her foot bounced again, and even in the dark, Pax shot her a glare. Morgan clenched and unclenched her good hand while she watched the signs on the highway telling them how close, or rather how far, they were from their destination.

"How much longer?" she muttered.

"No. We're not doing this. You are not five, and this is not that kind of drive. We'll get there as soon as we can get there."

"We're so close."

"I know."

Morgan clenched her jaw. Looking around, she hoped local police didn't find Lollie so she could be the one to slap the cuffs on her, but at the same time, she didn't really care so long as Lollie was in custody and not with another woman. Her heart raced. She thought about texting Fiona only to nix that idea two seconds later. They weren't dating. They weren't in any kind of relationship. Morgan certainly didn't want to be until she had a bit more separation from Lollie and that whole fiasco, but she felt she owed Fiona an answer on the case. As soon as they had her in custody, Morgan would call and tell her.

Only then would she have some good news to report and an actual legit reason for contacting Fiona. Without that, she couldn't even put into words why she wanted that connection. Yes, she liked Fiona, but whatever was between them had gotten so complicated so fast that all she wanted was to run in the opposite direction. Scratching the hair around the staples still lodged into her head, Morgan sighed.

"How—"

"Do not!" Pax warned.

"I wasn't going to ask that," Morgan stated with a touch of arrogance, except she had been going to ask that. So now she'd have to come up with a backup question. "How mad do you think Taylor is going to be that we're just leaving the state without telling him?"

"We told him. He just won't know until he wakes up and checks his voicemail. That's his problem."

Morgan nodded to no one but herself. Her foot still moved up and down in rapid succession, her hands clenched tightly in her lap. She was ready to go, ready to be in Casper already. It was another two hours before they arrived. They bypassed the local police department, having already talked to them multiple times in the almost six hour drive. They went straight for downtown.

Everything was quiet. It was too early in the morning on a night when it had been late. Trash littered the streets. Small stores were closed down. Morgan didn't dare leave the car without her vest. She plopped it on her chest and wrapped her warm winter jacket around her, zipping it up. The added weight made it more difficult to move, but she ignored it. It wasn't anything she wasn't used to after years of working for the bureau.

Pax and her separated and walked up and down the blocks. Morgan was three blocks away from the car, the cold seeping into her shoes and biting at her toes, but she pushed forward. Something had to hit her radar, something that would tell her where Lollie had been. She was about to turn around when she looked down one of the side streets. Pursing her lips, Morgan cocked her head to the side at the one store that had lights on.

She glanced back to where Pax had gone and didn't see him. Morgan took the chance and walked down the road. It took her half a block to get there, but when she looked at the sign above the business, she knew she was in the right spot. It was a coffee shop, and the piece of paper in the window told her the night before they'd had extended hours.

Morgan stood in front of the window and knocked. They weren't open yet, but it was clear someone was inside. She thought about calling Pax to let him know where she was, but she didn't. She had no new information to tell him. She was just following her gut.

A skinny man popped around the counter and stared at her. He waved his hands and shook his head, shouting, "We're still closed."

Morgan took a breath, pulled out her badge and plastered it to the glass door. "FBI."

He paused but opened the door for her to come in. Shaking off the cold from the outside, Morgan blessedly let the warmth back into her toes. He let out a breath. "How can I help you?"

"You own this place?"

"Yeah."

"Were you working last night?"

"No."

Morgan nodded. "I'm looking for an individual who may have come in here last night. Can you tell me who was working so I can contact them?"

"Uh...sure." He walked behind the counter and grabbed a clipboard. Skimming through it, he nodded. "Dawn Pearson closed for me. She's worked for me for years. And Henry Balask was here from two in the afternoon until eight last night."

"You only had one person closing?"

"Not unusual. We're pretty small." He set the clipboard down. "I open just about every morning."

Morgan swallowed. "Do you have cameras?"

"I do. I have one right over the cash register." He pointed behind him, and Morgan caught sight of the camera she had missed before. "I also have one by the entry."

"Can I look through the footage?"

"I guess. What makes you think whoever your looking for came in here?"

Morgan followed him around the counter and into the back office. She glanced at the door again and let out a breath. "Just call it a hunch. She's pretty coffee-obsessed and likes hole-in-the-wall places."

"Well, that'd be us to a T."

"I figured." Morgan's body vibrated as she followed him. She was ready for this case to be done and over with and to end. She wanted Lollie behind bars or in the ground. That was the only way she saw this ending. She wasn't going to give up until Lollie was done with her killing spree, and the only way that was going to happen is if Morgan intervened.

Morgan leaned over the owner's shoulder as she watched through the camera footage. Remembering the phone call, she pulled out her cell and looked up the time exactly when Lollie had called. Swallowing, Morgan asked, "Can you look just around when the store closed? The entrance camera."

"Sure." He fast-forwarded the video. There was nothing on it.

Morgan was about to give up, calling her hunch wrong, when she caught the flash of something outside the window. Narrowing her eyes, she stared at the small screen. "Keep the video running."

It was a full twenty-three minutes after the store was closed and the last customer was out that she saw Lollie's head pop in through the door. Twenty-seconds later, the lights went off and the barista locked and left the building.

"Who was that?"

"That's Dawn. She's the one who closed last night. Did everything properly like she always does."

"I need her address. Now."

"I..."

"Now."

Morgan stepped out of the office and had her phone to her ear with Pax's number dialed. Her heart was in her throat, her mouth dry, and her energy about ready to burst from the top of her head. Pax answered with a grunt. Morgan smiled.

"I got her. Head down to the little coffee shop off Fourth Avenue. I'll be outside waiting."

The owner came back with the address on a small piece of paper. It was just around the block. Morgan knew it. They'd driven right by it. She turned to him, issued her thanks, and left the building. She was already on the phone with the Casper Police Department to call for backup. They were going to need it.

When Pax got there with the car, he picked her up, and they drove to the police department, which was only a few blocks away. They witnessed the uniforms coming back to help them out. It was early in the morning, but a serial murderer always took precedent over patrolling the streets in general.

As soon as they got to the station, Morgan and Pax headed inside to speak with the captain on shift. They had to form a plan of action. Morgan wasn't going into this situation without a plan, and they didn't have much time. Pax let her take the lead, since she was better at communicating their needs and communicating with locals. He always said it was because of her sister, but she figured it was because he'd rather not deal with it if he had a choice.

"We need at least five uniforms. I'm not waiting to do this entry. She is armed and dangerous." Morgan spoke rapid-fire to the Captain Johnston. He seemed to be following along, but she didn't want to explain the whole case to him. "We've been following her for over a month now. She's killed seven women, attempted to kill another one. Agent Jones and I will go in first. She knows me, so it may distract her from killing the hostage."

"There's a hostage?"

"Maybe. Unknown if she's still alive." Morgan set her jaw. "We have to move quick."

"I understand that, Agent Stone." His tone came off as placating. Pax was ready to step in; Morgan saw his stance shift out of the corner of her eye, but she was taking charge, and she wasn't going to let someone else run all over her.

"This is my case, Captain. I have spent months working this case." It was a bit of an exaggeration, but he didn't need to know that. "I have profiled this woman from the beginning. We will take point. If we do not move quickly, she will be gone. I will not lose her again."

"Okay." He put his hands up. "You have seven uniformed officers as backup. What is the plan, Agent?"

Morgan wrinkled her nose and clenched her jaw. "Agent Jones and I will make entrance. Two of your officers will follow behind us. The rest will remain outside until the scene is clear. If she is gone, or if her hostage is dead already...we'll go from there."

"Simple enough. Let's go."

It was a flimsy plan. She wished she'd had far more time to talk it out, but she also knew Lollie hadn't given her much of a warning for a reason. Whatever she was planning, it was going to happen soon. Morgan and Pax got into their car, the uniforms following. No one had lights on or sirens. They didn't want to alert Lollie they were closing in.

After five minutes of driving, they were at the apartment. It was still in the downtown area, a brick building. There was a bookstore at the bottom floor that had lights off. The door inside to the apartments was around back. Pax parked toward the end of the alley. Morgan sent up a prayer, hoping God had more faith in her than she did.

She and Pax said nothing as they exited the vehicle, slowly closing the doors so they didn't make a sound. The uniforms followed the cue, Captain Johnston leading the way. Silently, they moved to the exterior door. It opened without a key.

They took the steps up to the third floor. Just like in Bozeman, they flanked the door. Morgan's heart pounded. Pax was right next to her, and she knew with him by her side, they would get Lollie this time. Both had weapons drawn. When Morgan looked behind her, she saw the officers filing around. Some were still downstairs, watching the other exits to the building.

With a breath, Morgan nodded at Pax. She was ready whenever he was. With her jaw set, her eyes forward, and her finger on the trigger of her gun, Morgan squared her shoulders, preparing for whatever would be there when they opened the door. Pax didn't wait one moment more. One of the uniforms carrying the Halligan bar stepped forward. Morgan shifted slightly to let him have room.

Ramming it hard into the door frame once and then twice, he hit exactly where he needed. Applying the pressure, he popped open the door, and it swung freely. One more glance at Pax, and Morgan barreled inside, weapon drawn, and hope propelling her.

## CHAPTER THIRTY

THE FIRST step she took into the apartment set warning bells off. Morgan slipped in quietly. There was a lamp on in the corner of the room, but no one in sight. She heard them in the next room over. Morgan knew from experience that Lollie loved waking her lovers up in the morning and knew that was when most of her kills happened.

The sun was still down, but it was close to six. Morning had arrived. Taking slow and steadying breaths, Morgan walked around the room. The uniforms filed behind them, clearing the rest of the room while she and Pax moved forward. The door was cracked open. Morgan strained her neck to look inside, not sure what she'd find. They hadn't exactly been quiet upon entry, so she was surprised there wasn't more rustling around.

When she peeked through the cracked door, her heart skipped a beat. Lollie was naked and straddling a woman between her legs, her hands on her neck. Straightening her back, Morgan kicked the door the rest of the way open and stepped into the bedroom.

"Hands up! FBI, put your hands in the air!" Her voice rang through the silent room.

Lollie didn't stop. She glanced over her shoulder, her face hardening as she tightened her grip.

"Hands up!" Morgan shouted again.

Once more, Lollie didn't budge. Pax filed into the room, moving rapidly to the other side of the bed. Uniforms came in after them. Morgan walked forward and nodded at Pax. He put his gun in his holster and reached to grab hold of Lollie and knock her off the woman. The woman's legs moved wildly under Lollie's body, and she clutched at Lollie's wrists, trying to get purchase to push her off.

Pax didn't wait, but as soon as he got close enough, Lollie let go of the woman and gripped a knife she must have hidden next to her on the bed. Morgan's finger twitched as Lollie jerked toward her partner. Morgan fired. The bullet flew straight and perfect, right where she had aimed, slamming into Lollie's shoulder and ripping through her flesh.

She lurched onto the bed from the momentum. Pax grabbed the knife and stepped back, holding it out for someone else to take. Morgan kept her weapon trained on Lollie while Pax gripped Lollie's good arm and dragged her to the floor. She hit with a thump.

Morgan slid her gaze to the woman and shook her head at her. "Stay on the bed. Don't move."

She complied. Pax put his knee down in the center of Lollie's back. Morgan wanted to be the one to slap the handcuffs on her, but in that moment, it was more important to just have them on. Pax reached to his belt and gripped the zip tie cuffs. He slid them onto Lollie's wrists and pulled tight. As soon as he had her handled, Morgan shoved her gun in the hostler at her side and moved to the bed to help their victim.

"I'm with the FBI," Morgan stated. "You're safe now."

She looked up at Morgan with wide eyes. Morgan turned toward the uniforms. "Get me a blanket or a robe or something, and get the medics here. Clear the rest of the apartment."

She didn't want the woman to move. Didn't want her to get up too fast after everything that had happened, but she very much related to the need to move away from the bed and from Lollie. Morgan helped her to sit up, wrapping the blanket around her shoulders and holding it in front of her. Morgan squatted down and softened her features.

"Are you Dawn?"

"Y—yeah." Her voice was hoarse, no doubt from being almost strangled to death.

"Don't speak just yet. I don't want you to hurt yourself."

"W—who is she?" Dawn ignored Morgan's request.

"Her name is Lollie, and we've been looking for her for close to a month now. But we've got her. She's not going to hurt you any more, okay?"

Dawn nodded and shivered. Morgan didn't want to touch her again and scare her or traumatize her even more. Morgan checked on Pax with a glance. He was still watching over Lollie who remained on the ground face down.

"She breathing?" Morgan asked.

"Yeah."

"I'm going to take Dawn here to the other room."

"Good idea," he answered.

"Come on," Morgan ordered Dawn. Helping her to stand with a hand under her elbow, Morgan led her into the living room and sat her down on the couch. The distance would no doubt help. "Tell me what happened."

"I—I don't know. We met last night. She was nice. We came up here, and I don't know. She just...changed."

"Okay. I'm going to have you go to the hospital and get checked out. I want to make sure she didn't do any serious damage to your throat."

Dawn looked down at her toes, tears slipping down her cheeks. Morgan's heart broke. She had been that woman, that broken, but she knew both of them were stronger than Lollie, and no matter what they would pull through this. She left Dawn with a uniformed officer while they waited for the paramedics to arrive.

She went back into the bedroom and squatted down next to Lollie. Pursing her lips, Morgan let out a breath. "Did you think you could just change your name, steal her identity, and then this would be over?"

"I love you."

Morgan rolled her eyes. "You just might, but that doesn't excuse what you have done here tonight, what you did to me, or what you did to any of the other women you have met in the past few months. It doesn't excuse the fact that someone has been sitting in jail for a murder you committed."

"I haven't killed anyone."

"You're right. You are innocent until you are proven guilty, but I'm pretty damn sure you'll be proven guilty."

Lollie didn't answer.

Morgan clenched her jaw and shifted from one foot to the other. "Really, Lollie. Did you think a new name would let you go free? Are you that stupid?"

"I thought you and I could be together then."

"I was right before. You are delusional."

Morgan stood up and walked out of the room as paramedics arrived. The first team went straight in to Lollie while the second team stopped with Dawn. It was going to be a long day indeed, but they had their suspect in custody, and the murders for love were done. Morgan knew they had the right woman. She'd have to file all her paperwork in the next week and send files up to have the individual convicted of one of Lollie's cases reevaluated.

It was a whole mess, a whole lot of paperwork, but she could get it done. It was all worth it in the end. Lollie was going away, and the streets were a little bit safer than they were before. It was as if a weight was lifted from her, and as she walked around the apartment to collect evidence, she took lighter steps, hopeful steps.

It had been a week in Casper, but she was finally finished with her paperwork. She was able to head home. Pax had left days ago, and she'd let him. He had a family, and she didn't. He could do what he needed from

Chicago while Morgan had tied up all the loose ends in Wyoming.

As Morgan stepped into the Denver airport, she let out a breath. Relief washed over her. Lollie had been transferred to a more secure jail to await whatever the lawyers were going to do with her. Morgan didn't really care so much as long as she wasn't released any time soon. It was as if a chapter had finally been closed, one she most definitely did not want to look back on.

Slipping into the uncomfortable chairs to wait for her flight, Morgan pulled out her cell phone. She had to make the call. Pax had told her she did, and she knew it, but she didn't really want to. Bolstering herself, Morgan dialed Fiona Wexford's number. It rang and rang and rang, and Morgan was pretty sure she was going to end up leaving a message, although this news was the kind she did not want to leave on a voicemail.

At the last minute, Fiona answered. "I didn't think you would ever call me again."

Morgan smiled. She hadn't thought she'd call again, but she wasn't about to share that bit of information. Blushing, and thanking the heavens Fiona couldn't see it, Morgan relaxed in her chair and ran her hand through her head, glad to finally have all the staples out. She'd given in and headed to an urgent care, demanding they take them out. The stitches in her hand as well.

"I arrested her."

"You what? Are you serious?"

"I see your little birdie didn't share that."

"They did not."

Morgan clenched her jaw, not happy she hadn't been able to get any more information from Fiona about who her source in the FBI was. Morgan sighed. "I arrested her earlier this week."

"Where?"

"Wyoming, of all places."

"How random." Fiona's curiosity was there, and it warmed Morgan's heart.

"Not so random. She was on the run, and she knew I wasn't far behind her."

"So why stop?"

Morgan licked her lips. "Long story."

"No. Tell me."

Morgan shifted in her chair, not quite sure she wanted to tell Fiona her secret. In every experience she'd had with Fiona, there had been no judgement. Not for kissing her at a crime scene, not for asking her help in doing her dishes or crashing at her house when she was scared to sleep alone. Not one moment of it. Taking a chance, Morgan told her.

"In Seattle, when I was there working the case—"

"When you were injured on the job?"

"Yes, when that happened. It was Lollie who did it. She was mad at me."

"You said that. But why? I don't think you ever shared."

"Do you want me to tell you or not?" Morgan bit out. She winced at her tone, but it was a struggle just to get the words out, and Fiona's constant interruptions weren't helping any. "Sorry."

"Don't. Just tell me what happened. I'll shut up. I promise."

Morgan let out a soft chuckle. "I met Lollie at a coffee shop. I didn't know who she was. She clearly didn't know who I was. We went on a couple dates. She was mad because she figured out I didn't live in Seattle, and she wanted a more permanent arrangement."

"Permanent like a coffin."

"Well, yeah, but she doesn't see it like that."

Fiona was silent. Morgan's heart fluttered, and she wasn't quite sure what to do or say next. Confessing that had been hard enough, but she still feared what Fiona might say, what she might do or think.

"Talk to me," Morgan whispered. "Don't go silent. What are you thinking?"

"I was thinking that I'm confused."

"Confused about what?" Morgan glanced at the ticket counter to check on her flight and see how much longer she had to wait for it.

Fiona grunted. "I thought, I guess without confirmation, but I thought you were interested in me."

Morgan snorted. Of all things for Fiona to say. "I am...I was...I am interested in you."

"Then why would you go out with her?"

"I didn't think you were interested in me. I'm not exactly...what's the word...I'm not exactly observant when it comes to things like that. I'm inept."

"You're oblivious."

"Yes! That's it. I'm oblivious. Thank you."

Fiona laughed lightly, the sound sweet to Morgan's ear, and she relaxed into her chair again. "I like you, Morgan."

"But you said you were dating someone."

"I am in a relationship, yes."

"Then this conversation isn't going anywhere unless you are in an open relationship."

"It's not, at least not in that sense."

"Then we shouldn't talk about it. I just wanted to call and let you know that she has been arrested. You can close your cases."

"Morgan..."

"I'll see you around, Wexford."

"When are you coming home?"

The single word was her melting point. Morgan stared at the screen above the ticket counter again and breathed a sigh of relief. "My flight boards in twenty minutes."

"I'll see you soon, then."

"Talk to you later, Wexford."

Morgan hung up. She'd wait until she was on the plane to do some more paperwork, to finalize her reports, and reacquaint herself with the trafficking case that was still ongoing. She'd focus on that for a while and leave the serial killers to someone else. She needed something a little less personal, even if it was equally as traumatic for all those involved.

When they called her boarding zone, Morgan grabbed her bag with her freshly de-stitched hand and straightened her back. She got into the throng of people ready to board, she pushed all thoughts of Lollie to the back of her brain. She'd deal with her again when she had to, when the trial started since she doubted Lollie would willingly admit to murdering seven people, but for now she could focus on something she could solve, someone she could save, and taking down Mr. Jimmy's sex ring.

## ABOUT THE AUTHOR

Adrian J. Smith has been publishing since 2013 but has been writing nearly her entire life. With a focus on women loving women fiction, AJ jumps genres from action-packed police procedurals to the seedier life of vampires and witches to sweet romances with a May-December twist. She loves writing and reading about women in the midst of the ordinariness of life. Two of her novels, *For by Grace* and *Memoir in the Making*, received honorable mentions with the Rainbow Awards.

AJ currently lives in Cheyenne, WY, although she moves often and has lived all over the United States. She loves to travel to different countries and places. She currently plays the roles of author, wife, and mother to two rambunctious toddlers, occasional handy-woman. Connect with her on Facebook, Twitter, or her blog.

### For by Grace (Spirit of Grace #1)

*If you just want to spend an afternoon losing track of everything else, this is the book to do it with. There's suspense, humor, and even a little hint of romance – A. M. Leibowitz*

Being a Sheriff's Deputy is not all about saving lives and arresting criminals, and each day Grace wonders if she'll make it home.

While kids at the schools Deputy Grace Halling visits see her as the knight in blue-cotton armor, people involved in the cases she is dispatched to have a different opinion. She has every confidence in her ability to do her job and arrest criminals. She easily takes down a knife-wielding woman and a drunken combatant teenager without hesitation. Everyone—victim, suspect, or witness—has a story to tell or to lie about, and Grace is never perturbed by their tales.

That all changes when she looks down the barrel of a gun. She loses confidence in her ability as a deputy, she loses trust in herself and fellow officers, and she struggles to stay afloat as shift after shift passes. Grace cannot find her rhythm of being a deputy again. And when the Police Chaplain unexpectedly barges into her life, her personal and professional lives are flipped upside down. Grace struggles to find her even ground, worrying that the next time she stares a murderer in the face will be the last.

**2014 Rainbow Awards Honorable Mention**

### Memoir in the Making

The first day of her junior year in college was supposed to go off without a hitch. But when Ainsley Jacobs sat in her memoir class with a professor she'd never had before, her life took an unexpected turn. She couldn't get her well-dressed professor, Meredith Frenz, out of her head.

Meredith had lived a lonely yet comfortable life for the past fifteen years, and despite flings here and there, she had no desire to jump head first into a relationship, especially one with her student. Despite all her thwarted efforts, Meredith was determined to keep to herself and push Ainsley away.

Forbidden love is often the most attractive.

CPSIA information can be obtained
at www.ICGtesting.com
Printed in the USA
BVHW092001080721
611250BV00008B/155/J